Includes Bonus Story of
Song of the Dove
by Peggy Darty

Journey of the Heart

DIANN MILLS

BARBOUR BOOKS
An Imprint of Barbour Publishing, Inc.

Dear Reader,

Journey of the Heart was my first published book, a dream come true. The characters and their journey played out vividly in my mind and refused to let me go. I envisioned a strong young woman thrust into the realities of life. She had the inner courage to accept her walk into maturity and faith in God. I also saw a young soldier who was committed to keeping others safe in wild, untamed west Texas. Together their faith and belief as young Christian pioneers fashioned a hero and heroine typical of those who settled our country.

But if it hadn't been for my husband who challenged me to write this first book, the story would never have gone beyond my imagination. Here began my passion for creating adventures for my readers.

I hope you enjoy my very first story.
DiAnn Mills

Chapter One

Katie Colter bathed her father's feverish body. For the moment, his labored cries had ceased, and he slept. Silence met her, and she held her breath until his chest slowly rose and fell. Putting aside the cloth and cool water, she touched his warm face. Her dear father seemed to grow worse instead of better, no matter how many herbs and liquids she forced through his parched lips. He'd grown so thin since the cough and fever raged through him.

Listening to his labored cries was better than watching him slip away.

With strength she'd not seen in days, he opened his eyes and reached up for her hand. She grasped it and kissed his fingers while tears trickled down her face.

"Soon I'll be gone," he said through a ragged breath.

"No, Pa. You'll get better."

"I want you to leave the Indian village." He closed his eyes.

"Why? This is my home."

"Your home is with the whites, not here among the Comanches. Go to Fort Davis now, before I die. This is not a fittin' place for a woman. Your Uncle Seth and Aunt Elizabeth will provide a home for you. Take the deed to the land and present it to Colonel Ross. He'll know what to do with it. Promise me you will do as I say." He opened his eyes and captured her gaze.

Grief swirled through her, agonizing, terrifying fear for today and tomorrow.

"Katie, promise me."

"What about Lone Eagle?"

"No, daughter. Leave now. I know the Spirit calls me home. Find your *rehoboth* at the fort. God does not abandon His children."

"Which spirit do you mean?" Did he refer to the Great Spirit? Because he seldom mentioned the God of her mother.

"The one true Almighty God, and in Him you should place your trust," he whispered.

She failed to understand, thinking his words were a result of the fever. "What is rehoboth?"

He squeezed her hand. "Promise me."

"Yes, of course." How would she do this thing he asked of her?

"I love you."

"And I love you."

He parted his lips to speak, but he drifted off into unconsciousness and never uttered another word. His chest no longer rose and fell, and his heart no longer offered the steady beat of life. His suffering was over. The Great Spirit had spoken through the wind rustling among the trees. Jeremiah Colter now lived in the spirit world of the great Comanche Indians.

Her tears dampened his chest. She desperately wanted to remain with her Indian family and friends. Desert Fawn loved her and wanted her to stay. Katie had dreamed of becoming Lone Eagle's wife, but that must be forgotten. She'd given her word.

Where was this God when her father died? How did Pa's God expect her to live without a mother or a father? How could his God do this to her? He must surely be a cruel spirit.

Comanche gods would not have allowed this to happen. Pa should have called out to them because their medicine was good.

Only strangers lived inside Fort Davis—strangers and white soldiers. She hadn't seen Uncle Seth and Aunt Elizabeth in seven years. Pa saw no purpose in visiting Fort Davis or his brother and sister-in-law. He had everything he needed at the Indian village and didn't require any aid from white folks. When her own father refused the white man's ways, why should she leave her Indian family to live among them?

Whatever Pa wanted her to find at Fort Davis, she didn't need. But she'd fulfill her promise.

Sergeant Peyton Sinclair scanned the horizon line of the Davis Mountains where the sharp peaks reached above the clouds and appeared to hold up the sky. His eyes trailed downward to the oak, juniper, and piñon pines that covered the high terrain and provided easy coverage for raiding Indians. Apache, Kiowa, and Comanche war parties easily moved about in Limpia Canyon, and too often they were not seen as they climbed the canyon walls enclosing Fort Davis.

From his lookout point, he scrutinized every waving bush and cottonwood for signs of hostile Indians. A deer leaped across a blanket of moss and wildflowers, and quail dressed in mottled black plumage skirted skyward in a rhythm of their own.

He wiped the sweat stinging his eyes and noted something moving across the valley floor. He focused his binoculars on an object heading directly toward the fort.

"Hey, Miles, I believe we have company," Peyton called to a soldier several feet away. He lifted his cap and raked his fingers through red hair.

"Comanche?" Miles said, spitting tobacco with his question.

"Can't tell," Peyton said. "But it definitely looks like a pair of spotted horses." He whistled.

"What is it?" Miles said.

"A lone wagon, and the driver is either a blond Indian or a white woman dressed in Indian clothes." Peyton focused on the wagon.

"I think the heat has finally gotten to you," Miles said, squinting to take a better look. He hesitated while his eyes studied the object. "You might be right, Sergeant."

"Of course, I am. It sure looks like a woman. . . . I wonder what's in the back of that wagon."

Miles waved to the soldiers stationed near the gate. "Wagon heading this way, and it's weighed down with something. Don't know whether the driver is Indian or white. This might be an attack."

Peyton and Miles watched the wagon creep forward until they determined two spotted horses pulled a heavily ladened buckboard. A young white woman held tightly to the reins.

"Who goes there?" Peyton called from his stance atop the gate wall. A handful of soldiers dutifully positioned themselves, ready for a confrontation.

The young woman pulled the buckboard to a halt and lifted her tanned face to Peyton Sinclair. She wore a buff-colored Comanche Indian dress decorated with colored beads of royal blue and red. Blond hair, a shade lighter than her dress of fringed deerskin, hung loosely around her shoulders. She looked no older than sixteen or seventeen. A rifle barrel lay sealed in the palm of her right hand, and Peyton took heed of her finger resting near the trigger.

"Katie Colter, sir, Jeremiah Colter's daughter," Katie said.

"I've come to see Colonel Ross and speak with Seth and Elizabeth Colter."

"What's in the back of your wagon?" Peyton said.

Katie reached behind her and tugged at an Indian blanket covering a trunk, a few deerskins, and buffalo hides. "All my belongings, sir."

"Where's your father?" Peyton said.

"He died a few days ago," she said.

The soldier who had spoken to her ordered the gate open, and Katie drove the wagon into Fort Davis. All the strain of the past weeks seemed to hit her straight on. She seemed frozen in the moment when she had watched her father die.

She handed the reins to the sandy-haired soldier who first questioned her.

"I'm sorry about your pa." Sergeant Sinclair stared into her eyes. "Are you all right, Miss Colter?"

"Yes, I believe so. I'd like to see Colonel Ross," she said. "Can you tell me where to find him?"

"I can take you to him, but first can I get you some water or something to eat? You look real pale," he said.

"No, thank you, sir. I have to see the colonel." Katie fought the blackness threatening to overcome her. Maybe the weakness came from not eating or sleeping. She hadn't been able to tend to either one. Food didn't sit well in her stomach, and rest escaped her.

The sergeant reached to help her down from the buckboard, but she ignored his gesture and climbed down alone. She followed him past a row of decaying huts and rough, dark stone buildings with grass-thatched roofs to a small log cabin. Waving strips of dirty white cotton cloth served as window coverings that did little to keep out the elements. Her home with the Comanches had been much more suitable.

The sergeant knocked and disappeared inside. She waited, acutely aware of the gnawing discomfort in the pit of her stomach and the exhaustion that weakened her body and mind. Soldiers and civilians stared at her curiously. Some glared. One man spit at her feet. She blinked and turned from their view. Perhaps the conversation with Colonel Ross wouldn't take too long, and then she could visit with Uncle Seth and Aunt Elizabeth. Surely they would allow her to eat and rest, even if they didn't want her to permanently stay with them.

The fort's gate had closed behind her. Final, as though the past couldn't enter these walls. Familiar surroundings would have offered hope and compassion in her time of grief, but not these strange people living within the perimeters of the fort. *Her whole life seemed to have ended. Everything beautiful and purposeful had vanished forever. Would this ache for Pa ever go away?*

Now she understood why Comanche women cut themselves when they lost a loved one. If she thought it would lessen her pain, she'd gladly use the knife tucked inside her dress.

The soldier stepped from Colonel Ross's office and interrupted her thoughts.

"Miss Colter, the colonel will see you now," he said. "I'll wait outside until your business is finished. Pardon me for not properly introducing myself. My name is Sergeant Sinclair, Peyton Sinclair."

She nodded. "Thank you for seeing me to the colonel's office, Sergeant Sinclair."

"You're welcome, miss. Would you like for me to take your rifle?"

She drew in a deep breath. "I best be holding on to it myself, but I'd be obliged if you would keep an eye on my wagon," she said, capturing a warm gray gaze. Maybe he was trustworthy.

"Miss Colter, I'll stand right outside the door until you are finished with Colonel Ross. You have my word."

She paused to consider the sergeant's request. "All right." She handed him the rifle and stepped inside the colonel's small office. It smelled strongly of tobacco, a familiar odor, but it didn't cause her to feel any more comfortable. A sense of dread encompassed her senses each time she thought about talking to a stranger regarding her father.

A heap of papers was piled high on the colonel's desk. He sat slightly bent, preoccupied with a matter before him. Coffee-colored hair mixed with strands of silver curled at the temples and matched a bushy yet neatly trimmed beard. A pipe rested in the corner of his mouth, yielding an occasional spiral of smoke, and a military hat perched precariously on the corner of his desk. He wore the royal blue jacket of his uniform, but it was shabby, frayed at the seams, and in need of mending. A map of the territory was nailed to the wall behind him. Her eyes swept over the area she once called home.

"I hate paperwork," Colonel Ross mumbled, "and this report must go out with a rider in the morning."

She chose to remain silent until he decided to speak to her. Colonel Ross gathered the shuffled papers into one single stack. He muttered something under his breath and laid them abruptly to one side. Leaning back in his chair, he motioned for her to take a chair in front of his desk.

"Sergeant Sinclair tells me you're Jeremiah Colter's daughter."

"Yes, sir," Katie said, using much of her strength to sit

erect. "He died nearly a week ago."

The colonel merely nodded, and Katie surmised Sergeant Sinclair had already given him that information.

"And he sent you here—to Seth and Elizabeth Colter."

"Yes, sir. I came to your office first. Uncle Seth does not know Pa died."

"I haven't seen Jeremiah in years, and I dare say I've never seen you before. What's your name again?" The colonel picked up his pen. He pulled a wrinkled sheet of paper from inside a desk drawer and meticulously smoothed it out. Dipping the pen into an inkwell, he glanced up for an answer.

"Katherine Grace Colter," she said slowly while he wrote the words. "Pa died on June 12."

"How did he die?" The colonel sounded more compassionate than his earlier tone.

She watched him write June 12, 1857. She hesitated a moment, mentally reliving those last few weeks of her father's life. "Fever and chills, sir. Indian medicine wouldn't cure him."

Colonel Ross humphed. "Seldom does." Once more he dipped his pen into the inkwell and entered Katie's words.

"I have the paper stating the land belonged to my pa, and now to me." She produced a legal document from a deerskin bag.

"I'll take care of the transfer for you, Miss Colter. The last time soldiers rode by your place, it looked deserted. I gather you two have been living with Comanches?"

"Yes, sir." They'd still be with their Indian friends if not for his untimely death.

"My advice is to keep that bit of information to yourself. Folks here don't like hearing about whites preferring to live with Indians. Some of them had family killed and hurt in Indian raids."

"Yes, sir." The hatred was on both sides. Had he ever heard how the Comanches felt about white people invading their land?

Colonel Ross eyed her sharply. "I'm surprised Jeremiah didn't have you stay with them."

"He said it wasn't a fittin' place for a white woman."

"Smart man. And how do you feel about it?"

Silence penetrated the small office.

"I'll be keeping my opinions about Comanches and the like to myself, Colonel Ross," Katie said. "Just like you recommended." She swallowed her disgust. "Can you direct me to where my aunt and uncle live?"

He rose from his chair, scraping the chair legs over the wooden floor. "I'll have Sergeant Sinclair escort you." His voice bellowed out for the sergeant to enter.

"Thank you for your help," she said. "Will you let me know about my land?"

"Yes, Miss Colter. I'm sure you'll make a smooth transition into life here at the fort. Your aunt and uncle are fine people and will most assuredly welcome you."

Sergeant Sinclair still carried her rifle, but at the present she had little use for it. But she knew this soldier's name and rank if needed. While he spoke to Colonel Ross, she noted his average height and broad shoulders. Without a doubt, she could find him if he decided to keep her rifle.

Chapter Two

Katie followed Sergeant Peyton Sinclair to an area reserved for families. Most of the cabins had grass thatch for roofs, but other less sturdy structures had tarpaulins sheltering them from rain and sun. The sergeant knocked on a wooden door of a cabin that stood in good repair, and one she remembered from years before. Would Uncle Seth and Aunt Elizabeth really want her living with them—or would they reject Pa's request? If the latter, she'd return to the Indian village first thing in the morning.

Before Katie further contemplated the matter, the door opened and Aunt Elizabeth greeted the sergeant. The woman possessed a wide, genuine smile, just as Katie remembered. Her aunt looked a little plumper, and white frost wove through wavy brown hair.

"Katie?" she half questioned, half whispered. "Is it you, child?"

Katie couldn't help but return the smile. "Yes, ma'am."

"Oh my," Aunt Elizabeth said and instantly reached for her niece.

Katie couldn't remember when a woman's touch felt so comforting. Many years had passed since a white woman had embraced her with such tenderness.

"You're all grown up, child. And you look so much like

your mother. For a moment I thought I was standing in front of Mary. Goodness, where are my manners? Please come in— and where is your pa?"

She pulled away from her aunt's arms. "Pa died a few days ago."

The woman touched her heart. "Oh child, I'm so sorry. If only your uncle and I had been there to help you."

"He told me to come to the fort—to you and Uncle Seth, but if there isn't room—"

"Nonsense. This will be your home. We love you, and there's plenty of room."

Katie stepped inside onto a stone floor. The small home smelled of roast meat and bread. It tantalized her senses. "Are you sure you don't mind? I can go back to the village."

"No," the older woman said. "We have wanted you near us since your mother died. We've never known the laughter of children, and we'd love to make a home for you."

"Thank you, Aunt Elizabeth. Pa would have been pleased," Katie said, not really certain of her feelings. She'd forgotten the motherly ways of her aunt, and it felt strange to be near her.

Sergeant Sinclair excused himself with the promise of making sure Katie's belongings were delivered to her aunt and uncle. He would personally see to the care of her horses until her uncle instructed otherwise. Before he left, Sergeant Sinclair handed Katie her rifle. The door closed, and the two women were alone.

Katie stood silent, afraid to speak for fear she'd cry. She looked around at the fireplace and the rocker resting nearby. Aunt Elizabeth's cotton window coverings were clean, and everything looked neat and in its place.

"Sit down, child," she said. "You look mighty tired and

thin to the bone. Let me ladle you out some venison stew."

Katie moved to a bench beside a rough-hewed table. "Thank you, I am hungry."

"Good, you can eat, and then we can talk. Katie, you have the same green eyes and tall willowy shape of your mother. Jeremiah was truly blessed." She seated herself across from Katie. "It has been over seven years since I've seen you, and so much has happened in your young life. We didn't find out about your mother until weeks after she and the baby died."

Katie sighed. "It was a boy, and they were gone soon after his birth. I don't think Pa ever got over losing both of them. Within a few weeks, he started spending time with the Comanches. Shortly afterward, we deserted the cabin on our land for the village. I guess he became more Comanche than white."

"We always wondered why he joined up with them."

"I'm not sure. He said white people were a peculiar sort. They wanted to destroy the country, not be a part of it. I remember when Ma was alive, he worked the ground and tended cattle. He often spoke of his Comanche friends, but I never heard him say anything about wanting to live among them."

"What about you?"

Katie smiled, but her heart lacked mirth. "Oh, I always miss Ma, but the years have left more pleasant memories than sadness. In the Comanche village, an old Indian woman took good care of me. She was like a grandmother."

Aunt Elizabeth rose and sliced a generous piece of bread for Katie. She silently watched her eat, as though she understood Katie was absorbed in her own thoughts. "Tell me about Jeremiah. What took his life?"

She finished the bread. "He took a cold that never got any better. The cough and fever grew worse until he slept most of the time. Near the end, he took to talking out of his mind."

"How hard that must have been for you."

She shook off the despair, vowing not to shed any more tears.

"I'm so grateful you came to us."

"He wanted me here," Katie said. "And I promised him."

The door opened, and Uncle Seth stepped inside. He looked thinner and nearly bald. His eyes lit up the moment he saw her.

"I heard Katie had arrived," he said. She rose to greet him, and he gathered her up in his arms. "I closed the blacksmith when the news came. Katie, child, you are so lovely."

"I came because Pa died," she said and clearly saw the pain in Seth's eyes.

"I know," he whispered and held her tighter. "Colonel Ross told me the whole story." He glanced up at his wife. "We will do our best to make a good home for you."

Katie would have felt better if they had not warmly welcomed her. If either of them had any thoughts or misgivings, they hid it well.

Long after they prepared a bed for her near the fire and she attempted to sleep, her thoughts wandered. Her aunt and uncle shared many stories about her mother, and Pa's death brought tears and recollections of days gone by. They appeared glad their niece had come to live with them. Her emotions tore her between the aunt and uncle who called her family and the familiar Indian village. All the way to Fort Davis, she'd hoped they wouldn't have room or means to provide for her. She actually hoped they wouldn't want her. Now that they seemed excited to see her, she felt bewildered. Aunt Elizabeth and Uncle Seth's reception was not what she expected or desired.

Katie's mind slipped back to Lone Eagle. He had worked hard to convince his father that she would be a good wife for a chief's son. Comanches didn't allow intermarriage, but because Pa had saved the chief's life, the old Indian gave his permission. She hadn't told Lone Eagle of Pa's dying words, for he had gone hunting. Instead she told the Indian chief of her promise. Surely he would explain to his son why she had to leave. Lone Eagle loved her, and it pained her to think their plans were destroyed.

The warrior most likely had returned to the village by now, and she fretted over his reaction. Katie knew he'd be angry, and she couldn't blame him. After all, she had sworn her love and devotion to the handsome, ebony-eyed man. Her disappearance would look like she had lied to him—perhaps made a fool of him in front of the whole tribe. Sometimes his quick temper frightened her, but she had long since decided her love could soften this one small fault.

Tired and confused about the future, Katie pushed it all firmly from her mind until the morning. Pa always said poor decisions were made before sleep and wise decisions made with the sunrise.

A week passed, and Katie found herself settling into a new life at Fort Davis. Sometimes she felt confined in the walls of the fort, and sometimes she preferred the floor to the straw-stuffed mattress, but Aunt Elizabeth and Uncle Seth's love set her at peace. The times when she missed the village and earnestly desired to be with her Indian friends, she remembered Pa wanted her to have a new life. Strong in her convictions, Katie firmly pushed aside the old memories.

Had Lone Eagle found another maiden? Many Indian

women found him handsome, and some were jealous when he chose her for his wife. But she simply couldn't break the promise to her father. She must learn to live in the white man's world.

"You've been cooped up much too long," Aunt Elizabeth said one morning after the two had completed morning chores. "Let's go for a walk, and I'll show you around the fort. We can take lunch for Seth and have a little visit."

Katie appeared more eager than she truly felt, but for her aunt's sake she agreed. The grief wore on her heart, and she preferred being alone. The two packed the remains of the previous night's dinner—slices of roasted duck, green beans from their small garden, and thick pieces of freshly baked bread.

"I have the basket," Katie said from outside the cabin door.

"Katie, child, did you forget your bonnet?"

She stepped back inside for the loathsome head covering.

"Must I wear it?" she said. "I don't mind a tanned face."

Aunt Elizabeth touched her cheek. "I know, dear, but here we wear sunbonnets."

Katie obediently covered her blond hair and tied the bonnet beneath her chin.

"Perfect. We'll start our walk to the left. There's always new construction going on. See those six stone buildings? I'm sure you passed them on the day you arrived. Those are the soldiers' barracks, and behind them are cooking sheds where the men eat."

As the two made their way by the barracks, her aunt pointed out storehouses, stables, and corrals.

"And what is that wooden structure?" Katie pointed to a building longer than the barracks.

"The hospital, and it's usually full. On the way back from the blacksmith's, I'll show you the colonel's home. It's quite nice and even has wood floors. I'm pleased with our home, but some of the married folks live in very poorly built cabins. And, oh my, I imagine the soldiers' homes suffer from lack of a woman's touch."

The two continued until they reached the blacksmith. Near the forge, Uncle Seth spoke with a soldier who had his back to them. Upon hearing the women's voices, Sergeant Peyton Sinclair turned to acknowledge the women.

"Good morning, Mrs. Colter, Miss Colter," Peyton said, tipping his hat.

Aunt Elizabeth returned the greeting, but Katie merely nodded.

"Don't let us interrupt your conversation," the older woman said. "We just stopped by to bring Seth his midday meal."

"We've finished business," Uncle Seth said. "And now we're just visiting. Perhaps the sergeant would like to share lunch with me?"

Peyton thanked Uncle Seth but politely refused. "There will be plenty of food for me at the barracks. Thank you just the same." He faced Katie. "And are you settling in to life here at the fort?"

She wanted to be polite. The man had done nothing to her, but his title and his uniform intimidated her.

"I'm becoming accustomed to my surroundings," she said. "Uncle Seth and Aunt Elizabeth have made me feel welcome."

His gray eyes seemed to study her for a brief moment before he spoke again. "I'm pleased to hear a favorable report. I'd hoped you would adapt quickly." He directed his attention to Seth. "Mr. Colter, it's been a pleasure talking with you, and I'll inform the colonel that those horses will be shod in a day or two in time for the patrol. Good day, Mrs. Colter, Miss Colter."

Aunt Elizabeth watched Peyton disappear from the blacksmith. "The sergeant has excellent manners," she said. "He appears to be a fine man."

Katie didn't respond. The workings of the blacksmith interested her more than Sergeant Sinclair.

"Katie, is there something wrong?" Aunt Elizabeth said.

She looked up from the basin of peeled vegetables ready for the stew pot. She'd broken her resolve to not contemplate the past. "Not really, I was remembering things about the Indian village."

"It's natural to miss your home," Aunt Elizabeth said. "You've been introduced to a different life here."

"Yes, ma'am. Living in a teepee and wearing deerskin dresses and fringed moccasins are not the only differences. My diet has changed considerably. In the summer, spring, and early fall our fresh meat was barely cooked. We had berries, a form of bread, and roots. In the winter, we ate dried meat mixed with crushed berries, nuts, and seeds. Some of the things in the Comanche diet made me ill, so Pa always found something else for me."

"How unusual." Aunt Elizabeth tilted her head. "I'm glad your father helped you through the transition."

"We didn't have regular mealtimes, either," she continued. "We ate when we were hungry, usually upon rising and in the evening."

"And did Jeremiah follow Indian practices?"

She wasn't quite sure what her aunt meant. Neither did she know how much to say. Sometimes he rode with the warriors, but he never told her what happened.

"There's no need to answer," her aunt said.

"Oh, I can. He respected their beliefs."

"Well, I'm sure you left treasured friends," Aunt Elizabeth said.

Katie paused. "I do miss Desert Fawn. She was the woman who took care of me when Ma died. I know I'll never see her again, and I loved her very much."

"I'm sorry you're not happy here."

"But I am." She set the vegetables on the floor and hurried to her aunt. "Life in the village. . .well, it was different than here."

"Well, child, I guess it's good that you came to us when you did. If you had waited any longer, you would have most likely married a Comanche."

She avoided her aunt's face and deposited the vegetables into the bubbling stew.

"Are you already. . .married?" Aunt Elizabeth said as though the sound of the question would make it true.

She looking directly at her aunt. "No, Aunt Elizabeth. I'm not, but Pa promised me to a Comanche warrior."

Her aunt trembled. "How did he feel about your leaving the village?"

"He wasn't there at the time, so I told his father."

She touched Katie's shoulder. "Then you didn't have an opportunity to tell him good-bye or explain your father's wishes?"

"No, ma'am," Katie said, barely above a whisper. She swallowed a lump in her throat and blinked back the tears.

"Do you love him?" She gently squeezed Katie's shoulder.

Katie lifted green eyes to her aunt's face. She saw no condemnation, only compassion. "I think I do, but I also know my home is with you and Uncle Seth."

"Would you like to talk about this man?"

"No, it wouldn't do any good. I made a promise to Pa, and I intend to keep my word."

"If ever you want to talk about anything, no matter what it is, I'm here for you."

Katie thought through her words before speaking. "Thank you. Both you and Uncle Seth are so good to me. Some of the other folks here are not as friendly, and I understand how they feel with the Indians burning their homes and killing their families. What they don't understand is the Indians feel the same way about the whites. I'm confused because I see both sides."

Aunt Elizabeth stood by patiently as if ready for Katie to say more, but she had said enough. "I'll pray for God to give you strength. If it comforts you at all, God loves all of us equally no matter the color of our skin."

Katie turned to stir the stew. Again a lump settled in her throat and tears swelled in her eyes.

"Do you think he will come after you?"

Her aunt's words startled her. She hadn't thought about Lone Eagle coming to the fort. Katie well knew the accessibility of the canyon walls. Did he love her enough to consider such a feat? She refused to think about it. The idea of Lone Eagle wanting her badly enough to risk his own life seemed incredible. But in a warrior's eyes, she belonged to him. Once more, she attempted to rid her mind of Lone Eagle and the plans they had made for their life together. Still she missed her warrior more than she dared to admit.

Chapter Three

Uncle Seth and Aunt Elizabeth Colter devoted Sundays to worship and rest. They spent the morning in church, the afternoon in quiet Bible study, and back to church for Sunday evening services. Katie participated in church attendance but not the Bible study. She didn't remember much about "Book" except for a few stories from her childhood. She didn't want to be in church, and she didn't believe or grasp the preacher's words.

Often she pondered over this mysterious Father God. She considered asking her aunt and uncle questions about their worship, except she feared they would be appalled at her lack of biblical knowledge. Comanche gods had been as much a part of her life as the Indians around her, and she didn't know which gods were the right ones. Pa believed in the Indian ways, but on his deathbed he called for the white man's God to end his misery. A lot of good it did to call upon Jesus. Pa suffered more and died.

"Katie, may I ask you something?" Uncle Seth said one evening during supper.

She sensed a serious nature to his voice and immediately gave him proper attention. "Of course." She placed her fork beside the tin plate.

"Do you know how to read?"

"Yes, I do. Ma taught me until she died; then Pa did my lessons, including arithmetic, map reading, and lots of writing." She breathed an inward sigh of relief. "And Ma gave me French lessons and social etiquette, too."

He crossed his arms on the table and appeared to be deep in thought. "I. . .Elizabeth and I. . .wondered why you don't read the Bible."

She bore her attention into his face. "Pa buried ours with Ma. He said we didn't need it."

"How much do you understand about the Almighty God and His Son, Jesus Christ?" Uncle Seth said.

She was trapped, and words escaped her. She would not lie, neither could she bring herself to disappoint her aunt and uncle by admitting how little she knew about their religion.

"Katie, child. If you truly don't know God's Word, it's all right to say so," he said.

She took a deep breath and toyed with her hands resting in her lap. "I remember Ma reading me stories but little else. Sometimes Pa spoke about God and Jesus, especially near the end. Before that, though, he. . .he believed in the same gods as the Comanches."

Aunt Elizabeth gasped. Katie immediately regretted her last words. The older woman's hand reached out to take hers.

"I'm sorry, but I don't believe in your God," Katie said.

"Are you willing to learn?" Seth said.

"Yes, sir, if you like." But her heart cried out no. Their God was cruel.

"I imagine Reverend Cooper's messages are rather boring," Seth went on. "He's not the best of preachers, but he means well. I'm not sure what would be the best way to teach you about God. I think reading the scriptures, beginning with Genesis—no, Matthew then on through to the New

Testament. And if you read in the evenings, we could answer your questions as you go along. How does that sound?"

"And where do I get a Bible?"

"Oh, use ours until we are able to find one for you."

Katie hesitated, wishing she hadn't sounded so agreeable to learn about their worship. "I already have the Comanche gods," she began. "Why do I need yours?" Aunt Elizabeth squeezed her hand, but Katie did not look her way. Her gaze stayed fixed on Uncle Seth's face.

"I understand how you must feel. Everything that has ever belonged to you has been taken away. You've been uprooted from your home and told to live with an aunt and uncle whom you barely know. Now you must feel we are trying to force our religion upon you. Because we love you, we want you to experience the love of Jesus Christ and His gift of eternal life. Your aunt and I worship the one true God, the merciful Creator of the heavens and the earth, but you will have to find out about His love and mercy for yourself."

Anger mounted inside her, even though the years spent among the Indians had trained her to keep a calm composure. "Where was your God when my ma and pa died?" she said, trembling. "I don't see love and mercy in their deaths."

"I wish I had answers for you," Uncle Seth said. "But God has a plan and a purpose for those who love Him. There's a lot of pain and sorrow in this world, and without God this life is worthless. All I'm asking is for you to read His Word, and learn about Him through the scriptures."

"Out of respect, I'll read your Bible," Katie said. "And I will ask questions when the words confuse me." But she refused to believe in the love of a God who allowed pain and suffering.

"Thank you," Seth said, easing his back against the hard chair.

"I'll start tonight, if you like. But remember I'm doing this for you and Aunt Elizabeth. It's the least I can do since you are providing me with a home and treating me so well."

Seth sighed. "You are a blessing to us. We are pleased to have you here, so don't think you have to *do* anything in payment. We love you, Katie, and we're concerned about your spiritual life."

So began Katie's reading of the Bible. She found the stories and accounts interesting but remained skeptical. Questions were answered and passages reread to grasp the meaning. By the third day, she found herself looking forward to the nightly reading. It frustrated her that what she'd agreed to do out of obligation had begun to touch her heart.

Aunt Elizabeth insisted upon cleaning up after supper so Katie could read, but she refused. The evening hours offered ample time for Bible study, and she would do her share of the work.

Sergeant Peyton Sinclair often stopped to see Seth about business. Why didn't he tend to army matters at the blacksmith? Yet she enjoyed talking to him. He had a quick smile and kind eyes, both of which she appreciated.

"Uncle Seth," Katie began one evening after the sergeant had left. "Besides you, Aunt Elizabeth, and Sergeant Sinclair, most of the other folks don't appreciate me being here. Are you sure you want me to stay?"

"Of course. Who has spoken to you?" Seth's face reddened.

"It doesn't matter whom. I was just concerned that they may have said something unkind to you or Aunt Elizabeth."

"Don't you worry a thing about us," Seth said. "Neither of us have ever been prone to gossip and malicious talk."

Aunt Elizabeth poured him the remains of the evening coffee and joined them. "What do you say to them?"

She shouldn't have said a word. This wasn't their problem. "I promised the colonel that I wouldn't say a word about living with the Comanches or how I feel about my Indian friends. Sometimes people's words make me angry, but most of the time the criticisms hurt."

"For certain, you are a better person than they are," Seth said. "Tell me their names, and I'll speak to them."

"It doesn't matter. I don't want to cause any more problems for you than what already exist." She smiled at her beloved aunt and uncle. Their love warmed and comforted her every minute of the day.

One evening Seth questioned Katie about Indian religion.

"Tell me how our God is different from Comanche gods," he said, pulling a chair closer to hers.

She considered her answer for several moments before replying. She was naturally reflective and wanted to make certain her words mirrored accurate knowledge.

"Comanches do believe in a Great Spirit—similar to the God of the Bible, but they also believe the sun, moon, and earth have powers. They don't gather together and worship like folks here, because their religious beliefs are more of an individual experience."

"I heard certain animals and birds mean specific things," Uncle Seth said.

She nodded. "Yes, and they can talk if needed. Thunder is supposed to come from a huge bird and is very powerful. A wolf means something good and a coyote is more. . .mischievous. Of course buffalo and eagles are powerful spirits and are very desirable. A deer can be good or evil, a bear cures wounds, skunks cure serious wounds, and elks are a symbol of strength."

"How would a Comanche get these powers?"

"Older boys go off by themselves to have visions about what holds their guardian spirit. Their powers can be just about anything, depending on their vision."

"Do you think the practice is true?" Uncle Seth said.

Katie pondered his question. "I'm not sure what I believe. The Bible says your God made everything, and He has all the power. If I say the Bible is the truth, then there is no truth in the spirits of the Comanches. I don't want to let go of Indian ways—not yet anyway." She took a deep breath before continuing and hoped her words would convey the inner turmoil of two different worlds.

"Uncle Seth, I find it impossible to believe there is a God who is powerful but loving. Powerful and strong I understand, but it's very difficult for me to add loving and merciful alongside them. The parables and the miracles done by Jesus are interesting, and He certainly went about doing good. But if He was the Son of God, why did He walk with those people when most of them didn't listen to Him?"

"Whoa," he said with a chuckle. "Slow down just a bit. You're a smart girl, Katie, and I see you're thinking and wondering about God's Word. Let's first talk about all the traits of God; then you'll be able to understand Him better."

All evening Uncle Seth talked about the characteristics of a loving, powerful God. He explained how God created and loved all of His children. Even though they were wicked and deserved to die for their sins, He wanted them saved. God decided to send His Son, Jesus, to them. Jesus taught them how much God truly loved them and wanted them to be obedient. God loved them so much that He allowed Jesus to take the blame for their evil ways. Jesus died on a wooden cross so people could one day live in heaven.

She appreciated the simplicity of his explanation, especially when the Bible was often difficult to comprehend. "So Jesus died for the people living then and now?"

"Yes, for all times."

"It's a shame He died for nothing, because people are still evil. His bones went back into the earth His Father created."

"Not exactly. God raised Him from the dead after three days. Jesus now lives in heaven with His Father, and all who believe in Him will one day live with Him, too."

"I need to think more about this," she said at the close of the evening. "My head is spinning like a child's toy."

"Of course, we'll talk again."

Katie smiled. "I'm afraid I have disappointed Aunt Elizabeth by not instantly believing."

"She's concerned because she loves you."

"And I love her. . .both of you so very much. Thank you, Uncle Seth, for taking the time to explain your religion to me."

He touched her arm. "I'm always here for you. For the next couple of days, I'll be working late. Colonel Ross has need of me. You can always ask Elizabeth questions during the day."

She went to bed and woke the following morning with the same thoughts. She wanted to believe in God and accept Jesus as His Son for no other reason than to please her aunt and uncle. But she had so many questions. It made no sense. Her parents had died before their time. Did they now live in heaven with God? Couldn't God have simply spared them a few years longer?

Perhaps she was only being stubborn and rebellious, but this God didn't seem fair. She missed her parents, and she needed them. If she were honest with herself, she'd admit how much she missed her Comanche friends.

In the second week of her reading, Katie found the word *rehoboth* in the twenty-sixth chapter of Genesis. Seeing the word given especially to her by her father startled her, and she read it again. The verse stated that Abraham named a well Rehoboth. Slowly she read verse 22 for the third time, this time aloud.

"And he removed from thence, and digged another well; and for that they strove not: and he called the name of it Rehoboth; and he said, for now the Lord hath made room for us, and we shall be fruitful in the land." Katie closed the Bible. *Pa had believed in God, and he'd told her to leave the Comanches and find her rehoboth—to find her own well in the land so she would be fruitful.*

Perhaps Pa's cries for Jesus were not fevered ranting, but a request for God to take his spirit to heaven. A tingling in the bottom of her stomach frightened her. The sensation caused her to tremble, and she pushed all thoughts of her aunt and uncle's religion aside. Evil spirits might harm them if she did not fear them.

"Katie," Seth said one morning as he left for the blacksmith. "Sergeant Sinclair stopped by to see me yesterday. He asked if he could come calling on you."

Katie's eyes widened, and she heard Aunt Elizabeth laugh.

"I knew it," she said, still laughing. "I knew from the start the sergeant liked the looks of our Katie."

"It's your decision," Uncle Seth said. "I told him I needed to ask you first."

Her thoughts flew to Lone Eagle, but she dared not

say anything about the warrior. "I need some time to think about it."

"I'll tell him so." He smiled. "He's not the only one who has expressed an interest in you, but up until now I haven't felt a need to talk to you about courtin' matters. You're seventeen, right?"

"Yes, sir, seventeen last January."

"I didn't like the looks or the actions of a few others who expressed interest, but I like the sergeant. He's a good man and a respected leader."

"Can we talk about it this evening?" Katie's words trembled.

"Seth, you go on now. You'll have her in tears—embarrassing her so. She's just being a woman, thinking things through."

All morning long, Katie pondered over Sergeant Sinclair wanting to court her. This strange notion bothered her. What would Lone Eagle do if he found out a white man wanted to spend an evening with her? Katie well understood what courtin' meant, and she knew exactly what the warrior would do. Lone Eagle would kill him.

But I'm not in the Comanche village anymore. I am a white woman in a white man's world. Any feelings I ever had for Lone Eagle have to be forgotten. He will live in his world without me, and I must go on with my life without him.

At midday Katie offered to take food for Seth to the blacksmith. During their visit, she agreed for Sergeant Sinclair to come calling.

Chapter Four

Aunt Elizabeth hummed a lively tune while mending Uncle Seth's shirts. As a blacksmith, he burned holes in his clothes faster than she could keep them repaired. The sound of Katie's aunt's voice soothed the apprehension about Sergeant Sinclair's visit that evening while she kneaded bread. Katie needed a distraction to keep from thinking about what Lone Eagle would do if he knew about the evening plans.

Her mind slipped back to Lone Eagle's parting words—the last time she saw him before her father died.

According to the tribe's tradition, young couples were not supposed to meet in public, so they arranged secret places for their conversing. Lone Eagle usually intercepted Katie on her way to get water. It was a trip she had to make frequently, and she never failed to look for the warrior standing among the trees near the riverbank. It became a game because he never hid in the same place twice. This time he stood straight in her path.

"Nei mah-tao-yo *[My little one]*," Lone Eagle had whispered.

"Hein ein mah-su-ite? *[What do you want?]*" Katie said, pretending to be annoyed with the interruption.

Stealing behind her, Lone Eagle's arms encircled her waist then turned her to face him. They held each other for several moments, basking in the warmth of young love. He released her long enough to tell her of the gifts waiting at Jeremiah's tent. Three horses were a generous gift in compensation for a wife, but Lone Eagle wanted the white warrior to know how much Katie meant to him. If her father accepted the horses, then he agreed to their marriage. Lone Eagle told her he would be gone for several days. When he returned, the two would live as husband and wife. She well remembered the sound of Lone Eagle's deep voice, the longing in his ebony eyes, and the warmth of his arms embracing her. Only his quick temper bothered her.

With a punch to the bread dough, Katie faced confusion and fear. By now she would have been Lone Eagle's wife. His property.

Katie sensed her aunt's gaze upon her, and she turned to smile into the face of the woman. If Katie felt certain of anything, it was the love of her aunt and uncle. In a world where everything had been snatched from her, she cherished her aunt and uncle. Tomorrow they, too, could be taken away, but today they were alive and real. Today she could reach out and touch them, and their words and faces were permanently etched in her mind. Ma and Pa, Lone Eagle, and Aunt Elizabeth and Uncle Seth were all those she loved, and it didn't matter whether they were in the flesh—in her heart they lived on.

"I've taken the liberty to arrange something for you this afternoon," Aunt Elizabeth said. A sparkle lit up her eyes.

"And what might that be?" Katie said.

"One of my friends, Martha Jameson, has a daughter your age, and I asked them to come by for a visit. The young lady's name is Lauren. I hope you don't mind," she said. Now reservation rose in her voice.

Katie paused a bit and considered the idea of having a

friend her own age. Never had she experienced such a delight. "I think it's a wonderful idea."

"Katie, child, you amaze me how you think about things before you answer." She laughed and wiped her hands with her apron. "I know you inherited that trait from Jeremiah. Many times he would hesitate in replying to our questions—always deliberating every part of other folks' words."

"I guess I'm my father's child," Katie said, while sadness washed over her. "I try not to be impulsive. Pa said to always put yourself in the place of the one doing the talking. If you can think like they do, then you can understand their hearts."

"And what does this heart say?"

Katie pressed her finger to her lips. "I believe we need to make a honey cake and dust off the teacups for we have guests this afternoon. And thank you for giving me something to think about other than Sergeant Sinclair coming by tonight. I'm nervous."

"I'm here for whatever you want to talk about."

While they readied for the visit, Aunt Elizabeth talked endlessly about Martha and Lauren, their large family, and their love for each other. The appointed hour soon arrived. The small home smelled inviting with the warm honey cake and freshly brewed tea.

"They're here," her aunt said when a rap sounded at the door.

Katie tore off her apron and hung it on a peg beside the front door. She shook a bit, wanting friends but apprehensive of what they knew about her.

Aunt Elizabeth opened the door. "Martha, Lauren, it's so good to see you. Do come in and meet my niece, Katie Colter."

One look at Martha and Lauren Jameson, and Katie felt at ease. Any concern she may have experienced about her association with the Comanches disappeared when they hugged her and welcomed her to Fort Davis.

Martha towered over Aunt Elizabeth and Katie. She was a large-boned woman with white-gray hair and the telltale signs of hard work lining her face. Lauren didn't resemble her mother except in the kind mannerisms. She barely stood five feet tall, tiny framed, and her hair matched the color of desert clay. Lauren appeared to be no more than a child, when in fact she had just celebrated her eighteenth birthday.

Elizabeth ushered the women to their seats, brightening with the guests. Welcoming others into her home was indeed a gift.

"It's been so long since I've enjoyed a good cup of tea," Martha said, setting the delicate china cup back on its saucer. "You really didn't need to make such a fuss, Elizabeth. Lauren and I have been meaning to come calling on you and Katie."

Katie peered into Martha's soft brown eyes, as inviting and liquid as though pure love flowed through them.

"And I've been enjoying her company so much that I haven't properly introduced her to other folks. Katie is such a help, I don't know what I ever did without her." Pride rose in Aunt Elizabeth's voice as she cut each of them a generous slice of honey cake.

"I'm just so pleased that someone here is my age." Lauren's sky blue eyes held the same warmth as her mother's, and she laughed easily. "How do you like our Fort Davis?"

She must force herself to be congenial. "It certainly is different than living out in the wild with Pa. Aunt Elizabeth and Uncle Seth have been wonderful, and I'm learning new things every day. Are you with the army?"

Lauren shook her head, but Martha chose to reply. "No, we're just seeking shelter until the territory is safer. We have a farm a few miles from here, but Indians kept stealing our cattle and horses, and then they burned our barn. Luckily no one was killed."

Katie's stomach soured. If these women were aware of her life with the Comanches, they didn't reveal it. Had Pa been a part of this? She hoped not, but why deceive herself?

Martha continued. "But in answer to your question, Lauren is fixin' to be part of the army."

A warm blush rose in Lauren's face. "I'm getting married soon to one of the soldiers."

For a moment, Katie felt envious of Lauren's happiness, but she elected to ignore her jealousy and wish Lauren the best.

"As pretty as you are, Katie, it won't be long before a handsome soldier whisks you off your feet," Martha said.

"Oh, it will be a long time before I contemplate marriage." What would her new friends say if they knew about Lone Eagle?

"Just look at you." Martha laughed. "Those green eyes and blond hair will have every soldier and civilian within miles knocking on your uncle's door."

The woman meant well—she simply had no idea what a relationship with a white man meant for her. "I think I'll just wait to make sure I get the finest one of them."

Elizabeth's hand slipped around her waist as though her aunt sensed the turmoil going on inside her head and heart.

Martha extended an invitation for the Colter women to visit the Jameson household the following week. They could combine tea and talk over a quilting session for Lauren's new home.

As dusk settled, Aunt Elizabeth and Katie chatted about the afternoon guests.

"Did you enjoy Martha and Lauren?" her aunt said while the two prepared dinner.

"Yes, ma'am, very much. Their visit was much too short. I had few friends in the village. Indian girls were suspicious of me. Mrs. Jameson and Lauren treated me like family, although I wonder about their offer of friendship if they knew the truth about me."

"Do you want to forgo seeing them next week?"

Katie drew in a ragged breath. "No, I gave my word to Pa. This is what I must do."

She silently helped prepare the evening meal. Her mind replayed the afternoon with Martha and Lauren Jameson. Both mother and daughter had reached out to her in kindness. Surely they had heard about her association with the Comanches, but they neither questioned her nor shunned her company. Should she tell them?

Katie picked at the venison stew before her. Ever since the shadows of dusk had crept across the two-room dwelling, her thoughts twisted and turned about Sergeant Sinclair's visit. She wanted to please her aunt and uncle, but she would have nothing more than a friendship with Sergeant Sinclair.

"I shouldn't have given my permission for the sergeant to come courtin'," Uncle Seth said as he reached for another piece of corn bread. "It's too soon. Why, I don't know what I was thinking. Here you are grieving over Jeremiah, and I worry you with a soldier."

"No, Uncle, really it's all right. Sooner or later I would have to go through this, and today it has kept me from missing Pa. You were right in giving him approval." Why couldn't her heart believe her words? She wanted to be obedient and honor Pa, but the reservations in her spirit held her captive.

"But, I didn't know about. . .how you were promised to a Comanche warrior," he said.

Katie could not reply quickly. To please him, she cut into a piece of venison. While she slowly chewed the meat, her thoughts formed into words.

"You could have decided not to mention Lone Eagle, but the fact you did tells me you are sensitive to my feelings. You could have demanded I never mention the Comanches, but you chose not to criticize or ridicule the only life I've known. My gods are not the same as yours, and still both of you continue to love me and have patience with my hesitancy to accept your ways. I've never met anyone like you or Aunt Elizabeth. How could I ever protest anything you say or do?" She took a deep breath before she could continue speaking. "Sometimes I feel like a child with so much to learn, and other times I feel like an old woman with so much to forget. I miss the past, but I made a promise to Pa. If I had stayed with the Comanches, I would have learned to despise what I now love. Pa said that here I'd find my rehoboth. Without the Bible, how could I ever learn what he wanted for me?" Tears flowed freely down her cheeks, not those of anger or frustration but of pleading for understanding when she didn't comprehend all the changes in her life.

"God is working in your life, child," Uncle Seth said. "Even though you don't recognize it. Let me make this evening easier for you to bear. I'll tell the sergeant you aren't feeling well."

She shook her head. "I want tonight to go as planned. I can't run from people who are different, because too many folks have done it to me. Sergeant Sinclair is kind, and I look forward to getting to know him."

"You're a sweet, dear girl," Aunt Elizabeth said.

"Well, I don't think so." She glanced up. "And that's a fact. I'm much too stubborn, and I long for the ways of the Indians. The things I repeat to you are the lessons Pa taught me, nothing more. You two are both loving and wise. You don't judge me or pressure me about anything." She rose from the table. "Now, if you will excuse me, I'd like to get ready for the sergeant while you finish eating."

She stepped outside into the fresh air and breathed in deeply. She didn't want her aunt and uncle to think she was anything other than a seventeen-year-old orphan struggling with a new life. Uncle Seth and Aunt Elizabeth saw only her youth and naiveté in the white man's world, but they would cringe if they could read her thoughts, not necessarily rebellion but so many questions.

She understood the ways of a man and a woman and had been tempted to give up her innocence on more than one occasion.

She'd seen the scalps of white men, women, and children hanging from the belts of warriors and didn't voice her alarm to Pa.

She believed the land belonged to the Indians, and the white men were thieves to try and take it from them.

She still felt a need to return to the village, even if it meant breaking her promise to Pa.

And Katie knew in the white man's eyes she was a heathen and a pagan because she believed in Comanche gods.

Those things would disappoint the aunt and uncle who loved her dearly, and Katie couldn't bring herself to ever reveal her innermost thoughts.

No sooner was the table cleared and cleanup completed than Peyton Sinclair arrived. Hat in hand, he appeared more nervous than Katie. Uncle Seth must have felt sorry for the man, for he suggested the two young people enjoy the mild temperatures in an evening stroll. Once outside the confines of the small house and in the dim twilight where the two could hide their uneasiness, they were able to relax. Peyton's voice gained confidence, and soon their conversation flowed with the familiarity they had shared in the past.

"Is life here with your aunt and uncle agreeable?" Peyton said.

"I'm slowly becoming accustomed to it," Katie said. "Most of the time, I have to concentrate on the fact that I am white and not an Indian."

Peyton laughed easily. "I have never seen a blond Indian before."

She liked this man. "It's not what is on the outside of me, but what's in my heart."

"Miss Colter, are you always so melancholy and serious?"

She pondered his observation. True, she didn't laugh as much since Pa died. "I just think too much."

"I would consider it an honor to be able to make you smile more," he said. "You are much too lovely to spend the hours in sadness, but grieving takes time."

"Yes, it does," she said. The couple walked by two soldiers who politely saluted Peyton and tipped their hats to her.

"They will all be talking about you tomorrow," she said.

"Good." And in the moonlit shadows of evening, she saw him smile.

"They are probably betting whether I will take your scalp or not."

"Would you?"

"Probably not. I don't carry a knife here at the fort."

"Ah, not only is she pretty, but she has a sense of humor." He chuckled. "I'll give you my heart, but I'll keep my hair."

DIANN MILLS

"You have a selfish attitude, Sergeant Sinclair, although I will give it proper thought. What color are your eyes?"

"Do you want them, too?" he said with another chuckle.

"No, sir." Katie relaxed and enjoyed their bantering. "I only remember they are soft and kind—perhaps gray?"

"Yes, gray, and thank you for the compliment. I know yours are green. They remind me of a jade necklace my grandfather gave to my grandmother upon the birth of my father."

"What a beautiful story. My mother used to tell me they reminded her of an exotic stone, I guess the same thing." Katie laughed lightly for the first time. "Of course both of my parents complained my eyes gave away my stubborn streak, 'cold as stone' they would say."

The two walked a little farther in silence. "Sergeant Sinclair, would you tell me about yourself?"

"Please, call me Peyton."

"If you will call me Katie."

"Now that we are beyond the formalities, I'm not an interesting person," he said. "A soldier's life is long and repetitious. We begin duty at sunrise, and the day ends around eight thirty."

"Oh, but you were a little boy once. You dreamed of things and of places you'd like to go. And I'm sure you always imagined yourself a hero."

"I guess I did, but I think your life has been more exciting than mine."

A call for the sergeant captured their attention. A soldier rushed to their side, acknowledged Peyton's rank, and then explained the need for Peyton to see Colonel Ross immediately.

"I need to escort Miss Colter back home," Peyton said. "How crucial is this?"

The soldier glanced at Katie then back to Peyton. "Excuse

42

me, sir, but Comanches attacked another family of settlers. What's left of 'em are in front of Colonel Ross's office. I've already fetched the doctor for the wounded ones. He needs you right away."

"Who are these people?" Peyton said.

"The Lawrence family."

"They had twelve children," Peyton said, his voice cold and distant.

"Not anymore, sir. There's only three left. The rest killed and scalped by them cursed Comanches." The soldier shifted from one foot to another. "Sorry, Miss Colter. I didn't mean to upset you."

She ignored the implication. "Is there anything I can do?"

"Don't imagine so, miss," the soldier said. "You bein' a Colter and all."

Chapter Five

"Soldier, your remark was uncalled for," Peyton said. "You get on back to Colonel Ross and tell him I will be there shortly."

"Yes, sir." The soldier saluted. "I apologize for the remark, sir."

"Don't be apologizing to me. It's the young lady you have insulted."

Katie nodded politely to the soldier's forced retraction of words. She knew he meant exactly what he'd said. The soldier merely repeated what most other folks said and thought about her. She was Jeremiah Colter's daughter, an Indian lover, just like one of them murdering savages.

Confusion pulled and tugged at her heart. Didn't she believe the Comanches were right in defending their own land? And did she not love a Comanche warrior and long to be with him? Katie knew the answers to those questions were still yes, but the attack upon this family seemed different. Wrong. How could the Lawrences have defended themselves against an armed band of Indians? A family of fourteen had been diminished to three. She failed to see any reason or purpose in their murders. Why the bloodshed? What good could come from destroying a man's family?

"Peyton, I want to go with you," she said. "I want to help those who saw their loved ones die."

He stared at her oddly, as well as the other soldier. "It may be very ugly, and the colonel may send you home."

"I realize that, but I have to try."

No measure of direction could have prepared her for the horror of bloody, mutilated bodies heaped into the back of a wagon. Peyton told her not to look, but when a torch flashed in front of her eyes, she looked directly into the pile of bodies to avoid being blinded. Her stomach curdled. Terror and nausea swept over her while the image of the butchered family burned in her mind. Peyton grabbed her trembling shoulders and whirled her away from the wagon.

This Pa had spared her.

"Let me get one of the soldiers to escort you back home," he said. "This is no place for a woman. I should have had more sense than to allow you to come."

She lifted her chin. "The survivors—they need a place to stay away from this nightmare." She couldn't describe how she felt about needing to help when she didn't understand her own compulsion.

"Others can help."

"Then it's my turn."

"Where are the remaining family members?" Peyton said to a soldier.

The man pointed to a small boy holding a crying baby in the doorway of Colonel Ross's office. Another soldier deliberately blocked the boy's vision from the wagon.

"Wasn't there a third?" Peyton said.

"The doc is working on him. He's hurt pretty bad. Don't know how he loaded his family into this wagon and got them here."

"Sometimes need drives a man beyond what he normally can do," Peyton said.

Katie pushed through the crowd to the children. Instantly she knelt beside a dark-haired young boy.

"Come with me," she said. "I know a place you can rest." She reached for the baby, but he refused to let her go. "Let me help you." She stroked his hair, never taking her eyes off his young face. "I'll help you with the baby."

The boy appeared to be dazed—his eyes bore into the darkness.

"She's hungry," he finally said.

"We can get her something to eat. What's her name?" One hand continued to weave her fingers through his hair and the other rested on the baby's blanket.

"Emily."

"And what is your name?"

"Jacob."

"Well, Jacob. Let's go where it's quiet and feed your baby sister."

Jacob glanced toward the wagon, but the soldier moved within his eyesight. Slowly he relinquished the baby and set her in Katie's arms. She looked for a familiar face and caught the attention of the soldier who had first alerted Peyton to the tragedy.

"Can you walk me back to my aunt and uncle's?" she said, gathering up the shaking, cold hand of little Jacob.

"You're doing a mighty fine thing, miss," the soldier said as they moved away from the crowd.

"For a Colter?"

The soldier said nothing more.

Jacob Lawrence, age six, and his year-old sister, Emily, were the only surviving members of the Lawrence family. Their brother

Jason died before morning. No one knew how the two youngest members of the family escaped the murders, and Jacob seemingly chose to blot out the memory of the deaths from his mind. The parents and ten children were buried alongside each other in the Limpia Valley, where the wildflowers grew and blossomed each spring.

Katie found a sense of renewed spirit by tending to the children. The sadness and grief, which filled so much of her hours, vanished in light of caring for the orphans. She gave up her bed for Jacob, and Uncle Seth constructed a cradle for Emily. At night, when Jacob cried out with the nightmares plaguing his little mind, Katie held him close until sleep allowed him to forget. And when Jacob's sobbing woke Emily, Katie held them both. One night in the darkness she felt Aunt Elizabeth's arms around them all.

"Dear Lord, have mercy on these little children. Let them sleep in peace and open their eyes to Your love."

Uncle Seth's hand rested on Katie's shoulder, and his deep calm voice gave her strength.

"Oh merciful Lord, we praise Your almighty name. We thank You for preserving the lives of Jacob and Emily. We humbly ask that You bring healing to their minds, and grant them a heart that loves You."

Katie swallowed her tears and held tightly to the children. Seth's prayer frustrated her. Why did he praise the same God who had brought such misfortune to the Lawrence family?

In the days following, Aunt Elizabeth seemed to beam with the presence of youth and life around her. She fussed over Katie for the circles beneath her eyes but stayed up late fashioning clothes for Jacob and Emily. Katie teased her for balancing both children on her full lap while telling stories.

Martha and Lauren assisted in finding additional clothes and made frequent visits to check on all of those living in the Colter household. Even the soldier who had insulted her that tragic evening arrived with a candy stick for Jacob and words of encouragement for the Colters. And Peyton didn't miss a day, if only for a moment, to call upon all of them. He never came empty handed, even though his gift might be nothing more than a polished rock for Jacob. Katie found herself looking forward to his visits. His half smile and wit moved her to laughter time and time again. She couldn't remember ever feeling so content.

"Aunt Elizabeth, do you mind if I take the children to pick flowers?" Katie said late one morning. "I don't think they will be in bloom much longer with the fall weather."

"I have a mind to go with you, too," the older woman said.

"Good. Before we know it, cold weather will keep us around the fire."

The two gathered up Jacob and Emily and set out for the lush grasslands around Limpia. When Katie pointed out sunflowers in full bloom, Jacob let go of her hand and hurried to the thick of them. The women sat and allowed Emily to play in the midst of the wildflowers.

"I love this time of year, don't you?" Katie said.

Her aunt nodded. "Even if we know winter is on its way." She snatched up a yellow bloom from Emily's hand. "No, ma'am, not in your mouth. I don't know if these are poisonous or not, but I'm not taking any chances."

Katie shook her head at Emily. "I'd like to make you a wreath for your hair, but I'm afraid you would eat it."

"Go ahead, she'd look so pretty," Aunt Elizabeth said. "I'll keep it out of her mouth."

Katie called for Jacob, and the two headed for a patch of reddish-colored mountain sage. The little boy sat quietly and watched Katie twist and turn the vines and blossoms into a wreath. Katie sat it atop his head.

"Boys don't wear flowers," he said. "Give it to Emily." Jacob raced to her aunt and placed the flower ring on his sister's head.

"Beautiful," Aunt Elizabeth said. "How nice of you, Jacob, to think of your sister."

He grinned, and then something else got his attention. "Look over there." He pointed. "Here comes Sergeant Sinclair."

Katie didn't quite know what to think of Peyton joining them, but she did look forward to talking with him.

"That young man is smitten," Aunt Elizabeth said.

"Oh, Aunt Elizabeth, he's just interested in the children."

Elizabeth laughed and Katie's face warmed. "We shall see."

"Hello," Peyton called, and Jacob waved.

"We're over here in the flowers, Sergeant."

"I see," Peyton said as he bent down to Jacob's level. "And look at your sister." He removed his cap, and Emily tugged at his sandy hair.

"Katie made it," Jacob said. "And I put it on her head."

Peyton's eyes flew to Katie, and Aunt Elizabeth coughed quite noticeably.

"Unless you have urgent business, why don't you and Katie take a walk?" her aunt said.

"Me, too," Jacob said.

"Of course, you," Peyton said, ruffling Jacob's hair. "What do you say, Katie?"

"How can I refuse? Isn't this weather wonderful?"

Peyton agreed and the three walked on through the valley.

"I only have a little while," Peyton said. "I have drills yet to do."

"Well, all of us appreciate your checking so often on the children," Katie said. "They love seeing you."

"Do you think Jacob and Emily are the only reasons why I visit?"

A slow rise of color warmed her cheeks. Peyton glanced her way and laughed. "I like your aunt's biscuits."

She shook her head and wrinkled her nose at him. She understood exactly what he meant.

"And I like her niece," he added. "She has the greenest eyes and the blondest hair I've ever seen."

"Emily doesn't have green eyes," Jacob said, obviously hearing every word. "You must be talking about Katie."

"Are you sure, Jacob?" Peyton said, as though surprised.

"Yep, and I bet if you were nice, she would make you a flower wreath, too. It's 'posed to be just for girls, but maybe it would be all right for a soldier."

"Splendid, I'd like that," Peyton said, and they stopped there, surrounded by wildflowers, for Katie to weave a wreath for him.

"I thought you were short on time," she said.

"I have time for this." He grinned, and she turned her attention to the flowers.

"Take off your hat," Jacob said to Peyton once she finished. "Now let Katie put it on your head like she did Emily."

Embarrassment coursed through her with Jacob's insistence, but she obliged. As the wreath sat perfectly balanced on Peyton's head, Jacob called for Aunt Elizabeth to come and see. Peyton's face matched the color of her own.

How much she had grown to like Peyton Sinclair and his incessant teasing.

"Are you understanding tonight's scripture?" Uncle Seth said one evening after the children had gone to bed. Katie had read for some time, and now the Bible lay open on her lap.

"I've been reading about Moses and how God used him to deliver the Israelites from the hands of the Egyptians."

"And what about that passage do you find most interesting?" he said.

Katie considered the question before she replied. "God took Moses from his home in the wilderness and sent him back to his own people in Egypt because God had a job for Moses. He didn't want to talk to Pharaoh, but God told him to go, and Moses went. Moses believed that God would free the enslaved Israelites." *Do I believe these words?* "He was obedient to his heavenly Father." She closed the Bible and handed it to her uncle.

"Do you feel a bond with Moses?" Uncle Seth said.

Katie looked over at the sleeping children and listened to the crackling fire. Her eyes searched the face of Aunt Elizabeth, who had turned her attention from sewing to hear Katie's answer. Katie glanced back to the lined face of her uncle.

"Yes, I do. I think God wanted me to stop being selfish and lend a hand to someone who really needed it. He had to pull me away from the Indian village to help these children." She nodded toward Jacob and Emily. "But oh my, the burden it has placed upon you two. I must find a way to help provide for all of us."

"Nonsense, child. One doesn't look at gifts as being burdens," Aunt Elizabeth wiped a single tear from her eye. "All my life I prayed for children, and now I have three. God allowed Seth and me to love and care for three special people who needed us."

"It amazes me how your God might use me, an unbeliever, to carry out His plan," Katie said.

"But, Katie child, your stating God used you says you are a believer," Uncle Seth said quietly.

Katie paused and regarded Seth's words. *Have I started to believe the words of the Bible?* When did her heart begin to open up to God? Was it the night she first saw the children? She well remembered the hideous depredation of human bodies and the fury that burned inside her for the horrible injustices. At times reminders of Comanche spirits and gods triggered her thoughts, but she no longer dwelled upon them. She couldn't remember the last time she feared evil spirits might harm her aunt and uncle for the Bible reading. Slowly the superstitions had faded, and her mind lingered more and more upon the Word of God. Katie now scribbled scripture from Reverend Cooper's sermons and later looked them up in Uncle Elizabeth and Uncle Seth's Bible. Perhaps now marked the time to purchase her own. A few gold pieces lay in the bottom of her trunk. She needed a Bible, and she could give the remaining gold pieces to her uncle. It would buy provisions for all of them for a long time.

Had she really come to accept the same God as her aunt and uncle? She wasn't sure, except His ways were becoming more of her own.

Almost two weeks later, Peyton paid an unexpected call to the Colter home. Usually he visited much later in the evening, when he had been relieved of his duties and could play with the children. Jacob and Emily had just fallen asleep for an afternoon nap when he arrived. Rather than accepting Aunt Elizabeth's invitation to step inside, Peyton stood in the doorway and asked her aunt if he could speak with Katie privately.

The seriousness of Peyton's voice alarmed Katie. Aunt Elizabeth gave her silent permission, and Katie followed him into the sunlight. She didn't question him, for he looked far too preoccupied with his thoughts.

"Katie," he began once they were several feet from the house. "The colonel wants to see you, but I want you to know that you have every right to refuse."

"All right," she said slowly, observing the concern in his gray eyes. "What does he want of me? Does it have anything to do with my land?"

"It has nothing to do with your land. One of the scouts, a Kiowa, says he needs to speak to you."

Her heart thudded. What could this mean? "About what?"

Peyton shrugged. "I don't know exactly, and he won't tell the colonel."

"That's strange," Katie said, attempting to sort out her thoughts on the matter. "I probably should ask Uncle Seth's permission first."

"I already have," he said. "At first he declined, stating he wouldn't have you upset; then he said you should decide."

Katie looked above her to the canyon walls where attacking Indians could easily surprise the soldiers. The vulnerability of the fort's location never frightened her before the night of the Lawrence murders. She'd always felt safe because of her relationship with the Comanches. It didn't occur to her that the friendship with the Indians would ever change until she saw for herself what hatred could actually do. Now she feared for all those people living in and around Fort Davis.

She despised the Lawrence murders, but their deaths didn't mean she could willingly pick up a rifle against a Comanche. She couldn't deny her past or love for her friends, both Comanche and white. But if the Comanches decided to attack the fort in large numbers, no one would be spared. Would they kill her, too?

Did her white skin mark her a victim, just like the Lawrence family? The land, always the land, echoed the war cry from both sides. If only the two could compromise for a peaceable solution.

Now a Kiowa Indian wanted to talk to her. Peyton said the man was a scout. He could easily spy for the army or the Indians, depending on who held his loyalties or promised the most in return. Many Comanches considered the Kiowa an inferior race, and she couldn't help but be suspicious of his motives.

Others would hear of this meeting, and they would start gossiping again. She shouldn't care what anyone said about her business, except it involved her aunt and uncle. Uncle Seth must have originally refused the colonel's request in order to protect his niece from malicious gossip. After further deliberation, Uncle Seth must have decided she should be the one to choose whether to speak to the Kiowa.

For the first time in her life, she didn't want to talk to an Indian.

"I don't have any idea what he wants, but I am willing to find out," she finally said.

Side by side, the two walked the short distance to the colonel's cabin. Inside, the Indian scout waited with Colonel Ross.

"Thank you for coming, Miss Colter," the colonel said with no trace of emotion. He motioned for Katie to sit down, and she obeyed. Not once did she give the Indian notice.

"This man is a Kiowa scout for the army. He states he has business with you," the colonel said.

She carefully observed the Kiowa. "I don't know him."

The Kiowa turned to her. "I must talk with you alone. This is important."

"If you have anything to say to me, then do so in front of these men." She would not be above reproach.

"I have a message from Lone Eagle," the Indian said in Comanche.

Every nerve in her body responded to the Indian's choice of tongue, but she masked her surprise and suspicion.

"Why should I believe you, a Kiowa?" she said in the same tongue. "You are paid by the army. Are you a spy?"

The Indian ignored her question. "Lone Eagle does not honor the promise made to your father."

The man spoke the truth, and she'd be a fool not to believe him. Only Lone Eagle's father, Swift Arrow, knew of Pa's dying words. Yet, she couldn't trust him.

"What promise do you speak of?" Katie said.

"To leave the Comanche village and return to your own people—as Jeremiah Colter requested before he breathed his last."

Katie nodded, still refraining from revealing any emotion. "Is that all of the message? All Lone Eagle asked is for you to tell me of his disapproval?"

"Lone Eagle says you must return to the village."

"I can't go back. I gave my father my word to live among the whites. I was with him when he breathed his last."

"Lone Eagle does not ask but demands as your husband. Your place is with him."

"The marriage was not consummated."

"Your father accepted the gift of horses. You are Lone Eagle's wife."

"I agree. My father kept the horses. But I left them at the village with the other gifts. My home is here."

"You cause great anger in Lone Eagle's heart. His hatred for the whites burns even more. You will die with the rest of the whites."

Chapter Six

Anger and fear raced through Katie's blood, and she fought hard to keep her emotions from spilling over.

"So those are Lone Eagle's words?" Katie said.

"Yes, all whites will die at the hand of the Comanches. Already Swift Arrow speaks to unite the warriors. They will be driven from the land."

Katie glanced at Colonel Ross, who did not understand a word of their conversation. She dare not turn and face Peyton. She did not want these two men dead or any of the others. Neither did she desire Lone Eagle killed.

"If I go back to him, would he reconsider his attack against the fort and the people living near it?"

"You think of yourself more important than you are," the Kiowa sneered. "Indian doesn't fight for a woman, but honor and the land of their fathers."

"I understand full well the desires of a warrior," she said. "But peace would be better. Tell Lone Eagle, I desire peace. Tell him I will break my promise to my father and return to the village if he will cease talks of war."

The Kiowa faced Colonel Ross and spoke in English. "I wish to leave now."

Colonel Ross nodded, and Peyton stepped away from the door. Weak and physically ill with the outcome of the meeting, she desired to leave the two men, too. How much of the conversation should the colonel and Peyton hear? What could the soldiers do in the event of an attack? She stood frozen to the wood floor. She didn't want the responsibility of knowing what the Comanches planned. . . . Perhaps if she explained part of the Kiowa's mission, reinforcements from other army posts could be obtained. The trail to San Antonio or El Paso was desolate and invited Indian raids. The dangerous passage marked the key reason the army first built Fort Davis. Leaders in Washington knew the peril of this part of the country and believed the fort lay in a strategic position. Anyone viewing the fort soon realized the canyon walls could very well imprison those living inside. But now wasn't the time to debate the army's lack of good sense. Katie didn't have the mind of the army. Colonel Ross might have the perfect solution to ward off an Indian attack. Defending civilians and the settlers were his lifeblood. His solution might be quite simple.

"Miss Colter, you look pale," Colonel Ross said, interrupting her racing thoughts. "Shall I have a soldier fetch smelling salts?"

Katie shook her head. She must say something about the Kiowa's threats.

"Colonel Ross. Are the words spoken in this room private?"

"Yes, Miss Colter, if you so desire. Sergeant Sinclair?"

"Yes, sir. Miss Colter's words are confidential."

"Perhaps additional sentries for the canyon walls might be a consideration." She trembled, while fear for others weighed on her heart.

Colonel Ross sat erect and appropriately gave Katie his full attention. "So the Kiowas are planning an attack?"

She folded her hands in her lap. They were moist and cold, like Jacob's hands the night she brought home the children.

"Not the Kiowas, but the Comanches." She secured eye contact with the colonel. "I don't think the Kiowa lied because his words held other matters of truth."

"Did he say when?" the colonel said.

"No, sir. He most likely didn't know for certain. You and I both know Comanche warfare is in stages—circling and striking when they have the advantage."

"Why did he have to speak with you about it?" the colonel said.

"I think, sir, his purpose was to see my reaction. Perhaps Swift Arrow wondered if I had abandoned all the Comanche ways."

"And was he satisfied?"

Katie gave Colonel Ross a wry smile. "I believe in peace."

"Is there anything else I need to be aware of? The conversation with the Kiowa appeared longer, and the sergeant and I would have to be fools not to note the tension."

She nodded. "The other matter had nothing to do with their talks of war."

The walk back home proved more of silence than words. Katie pondered every word spoken with the Kiowa. Granted, the Comanches had hit settlers and small bands of travelers for a number of years. More than once they'd climbed the canyon walls into Fort Davis and struck terror. The Comanches, with their strategic element of surprise, always kept the army at a disadvantage. She had little else to tell Colonel Ross. The Indians had threatened to wipe out the whites since they first arrived in the territory. The threat merely reinforced all of their actions in the past.

Certainly Lone Eagle could not be so upset that he increased the number of attacks to bring her back to him. The thought hardly made sense, unless his anger and revenge lay with pride—and Lone Eagle, as all other warriors, had a great deal of pride.

"Katie," Peyton began. "I'm sorry about today."

"There's no need for you to be sorry. It was my choice to speak with the Kiowa." She avoided his eyes.

"He obviously upset you."

"He would upset anyone."

"But why do I have a feeling the things you didn't tell the colonel are the most serious ones."

"Oh, Peyton." Katie attempted humor. "I believe you are being overly protective."

"Don't be coy with me," Peyton said. He grabbed her shoulders and whirled her around to face him. He trembled in uncharacteristic rage. "I want to know what the Kiowa said."

Katie felt her own anger race through her veins. "No! It's none of your concern, and besides, you're hurting me. Now please let go."

He instantly released his hold on her as though he had seized a forging iron. "I'm sorry," he said. "Katie, I never intended to hurt you. I had no right to demand anything of you."

"That's right, you didn't," she spat at him as fury raged through her. "I'll make my own way home from here, Sergeant Sinclair."

In the wee hours of the morning, she tossed and turned over the events of the day. First she would contemplate every word from the Kiowa scout; then she'd recall Peyton's demands. Her thoughts raced with such fervor that she failed to put either of the matters at rest. Tightly closing her eyes, Katie tried to divert her thoughts. Neither incident should rob her of sleep, but the resolution didn't stop the unrest rising and falling in her spirit.

She gave up trying to figure out why Lone Eagle sent a

Kiowa with his message. Lone Eagle could very well have held the man's family hostage until he returned with Katie's answer, or he could have promised horses or rifles in exchange. Lone Eagle wouldn't risk the life of another Comanche warrior, but he would consider the job for another tribe member.

The Kiowa couldn't be trusted, and she should have stated so to the colonel.

Why Lone Eagle sent a Kiowa was not important. She wanted to know why the message was sent at all.

The Kiowa spoke correctly in one aspect of it all. Lone Eagle would not unite other warriors over a mere woman. His position as the chief's son allowed him the privilege of leading war parties. If the warrior was convinced the white soldiers had his wife, his property, then he would go to any length to get her back. Yes, most assuredly pride and honor stood as the most logical answer for Lone Eagle to demand her return.

In the eyes of the warrior, she had abandoned her husband, and the whites were to blame.

Despite the warm quilt, Katie shivered in her sleep. What if Lone Eagle intended to punish her? Within the tribal laws, he had the right, especially if he now considered her a slave rather than an equal. Most likely she'd lost any respectability the day she left for Fort Davis.

The last words Katie spoke to the Kiowa rang through her mind. She asked for peace, and if joining him at the village stopped the Indian raids, then she would return to him. If she truly loved Lone Eagle, then why did a life with him suddenly sound frightening? Was the trepidation due to his forcing her into marriage? She remembered how it used to be with him. She couldn't wait to become his wife. What happened to those hopes and dreams? Was it the search for her rehoboth, the special place where she would prosper in the land, or had she resigned herself to a white man's world?

In the darkness, Jacob whimpered. Katie reached up and patted his back until he drifted back to sleep. Emily cried out, but moments later she, too, rested quietly. Katie's thoughts reflected upon Peyton and his unwarranted lashing out at her. He'd been furious when she refused to repeat all of the Kiowa's words. Oh, if she could only sleep and banish the events of the day.

Granted, Katie recognized her own stubbornness, and she often refrained from revealing her innermost thoughts. But she didn't see any reason to alarm Peyton about Lone Eagle's insistence that she return to the village. Uncle Seth did know of her involvement with Lone Eagle, but she firmly believed he would not reveal such information to anyone without her permission. Why would she want to tell Peyton about the warrior? It only invited more problems. She treasured their friendship and looked forward to his regular visits, but not at the expense of giving him every secret of her life. The problem lay with Katie and Lone Eagle, not Sergeant Peyton Sinclair.

"Katie," Uncle Seth whispered. "I haven't been able to sleep, and I could tell you were restless, too. Did something happen when you spoke with the Kiowa scout today?"

"Yes," she said softly. "I can't seem to get it out of my mind."

"Do you want to talk about it? We can go outside if you like."

"Oh, I hate to bother you with my problem."

"If it is important enough to keep you from sleeping, then I want to hear it."

The two silently moved outside and seated themselves on the front steps.

"What did the scout say to upset you?" he said and placed a comforting arm around her shoulders.

She leaned her head on him. The night air had turned cool, and she chilled. "Well, to begin with, he spoke in Comanche, so that meant the colonel and Peyton couldn't understand him." Katie told her uncle only of the Comanche threat to all of the white people. "I told Colonel Ross about the threat."

"Why did the scout tell you?"

"Probably to see if I was loyal to the Comanches," Katie said, inhaling the scent of him, a mix of the blacksmith and the outdoors. "But I assured both the scout and the colonel that I only wanted peace."

"I believe you spoke well."

"There's more. On the way back home, Peyton became very angry when I wouldn't repeat the conversation word for word. We had a bit of an argument, and I walked home alone. I know he meant well, but he hit my rebellious streak."

Uncle Seth squeezed her lightly "I'm sorry. I should have stuck by my original decision or accompanied you to the colonel's office."

"Oh Uncle, I don't blame you. It hadn't even entered my mind."

He kissed the top of her head. "I'll pray for both of you."

Peyton did not visit the Colter home the next day or the next. By the end of five days, Katie determined the depth of his anger had caused him to break ties with her permanently. She knew the children missed Peyton, for Jacob asked for him. Uncle Seth began taking the little boy on short excursions, filling his hours with new sights and sounds. She knew her aunt and uncle loved the children and wanted to adopt them. Perhaps Peyton's disappearance was good for them all. It provided a way for Uncle Seth to secure his relationship with Jacob.

She pushed any thought of missing Peyton from her mind.

Their argument proved she was better off without him. She didn't need another man to tear at her emotions.

"Is the sergeant out on patrol?" Aunt Elizabeth said one morning at breakfast.

Uncle Seth rested his coffee mug on the table. "No, I've seen him every day this week."

"Well, up until this week, he had made daily visits to see Katie and the children, but I haven't seen him this week."

Katie's face reddened. "Peyton and I quarreled," she said to her aunt. "I'm sorry. I had no idea he wouldn't come to visit Jacob and Emily."

"That's all right, dear. Maybe you two need time to mend your differences."

"Do I need to confront him about the matter?" Uncle Seth said. Even the children stopped eating when his voice raised.

"I'd rather that you didn't. Perhaps Aunt Elizabeth is right, and we just need time."

"All right, then, but I have no problem looking into the situation." Seth stated firmly.

Katie breathed in deeply. She didn't want her aunt and uncle fretting about her friendship with Peyton.

Sunday morning, Katie considered feigning an illness and missing church. Peyton always attended Reverend Cooper's services unless he was out on patrol, and she really wanted to avoid him. After further contemplation, she refused to give in to her own selfish desires.

Peyton was already seated when the Colters entered the wood and thatch-covered building and secured a bench near the front. During the sermon she found her thoughts straying. She missed Peyton, and she did want to mend their differences, but she wasn't ready to take the first step toward reconciliation.

At the close of the service, Peyton stood directly in her path outside the church. "You linger long enough, and he'll be gone for sure," Aunt Elizabeth whispered. Her aunt lifted Emily from Katie's arms, while Jacob already held Uncle Seth's hand.

Peyton held his cap in hand, and when she tried to walk by him, he stepped in her way. "I would like to talk to you," he said.

"Our last conversation ended rather unpleasantly." Katie stared at her family, who had stopped to visit with the Jamesons.

"I take entire blame for our misunderstanding," he said. "Again I apologize."

Katie faced him. He had such a kind face, but she didn't see the familiar sparkle, only a cloud. She'd told Jacob the sergeant had laughing eyes. Those eyes, which had attracted her to him with their warmth and sincerity, now appeared distant.

"It wasn't all your fault." Her eyes moistened, and a lump rose in her throat. "I do miss your visits to see the children, and they miss you."

"Jacob and Emily aren't the only reason why I came by the cabin," he said. "I enjoyed our little talks. Can I start calling on you again?"

She nodded, and a tear slipped from her eye. *Why am I weeping? It must be the warm day.* Peyton must have seen her display of emotion, and she regretted her transparency.

"May I stop by this afternoon?" he said, not taking his eyes from her face.

"Yes," Katie said, hearing her own voice tremble. "Do you remember when the children nap?"

"I do, and I'll be there early. I just wanted to see you for a few minutes before going out on patrol tomorrow morning."

Alarm soared through her, and she didn't attempt to disguise it.

"Is the Kiowa scout going?"

"No, he's been dismissed from his duties."

She breathed relief. "How long will you be gone?"

"Three or four days. It's a routine patrol."

No patrols were routine as long as men hunted each other. "How many soldiers are riding with you?"

"Eight."

"That's not very many, Peyton."

"We need to keep enough soldiers here in case of attack."

"I understand." She turned her head so he wouldn't see any more tears, but in doing so she caught sight of the Kiowa. The Indian stood watching both of them.

"What's wrong, Katie?" Peyton said. "You look ill."

"The Kiowa is still here. I thought he would have left the fort."

He turned to the Indian, but by then the Kiowa had walked away. Peyton focused his attention upon her. "I would do anything to wipe the fear from your eyes," he said, stepping closer to her. "Anything, Katie."

She avoided his gaze and glared at the back of the Kiowa. "Don't leave on patrol tomorrow. Can't Colonel Ross send someone else?"

"I have my orders. I have a job to do," he said. "Soldiers can't choose where and when they want to report for duty."

Chapter Seven

Katie trudged through the next two days, supplying extra activities for Jacob and Emily and insisting upon doing all the cooking. She claimed Aunt Elizabeth needed more time with the children, but in actuality Katie didn't want to think of anything happening to Peyton or the other soldiers.

On the third day, Katie tucked lunch into a basket and took Jacob with her to the blacksmith shop. She wanted the little boy to see Seth at work yet not be in the way of the fiery forge.

"Will you tell me a story?" Jacob said as they prepared to leave the cabin.

Katie remembered a story her father once told her. She grasped the child's hand and carried the basket with the other. "A small Indian boy received a spotted pony from his father. He was excited and looked forward to riding and training it, but the pony proved wild and couldn't be broken. After many weeks of attempting to ride the pony, the boy sought his father's advice. 'Pretend that you live inside the pony,' his father said. 'When you know the pony's heart, then it will be your friend.' The small boy worked hard and observed the animal and its habits. Slowly the pony began to eat from his hand and allowed the boy to stroke it. When the boy fully understood the pony, he no longer was afraid and made friends. The pony learned to love and trust the small boy, and one day it allowed the boy to ride it."

Katie's story sounded simple enough, but she wanted Jacob to see Indian children were much like white children. In her opinion, understanding between the Indians and whites was the first step to peace.

"I like the story," Jacob said. "Even if it is about an Indian."

Jacob watched Uncle Seth hammer and shape white-hot metal into horseshoes without so much as a single word. After an hour passed, her uncle asked the little boy if he had anything to say. Jacob's blue eyes grew wide, and soon a huge assortment of questions poured from his mouth.

At noon the three sat down together. Uncle Seth and Jacob talked constantly, but Katie's eyes darted back and forth to the front gate in hopes of seeing Peyton.

"The patrol will be back soon," he said.

She immediately glanced down at the unfinished food before her and felt her cheeks warm. "I guess I don't hide my thoughts well," she said.

"Not this time." He chuckled and stretched out his long legs. Within moments, Jacob stretched out his short legs.

They laughed at the child's imitation. Each time Uncle Seth took a bite of food, so did Jacob. At one point, a soldier walked by and her uncle waved. So did Jacob.

"I believe we have a blacksmith in the making," Katie said.

"You may be right." When she took another longing gaze toward the front gate, he spoke again. "Katie, child, I believe you like the sergeant a little more than you care to admit."

She hesitated before answering, as always, running his words through her head. "He's a good friend."

"All good relationships begin with friendship, and I already know how he feels about you."

"Did he tell you something?" Her curiosity sparked.

"Um, yes he did, and I fully approve."

"Well, what did Peyton say?"

"I'll let him tell you for himself. The question you need to ask yourself is, how do you feel about him?"

She wiped bread crumbs from Jacob's mouth. "I'm not sure," she said, searching deep within her for truth. "It's not a simple thing, Uncle Seth. You know how things would have been if I had stayed with the Indians." She glanced first at Jacob, who was listening to every word, then into the face of her uncle.

"Yes, I know very well. Elizabeth and I have discussed what could have easily happened if you remained living there. We don't keep secrets from each other, and we know you must be confused—not just about Sergeant Sinclair, but God, different cultures, grieving for Jeremiah, and how you feel about Emily and Jacob. The list is endless."

"Then you understand how torn I am?"

"Of course we do. Jeremiah was my brother, and I saw the same turmoil in him. It saddens me to see you in the same situation."

"How did you become so wise?" Katie said.

He chuckled, and so did Jacob. "I've never considered myself a wise man, but thank you. I think God gives us a measure of wisdom with each year we get older." He lightly touched Jacob's nose. "Much like a peppermint stick before a dose of bad-tasting medicine."

Shortly thereafter, Jacob showed signs of tiring. Katie suggested the two hurry home to check on Emily.

"Thank you for bringing lunch," he said. "Jacob, you can

come by and visit me anytime."

"We enjoyed watching you work. Right?" She smiled at the little boy, but he wrapped his arm around Uncle Seth and hugged him.

Sentiment seemed to strike Uncle Seth, and he pulled the little boy tightly to him. "You're a fine boy."

"Will you be my papa?" Jacob whispered loud enough for Katie to hear. "Will you be my papa and not let the Indians make you die?"

She had rarely seen a grown man cry. Even when her mother died, Pa had slipped away to weep. Yet, the tears from her uncle flowed unchecked, and she felt her own eyes do the same.

"God bless you, Jacob," Seth said. "I love you, child, and I'll do my best."

At home, before Katie had a chance to tell what she and Jacob had been doing all morning, Aunt Elizabeth stood Emily on the floor. "Look what our Emily did while you were gone. Soon she will be running."

This had truly been a wonderful day. Jacob reached out in affection to Uncle Seth, and Emily had taken her first steps. What a blessing for Uncle Seth and Aunt Elizabeth.

Katie caught herself repeating her thoughts. She had used the word blessing without considering that her thoughts indicated a belief in God. *Perhaps she'd been around people who believed in Him for so long that their speech had settled into hers. Or had she begun to trust the God of the Bible?*

On the morning of the fourth day with no word from the patrol, Aunt Elizabeth suggested Katie visit Lauren. When she attempted to prepare Jacob and Emily, her aunt said the children needed to stay at home. No doubt, her aunt wanted Katie to turn the waiting hours into girl talk. Reluctantly she agreed, knowing her aunt would have more work to do with Jacob and Emily underfoot.

The entire Jameson household, eight children in all, noisily welcomed her. When she saw Martha had all of them, except Lauren, in the midst of schooling, Katie apologized for the intrusion. She politely excused herself, but Martha wouldn't hear of it.

"Lauren, you and Katie just go about your visiting— perhaps a walk would do you both good," Martha said.

Katie shook her head. "No, Mrs. Jameson. I don't want to interrupt your teaching. Is there any way I can help?"

Martha wrinkled her nose at her. The gesture reminded Katie of one of the children laboring over a slate.

"Please?"

Martha laughed. Soon Katie sat on the floor beside one of the younger boys. He didn't look much older than Jacob, but still he managed to read a little. She helped him write his letters and do simple addition problems on a slate. It occurred to her that Jacob needed to be learning, and perhaps she should mention it to her aunt and uncle.

For the next two hours, Katie assisted Martha and Lauren in different levels of reading and arithmetic. Martha Jameson had taught school before she married and knew exactly how to assign lessons according to the ability of her children. As soon as a young Jameson could hold a piece of chalk or recognize a letter, she encouraged him to read and do numbers. Katie loved the way in which Martha praised her children's work and gently instructed those who had difficulty.

"My ma taught school before she married my father," Katie told Martha and Lauren.

"What all did she teach you?" Martha said, stepping over to the cook fire and stirring a pot of beans.

"The same things you teach your children: reading, writing, arithmetic, geography, social etiquette, and history. She also taught me French. Ma always told me that the world was a big place and filled with many experiences. She encouraged me to ask questions and to dream. I remember in the evenings Pa and I used to listen to her read the Bible. I had forgotten much of the Bible teachings until Uncle Seth encouraged me to begin reading it again."

"Did your schooling stop when your ma died?" Martha said.

"Just the Bible reading. When I started studying the scriptures here, it loosened my memory of what Ma used to read. My pa had graduated from a university in Connecticut and carried on my studies, except he added wilderness survival as well as the language and customs of the Comanches." Katie thought better of mentioning the Indians, but she'd already spoken of it.

Martha instantly picked up on Katie's discomfort. "Katie, I believe you received a fine education."

"Can Katie teach us about Indians and surviving in the wild?" the eldest Jameson son said.

Martha paused a moment, and all the children waited for their mother's response.

"If Katie is willing, she can teach you about those things, but first you must work hard on your other studies. And perhaps Jacob would like to join us," Martha said. "What do you think about that, Katie? Of course, you must ask your aunt and uncle's permission."

"It would be great fun," Lauren said. "And she could also teach me French, although I don't know if a soldier's wife will ever need it."

Pleasure excited from the top of her head to her tingling

toes. "I'll ask my aunt and uncle, except I'm not sure I would be a good teacher."

"You've been a wonderful help today," Martha said. "I believe you not only have the gift of teaching, but also the gift of patience and encouragement. God's truly blessed you with an abundance of special gifts. Make sure you thank Him by using those gifts for the benefit of others."

Katie could only listen and show respect for the woman's words. The thought of being useful made her feel good, especially teaching like her ma had done. But used by God?

Had this God really given her gifts? The thought seemed incredible that He would give gifts to someone who wasn't a believer. Did stubbornness play a part in her refusal to accept God and His Son, Jesus, or did she need some type of proof of His existence? *God, if You are truly there, show me so I can believe. I'm so confused about my life, and I don't know what is real or truth.*

Katie and Lauren finally slipped away from the Jameson household. Their time together would be short, but they were determined to make the most of it. Katie treasured the friendship with her and respected their differences in personality. Quick laughter, delightful spontaneity, and an unselfish, giving attitude were all a part of Lauren Jameson. No wonder a soldier had fallen in love with her. Lauren invited love and joy in every breath she took. Katie saw Lauren generously shower those traits upon everyone she met, and Lauren showed Katie what true beauty really meant. As the two girls walked about the fort, Lauren spoke to all they passed, if not with her voice then with a nod or smile.

"Are your wedding plans completed?" Katie said.

"Not yet. Mama has finished altering my dress, and I've been working on needlepoint every chance I get. Mama insists on so many things to be completed for our new home, but it really isn't necessary. Besides, I hate to burden her with extra sewing and the like to help me set up housekeeping."

"I know I'm being selfish, but I'm glad you'll be living close by," Katie said.

"No one could be more selfish than I am." Lauren patted her arm. "I want to be married now and get all this wedding nonsense behind me. Mama and Papa want everything to be perfect, but the day will be wonderful with or without the finery and party plans."

"They want to give you the best because they love you," Katie said. "My aunt is always talking about when I get married, we will do this or that. Maybe it's more fun for them than us."

"Probably so. I simply don't like to be the center of attention. It makes me feel uncomfortable." Lauren shook her head. Her mood seemed to lift, and she began to laugh. "Now tell me about you and Sergeant Sinclair."

Katie smiled at the teasing note in her friend. "There's nothing to tell. We're good friends."

"Good friends, my eye. He visits your cabin nearly every day."

"To see the children, or Uncle Seth, or Aunt Elizabeth." Fear of what Lone Eagle might do to Peyton and the others at the fort stopped her from thinking beyond friendship.

"Oh, you are storytelling, Katie," Lauren said. "I know for a fact the sergeant asked your uncle if he could come courtin'."

Katie attempted to give her a surprised look, but the mischievous twinkle in Lauren's eyes wouldn't permit it. "And how did you know about such a conversation?"

"Your aunt told my mother." Lauren tossed her head. "And some things a woman just knows—like affairs of the heart."

Katie couldn't help but burst into laughter at the dramatics.

"It's good to see you happy for a change," Lauren said. "I

have been praying for you to find joy in your life."

"Thank you. Since Jacob and Emily have come to live with us, my mind has been occupied with them instead of myself. And yes, seeing Peyton, I mean Sergeant Sinclair, keeps me busy as we become better friends."

"He cares for you very deeply," Lauren said.

"How do you know?" Katie said barely above a whisper.

"All you have to do is look at his face. It's the same way my soldier looks at me. It gives away everything they're trying to hide."

Katie didn't want to discuss Peyton any longer. If she knew her own feelings for him then she could respond more readily to Lauren. But didn't she love Lone Eagle? She thought real feelings of love never changed. Sometimes she wished she could push the Indian from her heart forever and allow Peyton to take his place. Could it be she feared Lone Eagle's temper as much as she cared for him? Or was she afraid to let another man into her heart? As much as she refused to admit it, she saw the caring in Peyton. A combination of guilt and perplexity forced her to refrain from any romantic notions. Peyton must remain a friend.

The Kiowa had seen her talking with Peyton. Their conversation must have looked as though they were more than friends, especially in light of making amends for their disagreement. Once more, fear and anxiety had cast a menacing shadow. The Kiowa spy would surely tell Lone Eagle about Peyton.

If she believed, she would pray. If the soldiers were attacked and Peyton was killed, it would be her fault. The words of the Kiowa echoed across her mind. As much as she hated to ever talk to the Indian again, she would have to find out Lone Eagle's answer. But now, deep in her heart, did she really want to leave her aunt and uncle? What of her promise to Pa? And how was she to find her rehoboth?

The ugliest thought of all sprung from Lone Eagle's threat to wipe out the whites. The warrior didn't say she would be to blame, but Katie knew Lone Eagle. Many times he revealed only a portion of his thoughts with the intention of waiting for a response. He didn't anticipate anything; rather, he allowed others to react before he proceeded with his plans. Lone Eagle had learned the lessons of cunning and wit in dealing with his enemies. Were the Kiowa's words intended to scare her into returning to the Comanche village?

Chapter Eight

The fifth day of the patrol's absence crept by much like a lingering fever, and still no word from the soldiers. Uncle Seth and Aunt Elizabeth prayed for the men during mealtimes and at bedtime. Katie bowed her head in respect to their God, but she didn't appeal to the Comanche gods, either. A lump rose in her throat, and she couldn't eat or sleep.

For the second night Katie tossed and turned, unable to relax or pull peace from the recesses of her mind. Racing thoughts became like nightmares, and she even imagined hearing the war cries of Comanches and the screams of dying men. Peyton said the patrol would be back in three or four days. When tomorrow dawned, it would be the sixth day. If only the men would return unharmed.

Night turned into morning, and Katie watched the chalky pastels of purple, pink, and orange spread across the sky. How could nature continue its unrivaled beauty and not be sensitive to the turmoil of the people around it? The Comanches relied solely upon the spirits of nature to guard and direct them in their dealings with the enemy. Whites prayed to a sovereign God to protect them from evil. Both claimed their way was the answer to life's purpose and meaning. She wished she knew which side possessed the truth. Sweet peace among the Comanches and the whites would be a true miracle.

Midmorning found her restless and irritable. When she grew frustrated in dealing with Jacob, she decided to take a walk. A heaviness rested upon the fort, as though the air carried some dreadful news. It seemed quieter than usual, not the normal hustle and bustle that resounded from corner to corner. As she moved about the various activities, she observed more soldiers posted in strategic points. Her eyes traveled upward to the canyon walls, and she searched for signs of Indians. Nothing moved out of the ordinary, but her heart pounded like war drums.

The scenic beauty surrounding the fort masked her inner turmoil. The ten-mile stretch known as Wild Rose Pass wound up from Black Mountain and looked down upon the fort. The pass was breathtaking, a welcome sight for any traveler who had weathered the desolate trail and warring Indians. The waters at the foot provided fresh fish, and Uncle Seth had taken Jacob there fishing on more than one occasion.

A band of soldiers and civilians drove wagons loaded with logs toward the fort. The armed men selected oak, pine, and cherry from the higher slopes to construct additional buildings within the stronghold. She wished they were the overdue patrol.

"What have your Comanche friends done with our soldiers?" a portly lady called out to her.

Katie recognized the woman, Mrs. Ames, an outspoken member of the church. She'd never heard a kind word from the woman and doubted if she ever would. Katie chose to ignore her. It would open her to more criticism and accusation. Instead she walked back home to tend the garden for Aunt Elizabeth.

If she believed in God, she could pray for Peyton and the others.

At least then she would feel like she was doing her part in the waiting. She sighed deeply and fought the familiar lump rising in her throat. *Oh God, if You are there, would You please bring the soldiers back safely? I don't know what else to say or do, but I ask if it is possible. Uncle Seth tells me that all things are possible with God, and he and Aunt Elizabeth along with lots of other folks are praying for them, too. I'd prefer a sign, something I could see and touch, but it's more important for the men to be protected.*

She no longer sensed anxiety overwhelming her, except she didn't know why.

Shortly after dusk, while her aunt and uncle and Katie quietly went about the evening chores, someone pounded on the door. Uncle Seth rose to receive the caller with Jacob trailing after him.

The sound of a familiar man's voice stole her breath.

"Peyton," Katie whispered. "Peyton!" She rushed to the door and nearly flung her arms around his neck but caught herself. Nonsense, she must contain herself. What would he think? "We were so worried about you," was all she could manage, for tears stung her eyes and strangled any more words.

"I think you're glad to see me." Peyton grinned.

"Are the others unharmed?" Uncle Seth said, ushering him inside.

"Yes, sir, God rode with us every step of the way and back."

"If you don't mind me asking, what delayed you?" he said. "Folks were mighty worried."

"One of the men got a stomach ailment, and it passed around to all of us. We weren't able to complete our orders, and by the time we all recovered, our supplies were nearly gone."

Jacob moved shyly toward Peyton, and the sergeant chuckled. "Have I been gone that long, little man? I did take a bath before I came here, so I shouldn't be offensive." He bent down to Jacob's side and gave him a hug.

"Emily is walking," Jacob said, returning the affection. Ever since he first hugged Uncle Seth, he'd been more open. "Here, Emily." He motioned sweetly to his sister. "Walk over here to Sergeant Sinclair."

Aunt Elizabeth stood the child on the floor, and she walked toward her brother's outstretched hand. Everyone clapped and cheered as she fell into Peyton's arms. Katie felt a pang of regret that she, too, couldn't have reached out to the sergeant.

"Why don't you and Katie visit outside?" Seth said. "It will give you two some time alone. She has been ornery as a she-bear ever since you've been gone."

Katie denied any such actions and followed Peyton into the evening air. "I am so glad you are safe," she said once the door closed.

"I could tell." He laughed. "For a moment I thought I was going to get Katie Colter into my arms."

The telltale warmth spread from her neck to her face. She was thankful for the darkness concealing her embarrassment.

Within a few feet of the cabin, he gathered her into his arms. "I've been wanting to do this for a long time."

Katie trembled uncontrollably. She willed it to stop, except the shaking continued. Peyton released her as though he had embraced a hot potato from a cooking pot.

"I'm sorry," he said. "I didn't mean to frighten you."

Katie licked dry lips. "I don't know why I am reacting like this. I was so worried, and I missed you the first morning you were gone." She hesitantly touched the cuff of his sleeve.

"But you don't want me to hold you?" Peyton's question sounded kind, but she could tell he was hurt.

"Peyton, I'm not sure of what I want or need. So many things are going on in my head, and I wouldn't want you to think my feelings weren't honest."

"I understand," he said. "I understand more than you may realize."

She relaxed slightly. Even though she knew Peyton had no idea what troubled her, his gentle words made her feel better.

"Can we walk a bit?" she said. "Or are you too tired?"

"No, I'm just fine."

"Would you tell me what happened while you were gone?" she said, to change the way of their conversation.

"It's most likely boring—vomiting soldiers doesn't say much about heroic feats of valor."

"You have a point, a good one I might add. But I just wondered if you met up with any Comanches."

"No. . .no problems at all. Like I said, nothing to report, only heat and empty prairie lands."

"Nothing seen or heard outside of these gates is boring— the land is beautiful and free."

"We did ride past your ranch," he said. "Everything looked fine. Just deserted."

"Then you were in the heart of dangerous country," She paused, while words and emotions jumbled into her head. "I asked God to keep you safe."

"And when did you pray for me?" Peyton said.

Katie considered the time. "Yesterday, about midmorning, I was out walking, trying to rid myself of a sour mood."

"Oh, missing me put you in a sour mood?" His tone quickly changed to a serious note. "Katie, did you say midmorning?"

"Yes, why?"

"God truly did watch over us," he whispered. "We were riding along the Teyah River when a peculiar feeling came over me. It was more of an urgency to turn the men around and ride out of there—fast. At the time, I felt foolish in giving the order, except now I believe the message came from God."

She stood speechless. She knew the area all too well. Comanches could have easily led them into an ambush. God did answer her prayer. And He'd given her a sign. She must tell Uncle Seth, tell him that God had answered her prayer.

"You're strangely quiet, more quiet than usual," Peyton said. "Are you all right?"

"I was thinking how God answered my prayer as soon as I spoke it. I've never confessed to believing in Him, and I prayed for you and the other soldiers out of desperation. I also asked Him for a sign so I would know if He was real. . . . He gave me both."

"Your aunt and uncle will be pleased," Peyton said. "I've been praying for you to find God, too."

"You have?" she said. "I'm a little confused about it all, but how can I not believe? I need to thank you for not giving up on me."

"A hug would be nice, but I'll wait until you're ready. I should get you back home before Colonel Ross sends someone to fetch me."

"Yes, of course, and I must tell Uncle Seth and Aunt Elizabeth everything." She did have good news.

"You, tell everything and not keep a bit of it to yourself?" Peyton laughed. "Now God would be performing a miracle."

Back at the cabin, Peyton excused himself with the promise of visiting the next day. When Katie told her aunt and uncle about her prayer and Peyton's report of the incident along the Teyah River, Aunt Elizabeth cried and Uncle Seth hugged her. The three prayed together, and her uncle led Katie to Christ.

The tension of the past days vanished at the close of the prayer. Not that the problems and fears disappeared, but the burden seemed lighter. Without being able to fully express her peace and joy, she opened the family Bible and found Psalm 40, where someone had clearly underlined the passage: "I waited patiently for the Lord; and he inclined unto me, and heard my cry. He brought me up also out of an horrible pit, out of the miry clay, and set my feet upon a rock, and established my goings. And he hath put a new song in my mouth, even praise unto our God: many shall see it, and fear, and shall trust in the Lord. Blessed is that man that maketh the Lord his trust, and respecteth not the proud, nor such as turn aside to lies. Many, O Lord my God, are thy wonderful works which thou hast done, and thy thoughts which are to us-ward: they cannot be reckoned up in order unto thee: if I would declare and speak of them, they are more than can be numbered."

The ache in her heart was on the mend. Her new heavenly Father would direct her through the days ahead. She didn't expect things to be easy, only that God would be with her. And like Emily, Katie took the first steps into the arms of her heavenly Father.

Chapter Nine

*A*fter Katie gave her heart to Jesus, she found a sense of peace and joy sprouting like wildflowers in spring. Uncle Seth said the Lord allowed gentleness and compassion to accompany her wherever she went. No longer did seriousness and sadness mark her every thought, and she responded to helping others more than before. Katie believed she must reach out to those who hurt. She wanted to soothe their pain, especially those who had endured tragic losses from the Comanches. The sensitive traits were real, and she couldn't deny them. The dilemma of making peace took precedence over who was right or wrong.

Seth told Katie that God put a special star in her eyes to light up the dark side of people. Every time she saw Emily toddle about on wobbly legs, it reminded her of holding on to God's hand while she stepped out in faith.

"Katie, child, do you plan to read the whole Bible tonight?" Uncle Seth said one evening after she had read late into the night.

"Are you tired of my questions?"

"You haven't asked me any for the past hour," Seth said. "You must be preparing a hard one."

"No, Uncle Seth." She laughed. "I'm reading Psalms. Well, really I'm memorizing a few of the shorter ones."

"Good," he said. "Having God's Word stored in your heart is the best guard against Satan."

Aunt Elizabeth handed Katie a folded sheet of paper. "Here are the passages I promised you. The scriptures listed here have brought me through many difficult times in my life. It's easy to turn to Psalms and praise God when life is good, but sometimes we need help when sorrow and grief seem to get the best of us."

"Thank you," Katie said, looking over the paper. "I'll always treasure this."

"It was given to me a long time ago when I had fallen into self-pity about Seth and me not having any children. I took to memorizing each one of those passages. God is so faithful. The adoption proceedings for Jacob and Emily are moving along just fine, and we are so blessed to have been a part of your acceptance of God's grace."

"I can see these verses will give me strength when Peyton is on patrol. I know God is watching over the soldiers, but I still feel anxious about them. When the soldiers are here, the feelings disappear. Then Colonel Ross dispatches another group, and I worry again."

"Jeremiah 29 says: 'For I know the thoughts that I think toward you, saith the Lord, thoughts of peace, and not of evil, to give you an expected end. Then shall ye call upon me, and ye shall go and pray unto me, and I will hearken unto you. And ye shall seek me, and find me, when ye shall search for me with all your heart,'" Aunt Elizabeth said. "Those words have always gotten me through the roughest of days."

"We all tend to worry and fret over things we can't control," Uncle Seth said. "It's a part of our nature. Elizabeth tells me that you delivered a loaf of bread to Mrs. Ames. I am so proud of you."

Katie smiled. "She had become so critical and outspoken about Pa and our dealings with the Comanches that her disagreeable nature had almost become a game. Sometimes I guessed at what she would say next. You are the one who told me true obedience to God means doing those things that may not be pleasant. I've been trying to look at her through the eyes of Jesus, and it has helped." Katie laughed. "Uncle, Mrs. Ames didn't know what to say when I handed her the bread. She just took it and shut the door in my face."

"But you did your part." He reached down and planted a kiss on her forehead. "Good night, child. Don't read too late. You need your rest."

Katie read and reread those biblical passages giving specific instructions about putting matters of concern into the hands of the Father. Even so, she still felt apprehensive. She hadn't seen or heard from the Kiowa, and she didn't know if his absence came as a curse or a blessing. Aunt Elizabeth said God warned His children about trying to solve their own problems instead of giving it all to Him. She said folks just didn't seem to listen when God knew what was best for them.

Martha added Jacob to her list of learners. When folks discovered Martha had once taught school, they asked to bring their own children. The parents paid her in food and chores while talk began of building a school. In the mornings, Katie finished helping Aunt Elizabeth so she could assist with the children's lessons. The hours Pa had spent instructing Katie on how to read maps and live in the wild proved invaluable to Martha. The older woman used Katie's knowledge as a reward for the boys when they proved reluctant to study.

As Lauren's wedding day approached, Katie helped stitch linens and clothing to add to the bride's trousseau. The girls grew closer and shared their heartfelt dreams about their own future families. Martha accused the two of giggling more than they worked, but she also encouraged them to spend time together.

Peyton visited the Colter cabin nearly every day. Katie never knew when he would come calling. Some days he arrived just before the children woke from their naps, and other days he came by in the evening. He always apologized for stopping by unannounced, and his visits were brief. She believed the short stays were due to her response toward his embrace. Had Peyton thought his touch was repugnant, when in fact she struggled with tender emotions? His presence brought on a whole new set of feelings, and it perplexed her more than she cared to admit. One thing she knew for certain—Peyton Sinclair was a good man, and she valued his friendship.

"Do you have a moment to talk?" he said one afternoon while the children slept.

Katie couldn't help but smile. "Of course I do. Shall we step outside?"

He opened the door into sparkling sunshine. They sat on a bench in front of the cabin.

"I wanted to thank you for telling me about your childhood with the Comanches," he said. "As a soldier, I tend to forget the Indians love and care for their families. It didn't occur to me that they participate in games and enjoy life much like we do. You gave me a whole new perspective on why they hate the white man. We are a threat to everything they hold sacred."

She valued his understanding. "I do have good memories,

especially of Desert Fawn and how she took care of me after my mother died. I do regret that the Comanches don't know the one true God. If they did, perhaps we all could live in peace."

"Sounds like a child's story," Peyton said.

"Yes, I guess it is. Even if we all believed the same, differences would occur."

"True. Maybe we could sit down and discuss problems without killing each other."

"Perhaps one day."

"Katie, were you given an Indian name?"

"Yes." She recalled the first time Jeremiah whispered it in her ear. "Swift Arrow gave it to me after he and my father became friends. I suppose you want to know what it is."

"Of course."

"Yo-oh-hobt Paph. It means yellow hair."

"It suits you," Peyton said with a wide grin. "Did your father call you this openly?"

"Most of the time. He called me Katie when we were alone and especially near the end." Uneasiness settled on her, as though his conversation was leading to a disagreeable topic.

"I have a new curiosity about the Comanches," he said.

A bird sang in the distance, and a dog barked. "And what's your question?" she said. "I might not be able to answer it."

"I thought you were the expert." He chuckled, but she didn't relax. "I'm sure you won't disappoint me. I've heard that Comanche war bonnets were made entirely of eagle feathers."

A hint of relief swept through her. "You heard correctly. Other tribes dye turkey feathers for their war bonnets, but to a Comanche that would be a disgrace."

"See, you did know the answer," Peyton said. "And I thank you."

"The Comanches are a proud race," Katie said. "They won't be driven from this land without a fight."

"Excuse me if this offends you, but Katie, do you miss them?" He studied her face.

She refused to believe he intended to insult her, but his curiosity reinforced her earlier misgivings. "Sometimes I think about the people I grew to love, but my home is here. I'm happy and I belong with Aunt Elizabeth and Uncle Seth. What more could I want?"

Peyton turned to the mountains. "Sounds to me like you have everything you need." His tone was oddly cold.

Katie's gaze flew to his face. What was that she saw?

Katie carried a basket of corn bread, roast duck, and apple pie to Martha's family. Most of the children had been down with colds and fever, and the food would be welcomed for the evening meal.

As usual when Peyton rode patrol, her thoughts turned to the increasing number of Comanche raids. The news inevitably devastated her as much as the families of the injured or killed. The horrible injustices done to innocent families and the thought of old familiar faces seeking out white settlers made her feel responsible. The incidents were not her fault, but guilt washed over every part of her. She worried and fretted until Peyton rode through the front gate. Why did he have to lead every group of soldiers who checked on Indian activity? But by the time she saw him again, the question slipped her mind.

She continued on her walk, but as she passed the colonel's

office, she spied a shiny rock near the side of the small building. She smiled and stepped closer. It would certainly gain Jacob's attention. She stooped to pick it up and heard voices.

"Two more families were found murdered and their homes burned to the ground," one soldier said. "Besides being scalped, the whole family, even the children, were tortured before they died."

She shuddered. Peyton never shared the grotesque details about his encounters with raiding Indians. Should she be grateful to him for shielding her from the truth? Her thoughts spun wildly. What if she were still with the Comanches, and soldiers attacked them? Lives taken were wrong no matter what the circumstances.

"Pardon me, sir, but we need to wipe out the whole Indian nation—women and children, too. I'm for burning their villages to the ground. Let them get a dose of their own medicine," another soldier said.

The colonel cleared his throat. "It's the land. The Indians believe we have no right to be here, and they are going to do their best to drive us out. Our job is to stop the raids so folks can live here without fear of losing their lives. Sooner or later those savages will realize that there are a lot more of us than them."

When would this ever end? If God was in control of all things, then why didn't He soften the soldiers' and the Indians' hearts to stop this senseless killing? Why couldn't both sides simply talk and work out a peaceable solution? Her father had traded furs, food, and horses for their ranch. It seemed fair to her. Why couldn't those at the fort see that reasoning?

"Lone Eagle appears to be leading more raids than his father. Reminds me of a rattler—ready to strike when you least expect it," the colonel said. "I wonder if he's human, and

I'd like the honor of blowing a hole right through his chest."

With Colonel Ross's statement, Katie breathed in sharply. He spoke of the man she'd once planned to marry. Lone Eagle was a warrior like the colonel's soldiers, a man who refused to let the white man destroy his people and their way of life. Perhaps he'd merely been a young girl's infatuation, but she understood what drove him to kill. While his actions churned her stomach, so did any man who took the lives of others.

What were Peyton's actions when on patrol? Did she even want to know?

"When is Sergeant Sinclair due back?" the first soldier said.

"Yesterday," the colonel said. "He's a good soldier, and I would hate to lose him. I want to know the moment he returns."

She'd heard enough. She hurried around to the front of the colonel's office and walked briskly toward the Jamesons' cabin. Her heart lifted a prayer for Peyton's safe return and an end to the bloodshed.

On the way back from her errand, she heard a commotion at the front gate. Peyton and his patrol had returned safely. He waved, and her heart soared. What had happened to her? Before coming to the fort, she'd promised her heart to Lone Eagle. Now another man caused the same feelings. Had she become fickle?

The day of Lauren's wedding came, and Katie was as excited as the young bride. Katie had sewn, baked, and assisted in the events leading up to the day ever since she met Lauren. The groom's name was Miles Barrett—a comely man who had earned the reputation as an excellent soldier and was well respected among the civilians. He accompanied Peyton on most of the patrols, and Peyton had remarked more than once on his clear thinking in the line of duty.

Lauren and Miles were clearly devoted to each other, and both of them had dedicated their lives to the Lord. For Katie, this marriage stated one more reason why the Comanche dispute needed to be resolved. Lauren shouldn't be afraid when Miles rode out on patrol.

Except for the soldiers guarding the fort, most everyone planned to attend the wedding ceremony. When Reverend Cooper saw the number of folks gathered to seat themselves inside his small, hut-like church, he immediately moved the wedding outside. Roughly constructed benches were snatched up like kindling and arranged in the open air. When the benches could fit no more guests, families stood together noisily waiting for the bride to make her appearance.

Excitement brewed in the air. She didn't ever want to return to the Indians. Here dwelled her family and her God.

Lauren and Miles's wedding served to remind Katie of how close she came to spending the rest of her life with a Comanche warrior. She searched the crowd for the Kiowa, and all the while the old gnawing fear crept over her again.

"Are you looking for someone?" Aunt Elizabeth said.

Relieved that the Indian was not among them, Katie pushed away any thoughts of Lone Eagle demanding she return to him.

"I just wondered about one of the soldiers, but he's not here," she said. If Lone Eagle truly meant to threaten her into obedience, the Kiowa would have long since found a way to tell her. How good that Aunt Elizabeth could not read her thoughts. "This is simply wonderful," she said.

She turned her attention to the bride walking toward them. Lauren's father held his daughter's arm while she steadied a Bible with her other hand. Martha and Aunt Elizabeth had searched frantically for a bouquet of wildflowers to arrange into a bouquet, but Lauren insisted upon carrying her Bible with several satin ribbons instead.

"Isn't she beautiful?" her aunt whispered as Lauren brushed by them.

Katie could only nod. Her eyes moistened for her dear friend.

"Look at her dress, Katie. I'd never seen it on her before." Aunt Elizabeth sighed. "Martha said it was her grandmother's wedding dress. Mercy me, it hugs her waist just right. I declare she looks more like a precious china doll than a prairie bride."

The dress's color had faded to ivory along with the many yards of delicate lace, yet the shade of the wedding gown enhanced Lauren's hair and sky blue eyes. Pearl buttons lined a high, lace-trimmed neck and lay within the scallops of the neck, sleeves, bodice, and layered skirt.

Katie listened to the parting crowd whisper "ooh" and "ah" as the bride fairly floated past them. Lauren's face glowed, and her eyes sparkled. Lauren was the most beautiful bride in the world.

As radiant as the bride appeared, the groom looked every bit as dashing. Every metal accessory on his uniform glistened.

"Looks to me like folks could see themselves in Miles's boots." Uncle Seth chuckled. "And he must have been up all night polishing the buttons on his uniform."

All the people who sat or stood near the young couple detected a slight trembling in the groom, especially as

Lauren moved closer to him.

Katie caught a glimpse of Peyton standing beside Miles as the best man. He took her breath away. Would she ever marry a man as fine as Sergeant Peyton Sinclair?

"Dearly beloved," Reverend Cooper began.

With all the planning of the past several weeks, the wedding ceremony ended all too quickly. The reverend delivered a short sermon on the biblical principles of a sound marriage, and Lauren and Miles whispered their vows. The crowd hushed to see them seal their promises with a kiss.

"And now I would like to introduce you to the new Mr. and Mrs. Miles Barrett. Lauren and Miles, you may greet your friends and family," Reverend Cooper said.

The soldiers cheered and other folks clapped. A chain of laughter echoed across the fort and over the canyon walls. The merriment had begun.

"Join us for food and fellowship." Mr. Jameson gestured toward the cabin where everyone was to gather.

"I've got my fiddle," a soldier shouted.

Aunt Elizabeth, Katie, and Martha, plus three of Lauren's sisters, assembled around two makeshift tables outside of the Jameson home. One table held all sorts of canned fruits, vegetables, preserves, delicate needlepoint items, tools, and even dry goods for the new couple to set up housekeeping. The second table held cake, pies, and fruit cobblers with a huge bowl of punch. The desserts were placed on several donated sets of dishes and even more sets of cups. Aunt Elizabeth and Martha served the food while Katie alternated with Lauren's sisters in pouring punch and washing dirty dishes.

At first all of them busied themselves in helping folks get food and drink, but when the line of guests dwindled, the servers relaxed and treated themselves. No sooner had Katie sliced herself a piece of apple pie than Peyton appeared.

"Have you eaten?" Katie said.

"Yes, ma'am," Peyton said. "You were inside the cabin when I went through the line."

"Good, because I'm starved."

"I think it's traditional for those who serve not to eat," Peyton said with a hint of a smile. "It's a custom that is strictly enforced."

She glanced up, eyes open wide, embarrassed at the thought of breaking a social rule.

"Especially apple pie—that's always for the best man."

"And you're teasing me." Katie shook her finger at him. "I don't know how you can tell such tales with a straight face."

"Years of practice. Can you get away for a little while?"

Katie looked around and saw nothing for her to do. "Aunt Elizabeth, will things here be all right for a while?" she said.

"Certainly, you've done plenty for one day."

Katie and Peyton left the crowd of people behind and made their way through the front gate to the beauty of Limpia Valley. They talked of the wedding, the cooler weather, and Emily and Jacob's latest accomplishments. Jacob loved learning, and he'd already learned his letters. Emily spoke new words almost on a daily basis. Both she and Jacob called her aunt and uncle, Mama and Papa.

Peyton pointed in the direction of Black Mountain, the tallest of its kind, and the beautiful Wild Rose Pass.

"See up there." Peyton pointed to Black Mountain. "When I see the beauty of that canyon pass, then I know I'm nearly home."

"I wish you could send me a signal, so then I could stop praying and fretting about you," Katie said.

"Did you know that you are the first person I rush to see

after I've reported to the colonel?" Peyton said. "Of course I clean up first, or you would smell me coming." They had stopped to admire nature's sculpture and enjoy the unseasonably warm fall temperatures.

"I wasn't aware of such things." Katie pretended to be unimpressed. "But thank you, especially for the bath."

A slight breeze met their faces, and the two quietly enjoyed the refreshing touch of fall. Soon winter, with all of its whistling winds and freezing temperatures, would keep them huddled around a warm fire.

He took her hand and together they strolled by the stream that fed Limpia Valley. "After being a part of Miles and Lauren's wedding I now wonder how Comanches marry."

"It's quite different," Katie said. "Comanche couples are not supposed to ever talk, but they usually devise ways to meet in secret. If a warrior has serious intentions, then he simply presents the maiden's family with gifts, usually horses. If the parents accept the gifts, then the couple begins living together and they are considered married. Sometimes the warrior will try to sneak into the bride's tent to snatch her away. Providing he's successful, then he has a wife."

"I think their way sounds better than ours," Peyton said, obviously amused. "Except you must have a lot of horses to win your lady's hand. What if the girl doesn't want to marry the warrior?"

"She can urge her parents not to accept the gift. But if her parents approve, she's stuck with her husband."

"I change my mind," Peyton said. "I like the idea of courtin' a girl instead of buying off her parents."

Katie laughed, and he squeezed her hand.

"You're on my mind most all of the time." Peyton faced her squarely, and his endearing look caused her heart to pound furiously. She didn't tremble like before but silently captured her own feelings and admitted to herself much more than a mere attraction to him.

"I would like to pull you close to me," he said softly. "Except the last time I frightened you."

She turned away then bravely met his ardent gaze with her own shy longings. "I won't stop you this time."

Peyton reached to hold her close, and she felt his breath brush against her cheek. She hoped he didn't hear the rapid beating of her heart, for she felt certain it would give away the secrets she needed to safeguard.

"We need to talk." He wound his fingers through her hair. "There are things, important things I must tell you." He gingerly released her and stepped back, studying her. "Katie, I care for you very much—more than caring, I love you."

She opened her mouth to speak, but his fingers silenced any response.

"Wait, let me finish, because I may not have the courage to tell you this again. Love for you hit me hard the night we learned about Jacob and Emily's family. Any other woman would have steered clear from such a nightmare, but you bravely insisted upon coming with me. When I saw the look of compassion upon your face at the sight of Jacob holding his little sister, I knew God had set you apart from all other women for me." He paused before beginning again. "Even though you didn't have Jesus in your life, a lot of folks, besides myself, were praying for you. And when you did accept Him, I realized God *had* put you into my life for a purpose."

"But there are things you don't know about me," she whispered.

"I know enough to see God's purpose in the both of us together," Peyton said. "And I, too, have things to tell you—some of which I regret, but they must be told." He gently grasped both of her hands and held her at arm's length from him. "I'm not proud of what the army has always asked of me, Katie, and one of the areas of duty has caused me to deceive you."

She could only stare at him in fearful wonder. Had he led patrols of men to destroy old men, women, and children living in Indian villages? Had Lone Eagle been killed? Peyton didn't know of her relationship with the Comanche warrior, unless Uncle Seth had told him. Had Peyton been transferred to another post and was now hesitant to tell her? His face appeared pained, and she couldn't imagine what could possibly disturb him so greatly.

"Peyton, my feelings for you are new, and despite my awkwardness in all of this, I want you to understand you can tell me anything. . .because I care for you very much. I've fought any type of emotion for you, and I can't believe I am admitting it to you now. What I am trying to say is it sounds like we both have things from our past to tell the other, but it shouldn't change how we feel." Katie wiped the tears slipping down over her face and trembled. She stepped into his embrace, and he wrapped his arms around her. "Peyton, I feel so guilty and ashamed about living with the Comanches. Uncle Seth and Aunt Elizabeth say I shouldn't, but every time I see someone who has been hurt by them, I despise myself."

"Sweetheart, God knows your heart. How can you blame yourself for their actions? You were a child living with those who treated you with love and kindness."

"And I loved them."

"Is not love the greatest commandment? Don't ever regret the time you spent with them. You learned how they think and what they feel. Too bad the rest of us can't do the same thing. Maybe then we would have peace. Katie, listen to me for one moment. I have not been truthful with you. . . ."

A shout from the distance alerted him. A young boy rode in their direction. The couple watched the rider approach and recognized Lauren's brother.

"Miss Colter, you're needed at the reception," he said breathlessly. "Lauren is ready to toss her ribbons to the next bride, and she won't budge an inch until you get there."

Chapter Ten

Katie caught Lauren's ribbons. She blushed and denied any truth in an upcoming wedding with Sergeant Sinclair, but Peyton only grinned and refused to comment. As the wedding celebration continued until after dusk, Peyton and Katie didn't find an opportunity to speak further. Once they attempted to leave the festivities for a few moments, except Miles spied them and urged them to stay a while longer.

Evening shadows forced everyone to their homes, and Peyton reluctantly informed Katie of a patrol scheduled to ride out before sunup. The soldiers would be gone for three weeks, escorting several wagons carrying provisions and supplies through Comanche territory.

"Don't you go getting into a sour mood," he said. It had become his favorite parting remark, and the words always made her smile.

He walked her to the cabin door. "I will do my best to stay sweet."

Peyton said good night and started to walk away, but he abruptly turned to face her. "Katie, I have never kissed you. I've certainly thought about it enough. Every time I'm ready, something or somebody interrupts us."

"There's nothing stopping you now," she whispered.

"Unless you don't want to."

"Oh, I want to. Guess I'd better take advantage of the dark while I can."

Katie thought her heart would burst through her chest. Surely Peyton could hear it flutter as his lips descended upon hers so slowly and gently, as though he wanted the kiss to last forever. He took her face into his hands and brushed a kiss to her forehead, the peak of her nose, and lightly against her lips.

"I love you, Katie Colter," he whispered and then he was gone.

Late into the night her mind lingered on the events of the day. What a perfect day for a wedding, and she felt so happy for Lauren and Miles. What had Peyton wanted to tell her that was so important? It had seemed urgent. Peyton stood for all that was right and good, but maybe something had happened during a battle.

Katie didn't intend to cry with his departure, but alone on her mat she muffled the tears. She had been ready to tell Peyton about Lone Eagle and the Kiowa scout. Her tears fell in fear for his safety. Why hadn't she told him about her relationship with the warrior? Now she must wait to uncover the ugly truth about herself and hear what he wanted to say.

As before, Katie threw herself into any work or activity that would keep her mind occupied until the patrol returned. She comforted herself by memorizing psalms, allowing their words to flow through her until she felt the blessings of praising God. Many times she daydreamed of Peyton and his endearing words of love. She prayed for guidance and direction with Peyton, certain God wanted them together.

"Katie, child, you certainly have been smiling a lot here

lately," Aunt Elizabeth said as they tidied the cabin. "Does the sergeant have anything to do with this?"

"Well, I don't know." She tried to appear surprised at her aunt's statement.

"Yes, you do." Aunt Elizabeth attempted to conceal a smile. "You have the glow of a lady in love."

"Do I?" Katie said then laughed in spite of her resolve to appear coy.

"So, tell your dear aunt what happened the day of Lauren and Miles's wedding. You have been radiant ever since."

"You don't think it's because I'm happy for Lauren?" Katie said, picking up a corn husk broom to sweep the rough stone floor.

"No, miss. So you might as well tell me—I won't stop pestering you until you do." Her aunt stood with one hand on her hip and pointing her finger with the other.

Should she tell Aunt Elizabeth? She hadn't told a soul about her and Peyton's conversation. "Well. . .it's very good. . . . He told me he cared for me, and I told him I felt the same."

"Something tells me those weren't the exact words."

"Probably not, but they are pretty close." Katie laughed. "Honestly, Aunt Elizabeth, both of us feel God has put us together, and we are very happy."

"Any mention of marriage?"

"Not the word marriage, but a hint of it." Katie lifted her chin stubbornly. "And that's all I can say until Peyton gets back and we have time to talk."

"I'm so happy for you," Aunt Elizabeth said with tears in her eyes. She shook her head as if to ignore the drops falling down her cheeks.

"I still have to tell him about Lone Eagle. And I will as soon as he gets back."

"Yes, it's best to be honest about everything with those you love," Aunt Elizabeth said. "Seth and I started our marriage with that belief, and I believe its sound advice for all couples."

Admitting out loud her love for Peyton made it real. The words spilled out like a bubbling waterfall, and she didn't care who could see or hear it. The patrol couldn't arrive home too soon.

Three weeks turned into four and still no word from the supply train or the army patrol. Katie gave the soldiers three more days' grace to allow for broken wheels or any other reasons why they would be delayed. On the morning of the fourth day, she chose to go see the colonel herself. After all, Colonel Ross should know why they were late, and he might answer her questions.

She nervously knocked on the officer's door. When she didn't hear a reply, she knocked again a little harder. Each time her knuckles rapped against the wooden door, her impatience mounted.

"I said, come in," the colonel bellowed behind the door.

She stepped inside and noted Colonel Ross hadn't reduced the stack of papers on his desk from the last time she was there. In fact, the mound of documents looked larger. He glanced up, and surprise etched the lines around his eyes.

"Miss Colter, excuse me. I didn't expect it to be you. Do sit down."

She seated herself on the ladder-back chair in front of the desk. "I won't take much of your time, Colonel Ross. I just have a few questions." She took a deep breath and willed her voice to stop shaking.

"You can have all the time you need. Is it about your land?

If so, I haven't gotten the paperwork back from the territorial land office." He leaned back in his chair and eyed her curiously.

"It's not about the land," Katie said.

"I didn't think so. You look too upset."

"The patrol is very late," Katie said as slowly and precisely as possible. "I was wondering if you had heard any word from them."

The colonel sighed deeply and picked up his pipe. "No, I haven't, but as soon as I do, I will be happy to inform you of their status." His manner was so formal that she wondered how many others had requested the same information.

"I realize you are busy, I'm just concerned."

"Your interest is understandable. Any number of reasons could delay them."

She rose to leave with no more assurance of the patrol's safety than when she entered his office. "Thank you, sir, for your time. I will continue to pray for their safe return."

"I'm sure the men appreciate your prayers, Miss Colter."

"Colonel?" Katie said with a degree of hesitancy. She latched on to the back of the wooden chair as though it would support her impending question.

"Yes."

"Why does Sergeant Sinclair accompany every one of the patrols?"

"Well, that's simple," the colonel said. "He's the only enlisted man who speaks Comanche."

Her face paled. She fought a sick feeling in the bottom of her stomach, and the room seemed to spin. It couldn't be true, but she'd heard Colonel Ross state so: Peyton spoke Comanche. No wonder he rode with every soldier who rode in and out of Fort Davis. His skills were vital in conversing, even surviving, with the Indians. Obviously the Kiowa scout didn't know Peyton spoke Comanche, or he wouldn't have spoken with her.

"Why wasn't I told this the afternoon Peyton escorted me to your office? Surely you remember when the Kiowa asked to speak with me?" Her voice sounded distant as though someone else spoke through her lips.

"I didn't feel it necessary," the colonel said.

"You didn't feel it necessary." Her voice rose. "Did you think I might reveal some valuable information you could use against the Comanches?"

"I believe you misunderstood—"

"I do understand, Colonel Ross. You wanted to make sure I wasn't some kind of a spy. Goodness, Jeremiah Colter's daughter must have been sent here to get information for the Comanches. Was the Kiowa's request a trap? And is his absence from the fort a way to make the meeting look real? Thank you, Colonel, for the confidence. I'm sure your interpreter gave you a favorable report."

Chapter Eleven

Katie didn't remember walking home after the meeting with Colonel Ross. Neither did she recall anyone she passed. Her thoughts were fixed on the colonel's truth and the likelihood of Peyton befriending her for the army's use. She didn't want to believe he would deliberately use her affections to gather information for the army, but the colonel's words made it appear so. Blinding, stinging tears humiliated her, and anger burned like a raging prairie fire.

At home Aunt Elizabeth tried to get her to explain what happened, but she simply paced the floor and shed tear after tear. Finally she picked up Emily and attempted to rock her. When holding the toddler didn't bring comfort, she held Emily close and wept more. Jacob patted her on the shoulder and whispered, "It will be all right," much like she had done with him.

"Has something happened to Peyton?" her aunt said, kneeling beside the rocking chair.

She shook her head.

"I can't help you if you don't tell me what is wrong." She pulled a wet strand of hair from Katie's face and tucked it behind her ear.

Katie took a deep breath. "I just found out that Colonel

Ross and Peyton arranged a meeting with a Kiowa scout to see if I would send information back to. . ." She couldn't finish with Jacob standing so near.

"Surely not. It has to be a mistake."

"The colonel just told me," she said between sobs and carefully retold the accounting, making sure to leave out certain words that would alarm Jacob.

"There has to be a reasonable explanation, surely a misunderstanding," Aunt Elizabeth said. "But right now, you need to get alone with the Lord. You will be miserable until you pray and find the courage to forgive both of them."

"Forgive them?" Katie startled. "How can I ever forgive or forget?"

"Not on your own strength, but with the power of God." Her aunt picked up a brown package and placed it in Katie's lap. "Here, we've been saving this for you. It's a new Bible, a gift from your uncle and me. We planned to give it to you this evening, but you have greater use for it now."

Aunt Elizabeth lifted Emily from Katie's lap and watched while she untied the heavy string around the package. Katie drew a brown leather Bible to her chest and mouthed a tearful thank-you.

"Go on into our room," her aunt said. "Spend time alone with the Father. Only He can comfort you."

Katie seldom entered her aunt and uncle's bedroom. She and the children slept in the main part of the two-room cabin and found no need to step inside her aunt and uncle's small bit of privacy.

Sitting in a wooden chair on which a quilt had been draped over the back, Katie wiped the tears from her eyes and silently prayed before opening the Bible.

Oh, heavenly Father, I hurt so badly. I feel like my whole world has just fallen down around me. I don't know why Peyton didn't tell me he spoke Comanche, and I don't know why he couldn't trust me enough to tell me he understood the Kiowa's words. I feel so horrible, and the ache in my heart is worse than when Pa died. At least he didn't have a choice, but Peyton chose to deceive me.

She stopped in the middle of her prayer. Peyton had used the word *deceive* when he tried to tell her something before he left on patrol. It had to be this; nothing else would have affected him with such urgency. Opening the Bible, she prayed for God to speak to her through His Word.

The dedication page was empty, and Katie decided to ask Uncle Seth and Aunt Elizabeth to complete it. If they had gone ahead with their plans to present the Bible to her that evening, the blank lines would have been filled.

Leafing through page after page, she read passages that comforted her but none that pierced her heart. Then 1 Corinthians, chapter 13 caught her eye. Katie read it once and wept in the knowledge of God's love for her and His infinite understanding of her feelings. She reread the description of love, blinking back the tears and thanking God for His Word. Verse 8 spoke directly to the pain in her heart. "Charity never faileth: but whether there be prophecies, they shall fail; whether there be tongues, they shall cease; whether there be knowledge, it shall vanish away." And on to verses 12–13: "For now we see through a glass, darkly; but then face to face: now I know in part; but then shall I know even as also I am known. And now abideth faith, hope, charity, these three; but the greatest of these is charity."

Katie closed the book and let it rest upon her lap. What Colonel Ross and Peyton did was wrong. They had deceived her in order to see if she would willingly side with the Comanches. Had the colonel and Peyton contrived the

Kiowa's questioning? She quickly dispelled the latter thought. The Kiowa spoke of matters known only by Lone Eagle and herself.

She sat upright—Peyton knew of her relationship with Lone Eagle. He had heard the Kiowa issue Lone Eagle's demands, and he clearly heard her answers. Peyton had known all along and never said a word. It was as though it didn't matter to him. *That's why he was so angry that day.* The guilt she bore for not telling him about the warrior didn't seem to matter now. Yet, beyond any measure of doubt, Peyton clearly understood her loyalties. She'd feared rejection from him when he learned the truth, and he had already heard the truth from her own lips.

Now she saw why the Kiowa had been released from his duties at the fort. The Indian could not be trusted. If Peyton did use her, why did he later pursue a relationship? Betrayal cut so very deep.

How much of the conversation did Peyton reveal to the colonel? Humiliation spread through her—the commander of the post knew intimate information about her. Perhaps Peyton kept some of the knowledge to himself. In any event, Katie must forgive them for purposely misleading her. And no matter the outcome, she must ask Peyton to forgive her for not telling him about Lone Eagle from the very beginning.

Katie closed her eyes and prayed for guidance. She leaned back against the quilt and slept.

She woke to the sound of Aunt Elizabeth's voice calling her to waken.

"Yes," Katie said. "I fell asleep. I'm sorry."

Her aunt pushed aside the blanket separating the two rooms of the cabin. "Peyton is here with the colonel. They're waiting to see you."

The news cleared any sleepiness lingering in Katie's mind. "They both are here to see me?" she whispered.

"Yes, child. I invited them in, but they decided to wait outside."

She stood and laid her Bible on the bed. "I guess I'd better see what they want." Then she added, "Peyton is all right, isn't he?"

"He looks tired, but healthy." Her aunt touched Katie's cheek. "I'm going to take the children to visit Seth."

"No, please. I can talk to them outside or go to the colonel's office."

"You aren't the only Colter who is stubborn," Aunt Elizabeth said. "And I've already told Jacob we would be leaving for the blacksmith."

She saw little use in arguing. Her aunt ushered the men inside, poured them coffee, and left with the children to see Uncle Seth.

Katie avoided eye contact with both men. She no longer felt like crying or shouting accusations. It seemed simpler to hear why the two had chosen to visit.

"Colonel Ross, I owe you an apology for my outburst in your office today," she said.

"Under the circumstances, I don't believe an apology is necessary."

"There's no excuse for my rudeness, and I am sorry. Colonel Ross, Peyton, you didn't need to pay me a call." She turned to Peyton for the first time but still avoided his gaze. "I'm glad to see you returned safe and unharmed. Are the other men all right?"

Peyton sighed. "Yes, just exhausted."

The men sat stiffly at the table, but Katie chose the rocker near the fire. Would she ever feel comfortable with either of them again?

"Miss Colter, Sergeant Sinclair and I are the ones who owe you an apology for what appears to be a misunderstanding or rather an oversight on our part. My reasons for accompanying the sergeant are to tell you myself that there was no pretense in the meeting you had with the Kiowa. The scout came into my office and stated he needed to speak with you. I sensed an importance in the matter and sent the sergeant to fetch you. In case you may have questioned my motives, I do not speak Comanche. Therefore, I have no idea what transpired in your conversation. The sergeant told me you relayed perfectly the Kiowa's words, and I chose not to ask anything more about the subject but to take heed as you suggested. As I said to you after the Kiowa left my office, I appreciate your concern for the welfare of the people living here at Fort Davis. I chose to allow the Kiowa to come and go here to use his treachery against him, and I purposely provided him with false information."

The colonel stood from his chair. "I sincerely hope you will give this young man an opportunity to clear up this unfortunate incident."

Katie nodded and escorted him to the door. "Thank you for everything you just told me and for coming by to see me," she said. "I am sincerely grateful, and again I apologize for earlier today."

Once the door closed, she leaned against it. She sensed Peyton's eyes on her, but she couldn't bring herself to face him.

"Am I so repulsive that you can't look at me?" he said, his words harsh and cold.

She forced herself to meet his gaze. Worry lines dug across his forehead. "No, I really don't know what to say or do. I've been angry, I've been hurt, and now I'm confused and ashamed."

"Why are you ashamed?" he said.

Katie took a deep breath. "Because I was busy feeling sorry for myself, and I forgot to consider the information you found out about me."

"Are you talking about your relationship with Lone Eagle?"

"Yes, and I should have told you about him the first night you asked to come calling." She remained against the door as though it helped her from crumbling before his eyes.

"And I apologize for not telling you of my ability to speak Comanche." Peyton's face softened. "I know it's no excuse, but I tried on several occasions."

"The afternoon of Lauren and Miles's wedding?" She moved away from the door and sat across from him at the table. "Because I wanted to tell you about Lone Eagle then, too. I didn't want to keep it from you any longer."

Peyton shook his head as though he attempted to clear his thoughts. "I did try the day of the wedding. Katie, if I learned anything the night you met with the Kiowa, it was how you were willing to go back with him to save the lives of people here. How could I be angry at your unselfish gesture?"

She stared at her hands neatly folded in her lap. "I never looked at it quite the same way as you do. I kept remembering Jacob and Emily's family and wanted to see it ended. You see, I'm not afraid of Lone Eagle, and at one time I believed I loved him. I don't want to ever go back there, but if I had to, it wouldn't be a terrible sacrifice."

He reached across the table and wrapped his hands over hers. His voice sounded raspy, and when she met his gray gaze, she saw emotion steal across his face. "Promise me you won't ever go back to him."

"I can't, Peyton." How could she make him understand? "I can't promise you something that might endanger innocent lives. I love you. I love you with all my heart, but I couldn't live with myself if one person was injured or killed to ensure my happiness."

"Must you be so noble?"

Katie lifted her hand to his cheek. "I'm not noble, no, nothing of the sort. I'm trying to live my life as God would want, and I'll go wherever He leads me."

"Away from me, away from a life together?" he said.

"I pray it won't come to a choice." Hot tears filled her eyes. "I don't want to live my life with one man and love another."

Chapter Twelve

*L*ong, uncomfortable moments followed with the sounds of outside activity deafening the roar in Katie's heart. She wanted to tell Peyton the many things she dreamed for both of them and the countless hours spent watching the fort gate and praying for his safe return. The look on his face silenced any words of endearment. She'd seen the same expression on his face the night she refused to tell him what the Kiowa had relayed to her. They had quarreled then, and she didn't want to fall into the same pit again. Arguing solved nothing; it only deepened the problem.

She ordered herself to say nothing more in her own defense but allow Peyton to express his indignation. Except this time frustration and anger weren't the only emotions tearing through him. She saw a mixture of love and hate intertwined to add confusion to his passion. Dare she hope the hatred was not intended for her?

How would she face another day if Peyton despised her? He risked his life every day he rode outside the safety of the fort. She waited for him to speak, but she must hold on to her convictions.

"The Kiowa should have tried to contact you by now," he said, his brows narrowed. "He could have used any excuse to gain entrance into the fort."

"I agree," she said. "I look for him every day."

"Then marry me now, Katie. Marry me before Lone Eagle has a chance to use his power over you."

She blinked back the tears, reaching deep for strength. "Don't you see? It wouldn't change a thing but make matters worse. In his eyes, I am his wife."

"It wasn't consummated," he said.

"Did you memorize every word of the Kiowa's conversation?"

"And if I did?"

"Then you understand my leaving the village hurt Lone Eagle's pride."

"I don't care about his pride! What kind of a man would want a woman who didn't want him?" Peyton pounded his fist into the table as though the physical action would make her listen to him.

Katie vowed not to lose her temper, and silence exploded from the four walls of the cabin.

Finally she spoke, but her voice cracked. "I grew up with Lone Eagle. I know him. He would use the lapse of time for his own benefit. He's known among the other warriors for his shrewd and cunning ways. Waiting is one of his favorite games. My fear is he will do nothing until he thinks I no longer believe he will send word. That's when Lone Eagle will take his stand. Peyton, it's not an affair of the heart for him. It's a way of life, and he must win. No matter if he loved me beyond any doubt, Lone Eagle would still be a warrior. By waiting to speak until I have made other plans"—Katie paused and felt herself grow warm with the implication of her words— "he causes me to fall into his trap, and then he will wage war. Lone Eagle does not make idle threats or speak empty words, for that would discredit him in the eyes of his people."

"Remember when the Kiowa said Swift Arrow and Lone Eagle would not declare war over a woman but over honor and the land of their fathers?" Peyton said. "He's using his power to force you back to him."

Katie slowly nodded her head. "Yes, but I am his property, and in Lone Eagle's eyes his wife has run from him."

Peyton stood and paced the room. "I will see that murdering Indian burn in—"

"Peyton, calm down. He may not be here with us, but he's succeeding in causing you to react in anger instead of logic."

"And what would you have me do?" Peyton swung his attention to her. "Sit back and allow Lone Eagle to decide your future, our future? I am a man, Katie, not a child who allows others to make his decisions for him."

"We could pray. We should turn this whole thing over to God and allow Him to work it out. I'm a new Christian, but I've seen the value of prayer."

He walked to the door. "I can't pray right now. I'm too angry, and the thought of you allowing a murdering savage to determine our happiness is more than I can handle." He lifted the latch and closed the door soundly behind him.

She glanced around the empty room. *What do I do now, God?*

"Trust Me, Katie," came a clear, quiet answer.

Katie spent the remainder of the daylight hours contemplating what she should do about Peyton. She prayed for him and asked God to be with him, but little else could be done. Peyton needed to search for his own answers and allow God to work in his life. She must *wait for Peyton to come to her. Waiting. . .that's what Lone Eagle did best, not her.*

The Comanche warrior held her future, and she never

doubted for a moment that the Kiowa had delivered her message. Lone Eagle deliberately chose not to send a reply. He stalked his prey well, and now he watched and waited for her next move.

But she wasn't his wife. She was still untouched.

Pa told her once that love could easily change to hate and hate to murder. Pride usually controlled a man's emotions, especially those affairs of the heart.

Katie had admitted her past love for Lone Eagle. She couldn't deny those feelings or pretend nothing ever happened. She'd worshipped him. Everything about the Comanche warrior had intrigued her: his hair—the color of the crow, his deep, penetrating eyes that had always held tenderness for her, the magnificent way he carried himself. He stood for the virtues held high by every tribal member. He fought bravely, and others told of his mighty acts in battle. As Swift Arrow's eldest son, Lone Eagle spent many hours with his father learning how to lead the tribe. His mother loved him above her other children. She sewed for Lone Eagle and cooked his favorite foods. The warrior knew his guardian spirits and regularly consulted their medicine. Comanche families wanted him to notice their daughters and befriend their sons. Lone Eagle rose as a son among sons, a warrior among warriors.

Her thoughts of love for Lone Eagle had led her to believe he was perfect. He did have a bad temper and a vindictive nature. How could she have overlooked the way he oppressed weaker warriors or shunned Indian maidens who were plain? Jealousy and arrogance clasped hands with Lone Eagle, and he never let her forget he would one day be chief of the Comanches. When they were alone, Lone Eagle showered her with affection. Katie never doubted his love or devotion, but many things had changed since she came to live at the fort. Her love for Lone Eagle began to diminish when she viewed how the people around her cared for each other. They worshiped the one true God—a God of love and compassion.

God, please help me. Katie shuddered. *Because I don't want to ever go back to him.*

Colonel Ross sent Peyton on another patrol, but Peyton failed to inform Katie. Neither did he tell her good-bye. In fact, she realized Peyton purposely avoided her, and Katie found out about the patrol through Lauren. This time the soldiers would be gone a week.

She prayed for Peyton's safety and for them to be able to talk upon his return. He had to have made a decision about the two of them by now. Maybe the silence provided an answer. The ache in her heart refused to go away. She hurt in the mornings and even more at night. Aunt Elizabeth and Uncle Seth continued their comfort and encouragement. Their wordless gestures told her they shared her pain. They cared for Peyton, too, and it didn't help when Jacob asked about his soldier.

"Jacob, would you like to go fishing?" Katie said when the small boy asked again about Sergeant Sinclair.

He didn't need to think twice. "Yes. Can we go now?"

Katie smiled and ruffled his hair. "Of course. I heard Uncle Seth say he had a taste for fish."

"I'll catch them all." He straightened his shoulders. "And I'll dig for worms."

The day had a bit of chill to it, and Katie made sure Jacob wore a coat. Together the two carried poles and a wooden bucket to bring back their catches. She hoped the sun would peek through the bleak sky to warm them a little, but the clouds seemed to carry the threat of snow.

Limpia Brook rippled noisily while Katie helped Jacob find worms. She'd tucked in a few slices of bread in case the fish needed encouragement to swallow the line.

"Indian boys catch fish with their hands," she said.

He attempted to snatch up a swimming trout, but the fish proved faster than his little hands.

"The water is too cold," Jacob said. "My fingers are froze."

Katie warmed them with her own hands, and soon he was ready to try again.

"Let's try catching fish the Indian way when the weather is warmer," she said with a laugh. "Today we can fish like the soldiers and Uncle Seth." Katie handed him a pole, and he took it reluctantly. "I bet my fish will be bigger than yours."

"Boys can fish better than girls."

An hour passed and still no fish. Jacob was rapidly becoming discouraged; then something nibbled at his line.

"Look, Katie, I've got one," he said.

She helped him bring in a good-sized trout and land it in the bucket.

"Now, it's your turn," he said, "but I know mine is bigger."

A short time later, Katie brought in one that measured slightly shorter than Jacob's fish.

"You won." She squeezed his shoulders. "I think we have enough for supper. Shall we take these two home?"

Jacob nodded. "Yes, I'm cold."

Once inside the fort, Katie heard the sound of soldiers and saw the army patrol enter the front gate. From the distance they looked tired and dusty, but nothing out of the ordinary. Then she spotted two soldiers tied across their saddles, and three others wore makeshift bandages. Peyton wore one of the bandages around his shoulder. From her stance, she saw bloodstains.

"Peyton!" Katie cried, leaving the fish bucket and rushing with Jacob to his side. "You're hurt."

He eyed her without the tenderness she remembered from the past. "It's nothing serious, just a shoulder wound." He had yet to dismount his horse but rather surveyed the crowd. "Some of us weren't so lucky." She couldn't bring herself to look at the dead men, and surely Jacob did not need to be a part of this crowd. Besides, Peyton's tone didn't invite conversation.

He's still angry. And with the deaths and injuries of his men, I can't expect him to want to talk to me.

She stepped back while Peyton grabbed the saddle horn with his left hand and swung his leg around the horse. Awkward, silent moments followed as a crowd formed around all the men. Some asked questions; others tended to the wounded and dead. Katie heard a young boy cry out for his pa.

"I'm sorry," she said to Peyton.

She looked around to see if anyone needed help, but there were more than enough people assisting the others. She'd just be in the way. Taking a deep breath and breathing a prayer for the soldiers and their families, Katie and Jacob retrieved the bucket and walked home.

Late into the night, she woke to the sound of someone pounding on the door. Uncle Seth should answer it, especially in light of the hour, but the pounding persisted and she didn't want the children wakened.

"Who would want a horse shod this hour of the night?" Katie whispered to herself as she hurried to the door. "Who's there?" she said as quietly as possible.

"Peyton."

"Do you have any idea what time it is?" Katie said, perturbed at his late call.

"Yes, I can't sleep," said the voice behind the door.

"Well, I was sleeping just fine." She purposely laced her words with agitation. "What do you want, anyway?"

"To talk to you."

"Peyton Sinclair, are you drunk?"

"No, the doc gave me laudanum for pain, but I didn't drink a thing. Are you coming out to talk?"

"No! I'm not dressed, and it's not proper."

"It's dark out here, and no one is going to see. Can't you put on your coat and shoes?"

"Katie," Uncle Seth whispered, parting the blanket partition. "Who's out there?"

"It's Peyton."

"What does he want?"

"For me to come out there to talk. I've already told him no. I'm not properly dressed, but he won't listen. If he doesn't stop pounding, he'll wake everyone up."

"Is he drunk?" In the shadow of firelight, Seth crossed his arms.

"I already asked him the same thing. He says no."

"Katie, are you coming out?" Peyton called.

She shook her head in utter disgust. "Would you hush? You've already wakened Uncle Seth, and if you waken these children I'll put a bullet through your other shoulder." Katie glanced in Uncle Seth's direction. "What do I do?"

"I'll run him off if you want me to. . .aw, go on out and listen to what he has to say. I'm awake now, so if he's drunk or bothers you, holler out. I'll thrash him good if he touches you. Who knows? He may have something worthwhile to say, and it can't wait until morning."

Uncle Seth must have lost his mind, but she'd hear Peyton out. "Give me a moment," she whispered at the door. After grabbing her coat and tugging on her shoes, she stepped out into the cold. Soft, wet flakes of snow sifted through the dark and rested on her hands.

"It's snowing," Peyton said.

She might thrash him herself. "I know, the first one this year. Is this why you came to see me?" Exasperation nibbled at her.

"No, Katie. I've come on serious business."

She wished she could see his face; maybe then she could tell his mood. "Be quick about it, Peyton. I'm freezing."

"The last time we talked, things weren't finished."

"Today or before you left on patrol?"

"Before I left. You're not making this easy."

"Why should I? Never mind, I well remember our conversation." She wrapped her arms around herself.

"Do you want me to keep you warm?"

"No. And if you think you can get away with anything, Uncle Seth is waiting inside,"

Peyton must have thought her remark incredibly funny, because he broke into a fit of laughter.

"Would you hush before you wake the entire fort," she said. "I swear, if I find out you're drunk, I will. . .I will. . ."

"Scalp me?" Peyton said.

"Now, that's not funny. I'm going back inside."

He took her arm, and the sudden movement obviously caused a surge of fire to his injured shoulder because he winced.

She gasped. "Are you sure you should be out with your shoulder?"

"It's a little sore, but it'll be all right. I'm sorry, Katie. Please, wait a minute more. I need to talk to you."

She tapped her foot against the cold ground. "Go ahead, I'm listening."

"I've had lots of time to think about the two of us, and I

have a few things to say," he said.

Her heart beat wildly against her chest. For the first time since she came outside, she was glad for the blackness of night. How very hard to care for a man and be so angry with him at the same time.

"First, I love you and nothing is going to change that. Second, I'm as pigheaded and stubborn as you are."

Katie smiled in the dark. "Are you just now realizing that?"

Peyton sighed. "Third, I want to force Lone Eagle's hand on this. I think we can make him state his intentions about you. It's risky, but I can't expect you to marry me until I know you are free to be my wife."

Katie said nothing while she reflected upon his words. "What do you suggest?"

"Let's announce our engagement," he said in one breath. "The Kiowa is here. He said he needed to purchase provisions. We can be certain the message will get back to Lone Eagle."

"What if he orders you killed?" Katie said.

"I'll risk it. Besides, I can't live without you."

"Now, who is being noble?" Katie said, without a trace of humor. "Oh, I don't know what to say, Peyton. I want this finished with Lone Eagle, but I'm afraid for you."

"I've prayed about it," he said. "It doesn't do any good to argue with a praying man, especially one who is in love."

"I've prayed about us, too." She didn't feel brave or resolute, only tired of fearing what Lone Eagle might do. "All right, I'll agree to your plan, and we'll wait for Lone Eagle's next move."

"We will be better at waiting than he is," Peyton said, and Katie heard the conviction in his voice.

She would be a fool not to admit the alarm and fright washing over her whole body. She shivered, but not from the cold. Peyton's plan brought the whole nightmare to a peak. He

DIANN MILLS

could be killed. She could be killed or forced to spend the rest of her life with the Comanche warrior.

Lone Eagle's decision still held Peyton and Katie's future, but God held their destiny. No matter what happened in the weeks ahead, God would be with them. He knew their hearts, and He would protect them. Katie remembered the search for her rehoboth, and a peculiar peace settled upon her.

"Trust Me, Katie. Let Me guide you."

Chapter Thirteen

When Katie stepped back inside the cabin, she found Uncle Seth rocking Emily.

"I leaned over to kiss her and woke her up," he whispered. "What did the sergeant want at this late hour?"

She smiled. "He wants me to marry him."

Like a boy, Uncle Seth could barely contain his jubilance. Little Emily opened her eyes wide and sat up in his lap. "Now look what I've done." He chuckled.

Aunt Elizabeth appeared at their side, and Katie repeated the story to her. Her aunt immediately burst into tears and insisted she didn't think it right to give up one of her children so soon. "But if you have to leave us, at least it's to a fine young man." She hugged her close.

"I declare," Uncle Seth said. "I thought the man had indulged himself in too much whiskey, but instead he was drunk with love. And here I sat ready to teach him a lesson. He *is* a good man, Katie, and I'm proud to call him a son-in-law. I must be getting old, because I forgot he'd sought permission to marry you right after you two had your last spat. I should have known."

She could hardly believe her uncle's words.

"Yes, the sergeant came to me the day before he left on patrol and requested your hand in marriage."

In the next few days news spread quickly through the community, and Peyton and Katie met head-on all the questions surrounding the engagement. The two decided upon a Christmas wedding with the ceremony set for the afternoon of December 24. In less than six weeks, Peyton and Katie would be man and wife. It also meant Lone Eagle had less than six weeks to respond to the news.

"What if Lone Eagle chooses to do nothing about our marriage?" Katie said one evening after they had announced their plans. The two walked hand in hand back from a visit with Reverend Cooper. All day her excitement had mounted, and she had tried to discount it in light of Peyton's reasons for an early wedding date. She knew he loved her, but she regretted the reason for the ceremony centered on Lone Eagle.

"Then I get a wife for Christmas," he said.

"I don't want you to feel like you have to go through with this ceremony." In fact, she despised the ruse. "I feel like Lone Eagle is the reason you want to get married."

Peyton stopped and, with his uninjured hand, lifted her chin. "Lone Eagle is the reason I hadn't asked before. I needed to be sure you weren't still in love with him."

Warm tears stung her eyes. "Oh Peyton, I'm not sure what I once felt for him was anything but a young girl's infatuation. I don't deserve your love. I do love you, and I promise to be a good wife."

He leaned over and kissed her lightly on the nose. "Now, are there any more questions filling your pretty little head?"

"Yes, I have a lot of them. Where will we live?" she said.

"Let me think." He laughed. "Since it's Christmas Eve, I could ask the colonel to let us use part of the stable. The animals could keep us warm. Seems fittin', don't you agree?"

"I'm serious. I'd punch you except I might hurt your shoulder."

He laughed. "Truthfully, I have my eye on an empty cabin near the end of the civilian section. It needs a new roof and some fixin' up, but I can do it."

"Are you sure this is really what you want?" She had to be sure.

Peyton's answer came in a kiss.

"I want the two of us married and raising a bunch of children. I want to grow old with you and see our grandchildren play together. We will have a beautiful life together, but not until Lone Eagle releases his hold on you."

"What will we do if Lone Eagle puts me into a position where I have to go back to him?" Her words sounded more calm than she felt.

"You aren't going back to him," Peyton said. "Colonel Ross is the only one who knows about this. I've confided in him, and he has helped me devise a plan to capture Lone Eagle. This territory will be free of his murdering raids, and I will have Katie Colter as my wife."

More bloodshed.

With the early wedding date, Aunt Elizabeth grumbled and pointed out the lack of necessary items in Katie's trousseau. Peyton hadn't given her enough notice to plan a wedding or prepare things to take up housekeeping. Her aunt warned him to prepare for a lecture every day until the wedding.

Many folks congratulated the young couple. Some of those who had criticized her in the past now smiled politely. The contrary Mrs. Ames even made a point of stopping after church to express her congratulations.

DIANN MILLS

"If I had known so many people would be nice to you, I would have asked you to marry me the moment you rode into the fort," Peyton said after Katie received a gift of canned fruit from Mrs. Ames.

"In one breath, I'm so excited about the wedding," Katie said. "But in the next breath, I'm afraid of Lone Eagle's response. We shouldn't have to make wedding preparations around a threat."

"You're right and I agree totally with you, except we know God's hand is on our marriage. I don't believe He wants us to spend the rest of our lives wondering what Lone Eagle might or might not do. Our wedding date merely forces Lone Eagle to make a decision. Sweetheart, it's the only choice we have."

Every word he spoke was the truth. "When would you have proposed if Lone Eagle hadn't been a threat?" she said.

Peyton chuckled. "There's a whole lot of wisdom in proposing to a girl in the middle of a cold dark night. My timing would probably be the same. You would either have to say yes or freeze until you accepted. Lone Eagle had little to do with my proposal."

But Katie knew differently.

Peyton made certain the Kiowa heard the news. Within a week, the Indian disappeared from the fort. The young couple waited for Lone Eagle's reply.

Well-wishers invited the engaged couple to dinner, and Lauren and Martha stitched furiously on those special linens required in a young lady's trousseau. Katie searched through her trunk of belongings and found her mother's wedding dress. It fit perfectly with no alterations, and Katie wondered if anyone else ever knew such happiness. With tears, which seemed to dampen her face much more than usual, she thought how wonderful it would have been to have her mother see her

128

marry. The emotion rose again when she asked Uncle Seth to give her away. How she missed her father.

One evening during a walk, Peyton squeezed her hand. "Katie, I want to get out of the army."

Katie reflected upon his statement. It sounded like an answer to prayer. "Good. I worry so each time you ride out. My fears seem to chip away at my heart."

"Well, my enlistment is up in the spring, and I think I'm ready to settle down into civilian life again. Two reasons for my decision," he said.

"A wife who will worry every time you ride out?"

"How about a Comanche warrior who thinks she belongs to them."

"And may want you dead."

"There's more. I'd like to visit my folks in Illinois, and, of course, let them get to know my beautiful wife. I haven't seen them or my brothers in over five years. I miss them, and it seems right to go home for a visit."

"What then?"

"I've been thinking that God may want me to finish medical school."

"Oh my, I've never heard you say anything about wanting to be a doctor," she said.

"Well," he began. "It's why I joined the army. It's a long story, but one I suppose you need to hear." He rubbed his bandaged shoulder. Lately the wound had started to itch with its healing. "My folks wanted me to be a doctor, so to please them, I attended two years of medical school. I'd never been so miserable in my whole life. I thought the only thing I ever wanted to do was come out west and take up ranching. I sank into a horrible depression, and that was when an old friend of my father's talked to me about the Lord. Well, the hope in his message and the words of grace and mercy made me realize I needed a Savior. It didn't take long for me to give my life over to the Lord. My folks were elated. Not only were they going to have a doctor in the family, but they also had a Christian. It took a lot of courage to tell them of my decision to leave school. They were hurt and very disappointed. So I joined the army to give all of us time to heal. The trouble is I never saw a clear picture of what God intended for me until I met you. Then everything moved into place. I hope you will like being a doctor's wife, 'cause my mind is pretty set on it. I've saved enough money to buy us a small home and get me started back at school."

"But Peyton," Katie said. "I have a ranch, It's green and fertile and is bound to bring a good price."

"I forgot about your father's land."

"Our land. I could sell it, and then I'd have a perfect trousseau."

"Do you want to give up your land?"

"Of course—it should belong to someone who could raise cattle and horses. My pa used to talk about building a cattle ranch, but it never happened. I don't want to raise our children in Indian territory. I want them someplace safe. We've both seen enough tragedy in this land to last forever."

The idea seemed to have a sobering effect upon him. "What's wrong, Peyton? Is it because the land is mine?"

"No, sweetheart. With my savings, we can start better than I expected."

She wanted so much to marry Peyton and spend the rest of her life with him. To live out their lives without the fear of raiding Indians seemed almost too good to be true. God had blessed her with a good man, one who loved her dearly and demonstrated his compassion and gentleness in countless ways. Peyton would make an excellent doctor. How proud she felt! Now if Lone Eagle would just leave them alone so they could start their life together.

God, isn't there anything big or small I can do to hurry this along? Can Peyton leave Fort Davis sooner than the spring? I hate waiting; I don't know what Lone Eagle is thinking or what he wants from me. Am I being self-centered? Could it be my worries are needless? Help me to give it all to You and not keep pulling it back. Thank You for Peyton. He's so good to me.

She took a deep breath and asked God to forgive her for rambling. The truth of the matter was she feared Peyton's plan might get Lone Eagle killed or Peyton killed. She had no desire for the warrior to die. The idea sickened her. How could she want him dead? Lone Eagle had been her playmate and first love. Although she had been naive and foolish, the feelings at the time were real. The warrior said he loved her, and Katie had believed she loved him. Despite all the horrible injustices he had done, Lone Eagle had shown her a tender side. Nothing excused his murdering raids, but the good things about him did deserve a soft portion of her heart. She desperately needed him to reconsider his claims upon her.

With all her heart, she believed the whites and the Indians could live together if they tried to understand each other and make compromises. Honor and respect could prevail in the land if each promised to abide by a given set of rules. She refused to think of any more killing for either Indian or whites.

"Trust Me, Katie."

Chapter Fourteen

The chill in the air, the festivities of Christmas, and all the excitement of the wedding lifted Katie and Peyton's spirits. Neither wanted to concentrate on the gravity of the situation before them or discuss it. Ignoring Lone Eagle did not eliminate the problem, it merely postponed it. The Kiowa would arrive soon enough with the warrior's message. Katie decided to enjoy the celebrations of the season and the preparations for their new home as long as possible. She repeatedly told herself it did little good to worry and decided to say nothing unless Peyton mentioned it. Except each time Peyton wanted to speak of it, she refused to discuss it. Denial had never been a part of her makeup, but she felt compelled to push their problems away.

The two worked side by side preparing the cabin. With Miles and Lauren's help, they replaced the roof and muddied up the sides to keep out the cold. But there were times Peyton drifted into silence, and she didn't question his moods. They shared the same fears.

"I think we should name all our children from people in the Bible," Katie suggested one evening as they finished sealing the cracks inside the cabin. Peyton had built a fire, and the small structure felt warm and comfortable.

"Well, I had a different idea," he said.

She stopped with her small bucket of mud mixed with straw and eyed him curiously. "What did you have in mind?"

"I was thinking that I wanted our children to always remember their mother and grandfather once lived with the Indians," he said, continuing his work.

"And?"

"So I would like to name them after Indian tribes. The first one we'd call Comanche, then Apache—that sounds good for a girl, ah yes, and Kiowa, Sioux—another girl's name, Navajo, Blackfoot, Cheyenne, and on until we get a dozen or so."

She stood speechless. "Peyton, are you crazy? Why ever would you want to give a child such a name?"

"I like the sound of 'em. You know, those names just seem to roll off the tongue. For certain, all the folks would know the Sinclair children."

"That's for sure," Katie said. "Let's talk about this. I bet we could come up with good names that both of us would like."

"Nope, my mind is made up," Peyton said with his back to her. "I've already entered a few in my Bible."

"No, you haven't. You're tormenting me again. You should be ashamed."

"Me?" Peyton whirled around with mud on his fingers and a glint in his eye. "I have more: Caddo, Iroquois, Cherokee. . ."

"You will never be able to convince me of those names," she said in pretended annoyance.

Peyton stepped closer, threatening her with mud-covered fingers, but he stole a kiss instead. "I might reconsider after the first dozen."

Katie insisted upon helping Martha and Lauren with school during the mornings. The children made gifts for their parents, and one morning they all made sugar cookies. They rehearsed Christmas carols to sing on Christmas Eve as a part of the wedding and again later for church services. Their sweet voices always brought tears to Katie's eyes, even when the bigger boys grumbled about singing. During lunch she hurried back to the cabin while Jacob stayed with the other students until midafternoon. The hours sped by quickly as she and Aunt Elizabeth took turns caring for Emily, discussing the wedding, and tending to chores.

This morning Martha and Lauren insisted Katie return home and work on sewing projects for her new home. Martha reminded her there were only days left until the wedding. The cabin still needed work, and she looked tired. Needless to say, many items remained to be stitched and sewn.

Katie lifted the latch on the Colter cabin and quietly stepped inside. She had so many things on her mind, and Emily might be resting. She heard the sound of voices in her aunt and uncle's bedroom. It seemed odd for her uncle to be home in the middle of the day. Unlike other settlers at the fort, his position as blacksmith kept him busy while others searched for chores to keep occupied. Katie hoped he had not become ill.

"Seth, you can't put this off any longer," Aunt Elizabeth said. "She needs to be told the truth."

"I know, I know, but you have no idea what you're asking of me." His words were spoken as though he were tired or ill.

"I realize you have lived with this for over seventeen years," Aunt Elizabeth said. "But it's time to put the past behind you. Katie loves you, just as you love her."

"She will despise me if I tell her the truth. She thinks I'm a God-fearing man, when in fact I'm vile and loathsome."

"No, you're not," her aunt said. "You're good and kind and

decent. Seth Colter, don't let the guilt hurt you any longer. This thing has eaten at you for too long. It's time to get it out in the open. Both of you love each other, and God will work it out."

"She's about to be married," he said. "Why do I need to tell her at all? She'll have a husband, and they will be gone in the spring."

Katie pushed aside the blanket separating the two rooms. "Tell me what, Uncle Seth? What could be so dreadful that you don't want to tell me?"

An injured look passed from her uncle to her aunt.

"I'll do it," he whispered to her aunt. "It's about time I took responsibility for my own mistakes." He reached for Katie, and she gave him her hand. "We need to talk. There are some things you need to hear."

He pointed to the chair, and Katie took her place. A chill had swept across the room, and she pulled the quilt from the back of the chair and laid it across her lap. Once her aunt left the room, he sat on the side of the bed. Lines deepened around his eyes.

"Uncle Seth, are you ill? Would you like this quilt?" Katie said.

"No, dear. I'm not ill, at least not in my flesh."

She gazed at him, puzzled, and the troubled look on his face caused her more concern.

"This is hard," he said. "And there's no easy way to say it. I won't make excuses for myself or expect you to understand. I just hope you will be able to forgive me."

"Forgive you for what?" Had he and Pa quarreled and never talked it through?

Uncle Seth leaned slightly toward her, and she saw his eyes moisten. "Jeremiah, my brother. . .was not your father. I am."

His words echoed in her ears, hollow and empty. Her stomach churned, and she drew the quilt up tightly around her. She refused to believe him. Surely he'd made a mistake. *How could this be? Jeremiah Colter wasn't her father!* And her mother, so sweet and gentle. . . What did this mean?

Uncle Seth must have seen the shock and pain in her face, for he instantly chose to speak. "Child, neither was Mary Colter your mother. Your real mother died of pneumonia before you were six months old."

Why wasn't she ever told? Folks said she looked like Mary and even had some of her mannerisms. Jeremiah and Mary Colter were not her parents? Yes, they were. She knew they were. This had to be a dreadful nightmare. Uncle Seth had made a terrible mistake. How could he explain those years Pa raised her by himself? If she didn't belong to him, then why didn't he send her to Seth and Elizabeth when her mother died? If her uncle spoke the truth, then why hadn't Jeremiah told her about it? She was grown and had the right to know. Why did Pa speak of rehoboth and not of this horrible revelation?

She lifted her chin and swallowed the lump in her throat. "I don't understand what you're saying. I'm so confused."

"I should have told you the truth when you came to live with us, but I feared losing you."

She took a deep breath. "How did this happen? Why didn't anyone ever tell me?"

He shook his head as though denying the past. "I promised not to ever interfere with your life—never claim you as my daughter. I didn't think anything would ever happen to Mary and Jeremiah to leave you alone."

"Please, will you explain it all to me?" She needed to know the truth without delay.

Silence followed, and she fought the twisting and turning in the pit of her stomach. She looked into the face of her uncle, a face marred with sadness. He sighed deeply, and his eyes cast a faraway glance. He appeared to look through her to another time and place.

"The first time I met your mother was on Mary and Jeremiah's wedding day. Mary introduced Hannah as her younger sister, and I instantly fell in love with the most beautiful girl in the world. I'll never forget the first time I looked into those huge jade green eyes and met that sweet smile. She looked like an angel straight from heaven's gate. Katie, every part of you is Hannah, your real mother. Looking at you is like seeing her again for the first time." With Hannah's name upon his lips, his face brightened. "Anyway, I wanted to court her proper, but her pa refused until she turned sixteen. For weeks I marked off the days until I could start seein' her. She became the reason I lived and breathed. I couldn't think or talk for thinking about her. Soon afterwards I asked her pa if we could marry, but he said we would have to wait until she reached seventeen. Again, I began marking off those weeks until her birthday. At last we were married, and our lives seemed perfect. I thought we were the happiest two people on earth."

Uncle Seth struggled to gain composure. Her own feelings oscillated from anger to hurt, but when she saw the agony etched across Seth's face, compassion overcame any desire to hurl accusations.

"Please go on," Katie said, swallowing her tears. "Not just what you think I should hear, but all of it. If you are my real father, then I must know what happened. All my life, they told me they loved me. Neither of them ever let on that I wasn't their own child."

"They did love you, Katie. Don't you ever doubt Jeremiah

and Mary's devotion to you. I remember the day you were born. Why, those two were as happy as we were. Then my Hannah took sick with a cold and fever. Then it got worse. Before long, she couldn't get out of bed. One morning I woke up and Hannah lay beside me, not breathing but cold and still. I wanted to die myself. I turned my back on everything in this life, including you. In those days, I didn't know Jesus, so I blamed God for all my heartache. Child, every day you looked more like your mother, and instead of seeing it as a blessing, I saw it as an ugly reminder of not having Hannah. I took you to Jeremiah and Mary and begged them to raise you. In turn, I promised to never claim you as my daughter. It sounded simple, the best way to handle my grief.

"Jeremiah had always been the restless type—couldn't seem to get roots back home. He wanted adventure, and he loved the wild. All the education in the world couldn't satisfy his longing for it. He wanted to take his family west and carve out a home for them. Mary loved Jeremiah. She was afraid to head out across the wilderness, but she wouldn't try to stop him. No sooner had they arrived than Jeremiah wrote, asking me to join them. He wanted me to see the beauty of his new home. Jeremiah told me about traveling through mountains and deserts until he found this piece of fertile land along the Teyah River. His letter went on and on about the animals, birds, sunrises, sunsets, the mountains, and his fascination with the Indians. For my benefit, he added that a few families had settled into an area a few miles away, so the territory wasn't completely desolate. My brother knew my blacksmith abilities would be valuable to those folks. It sounded good to me, so I gathered up my belongings and moved out here. My first reaction to this dangerous land, filled with rattlesnakes and Indians, didn't compare to Jeremiah's, but I stayed. Yes, it's beautiful, but not quite what I had expected. Sometimes I thought he had gone crazy to bring you and Mary to such a godforsaken territory, but Jeremiah had never been happier. He'd made friends with the Comanches, Apaches, and Kiowas. He traded with them so he and Mary weren't bothered by raids. Some of the other settlers didn't like his way of mixing with the Indians. They criticized him rather than listened to his way of thinking. As a result, he stopped visiting the settlers, not that I blamed him. It made sense when he spoke of respecting the Indians, and he believed they were smarter than the white man when it came to survival.

"Both Mary and Jeremiah asked me to move in with them, but I refused. I'd long since regretted giving you to them, and it hurt too much to consider seeing you every day. Besides, I had a business, and folks weren't about to risk their lives to see a blacksmith. If I wanted to see the three of you, I had to travel to their ranch." Seth stood from the bed and studied her.

"I want to hear what happened next," Katie said.

He seated himself again, and Katie watched him wrestle with the words and the memories. "Two years later, I met Elizabeth. I don't know what she saw in me, but thank God she took the time to care. In those days, I was a miserable, short-tempered man, and Hannah still filled my waking and sleeping hours. I had nightmares where she repeatedly called out for you. Guilt began to eat away at me for what I'd done. One night I told Elizabeth the whole truth, and instead of condemning me, she told me about God and His wonderful love. He wanted to forgive my sins and set me free from the guilt and blame of abandoning my daughter. Before the evening ended, Elizabeth led me to Jesus. For the first time, I felt a flow of peace and love that softened my heart and opened my eyes to all the bitterness eating away at me. Elizabeth and I talked for hours. She helped me see that God had decided Hannah needed to be with Him, and it wasn't my fault or yours. Yet, I would have to abide by the promise I made to allow Jeremiah and Mary to raise you. A few months later, I asked Elizabeth to marry me. Jeremiah and Mary immediately saw the change, and both of them asked questions and studied the Bible. I thanked them for what they were doing for my daughter and asked them to forgive me for all the trouble I'd caused. After Mary died, I wanted you back, but Jeremiah refused. He said you were his, and he would never give you up. . .and then he died."

Silence filled the room. Katie heard the chatter of Jacob, and once Emily cried out, but Seth's words spun like a child's toy in her mind.

"I need some time to myself," she said, avoiding Seth's stare.

"I understand."

"I need to think through everything you told me. I don't know what else to say."

"Neither do I."

"Uncle, I. . .I mean, goodness, I'm terribly mixed up," Katie said, fighting to keep her composure. She couldn't look into his face.

"Saying I'm sorry isn't enough, and asking you to forgive me doesn't seem like enough, either. Reckon I'll let you alone."

Chapter Fifteen

Katie swept the remains of the dirt and debris from the small cabin she would soon call home. Outside the temperatures steadily dropped, and along with the wintry chill fell a heavy blanket of snow. She held her breath against the sharp cold and surveyed the new roof. Miles and Seth had been so good to help Peyton, or the work would not have been completed in time to stop the wind from searching for a hole in the cabin. Inside, the cabin needed only a few more repairs to make it livable for her and Peyton. She should have been elated, but her mood more closely resembled the dark, gray snow clouds lingering above Fort Davis. Stepping back inside to the warmth of the crackling fire, she watched the flames shoot upward as they snatched up dry pieces of wood and consumed them into burning ash.

"What's wrong?" Peyton said. He'd been hammering pegs to hang pots, pans, and other items necessary for cooking. Now he gave her his full attention.

"I can't keep anything from you," she said, attempting to sound light, but the weight of her thoughts pulled away the joy she always felt with him. The knowledge of her real parents shouldn't bother her so, but it did. She examined his work as though her concentration had been solely upon his wooden pegs.

"Sweetheart, your face shows your feelings."

"True Comanches don't reveal their emotions."

"Oh, I can recall many times when you hid behind your stubborn resolve," he said. "For example, I thought you tolerated me for your uncle's sake." He looked at her oddly. "This is serious, isn't it?"

She stepped into his arms and slipped her hands around his neck. "We need to talk," she said. "Or maybe I just need for you to listen. A part of me wants to cry and another part wants to scream and shout."

"Sit with me by the fire." He motioned to a buffalo hide spread out beneath him and pulled her to the floor. "Have you heard from the Kiowa?"

"No, this is completely different from our problem with Lone Eagle," she said. "Seth told me something earlier today that has me really upset."

"I can see you're grieved about something," Peyton said, placing his arm around her shoulders. "Are you ready to talk?"

"I'm going to try," she said, and she proceeded to tell him about the conversation with the man she'd always thought was her uncle.

"Do you despise him for what he told you?" he said once she finished.

"No, I'm not sure what I'm feeling, but it's not hate. Look at all the good he's done for me. I couldn't even begin to list all those things. Without him, I wouldn't have received Jesus into my life or understood many Bible passages. He has fed me and clothed me—asking nothing in return. And Peyton, you are the only man he gave permission to come calling. I guess I'm saddened to learn the perfect picture of my parents is tainted." She drew in a breath. "Or is it tainted at all? I've had two sets of parents. How am I supposed to react to this information?"

"Are you looking for someone to blame because you weren't told the truth?"

"Maybe, but I care about all of them. That's the worst of the problem. I can't seem to think things through." Katie rested her head on his shoulder.

"How do you feel about Jeremiah?"

How dear that his questioning was to help her sort out her own feelings "I loved him. He raised me as his own daughter and always told me how proud he was of me. He used to call me his Indian princess."

"What about Mary?"

"I think she must have loved my mother very much to take me into her heart. It all is so very tragic."

"Do you think Jeremiah and Mary regretted raising you as their own?"

When she recalled the wonderful moments of the three together, she had no doubts. "No, I am very sure they loved me. I remember the laughter and the good times we had together. Pa often brought us wildflowers, and Ma always made a big fuss. He liked to hear her sing, and she always had a song. Sometimes late at night, they would sit out on the front porch and Ma would sing. He would come and lift me from my bed and hold me in his lap until the precious sound of her voice lulled me to sleep. Yes, Peyton, I'm sure they loved me."

"So, knowing Seth Colter is your real father doesn't change the feelings you have for any of them?"

When he phrased it that way, the confusion vanished. "No, I guess not. If anything I should love them more for their devotion to me and keeping the secret. If I consider it all, Seth could have made my life miserable when I came here, but he put aside the past and welcomed me into his home. Today he told me that seeing me was like looking at my mother again. And then I consider Aunt Elizabeth, who could have resented me and sent me back to the Comanches, but she loves me, too."

"You might want to tell them those exact words," Peyton said, taking her hand.

"I know I should, but I feel so strange and uncomfortable knowing he is my real father and that I never knew my mother. I'm sure I can forgive my father for giving me up, but it will take some getting used to."

Peyton toyed with her fingers then kissed them lightly. "Katie, Seth Colter made a mistake when he gave you to Jeremiah and Mary, but they loved your parents and chose to make you a blessing. In his pain, Seth believed he could live his life as your uncle. He gave his word to ensure that very thing. He may have been grieving, yet he recognized his child needed a good home. Then he came to know the Lord, and his commitment to Jeremiah and Mary demonstrated real love. His feelings for you went far beyond the baby given to his brother and wife. Seth knew real love, an unselfish giving for the benefit of others. I'm sure it bothered him every day of his life, and I'm even more sure God became his only source of comfort and peace."

How she treasured this man. "Peyton, you always see things so clearly,"

"Not really. I'm a stubborn man, and I want things to go my way, but I pray God always puts me back on the right path."

Katie contemplated Peyton's words. She couldn't ignore the truth or deny Seth's confession. Their relationship might be awkward, but it was up to her to take the next step.

"You're right, Peyton. If God doesn't judge Seth, and He has forgiven him, I should do the same."

"Why don't you let me finish up here, and you can go see him?"

"Oh, it would be so difficult. I don't know if I am ready to face him."

"The longer you wait, the harder it will be."

Katie understood exactly what Peyton meant. She didn't want a wall built between her and Seth, neither did she want Jeremiah and Mary's memory tarnished with bitterness. Katie recalled Seth telling her that forgiveness led to freedom. The truth didn't change how others had loved her. It confirmed it.

She rose to leave. "I'll go now," she said. "One of my fathers needs to know I love him."

"Do you want me to go with you?" he said.

"No, I should do this myself. . . . Peyton?"

"Yes."

"I'm still amazed at how you always manage to see things so clearly."

He laughed and broke the seriousness of the moment. "It's much easier to tell someone else how to handle their problems than to solve your own. Remember, I ran away from mine. I joined the army rather than face my family's disappointment over my decision to leave medical school."

"You and I seem to face one dark situation after another," she said. "Do you suppose our lives will ever smooth out?"

"I hope so," he said. "Right now I'm praying we can get through the next two weeks."

And Katie clearly saw the concerned lines across his forehead. The Kiowa must come soon.

Katie heard the pounding of Seth's hammer shaping a piece of metal into something useful. She stopped to listen and noted the rhythm sounded faster than usual. Perhaps he had too much work to do and didn't have time to speak with her, or he might feel the blacksmith wasn't a fitting place to talk about delicate matters. She could easily put off this conversation until another time.

She forced herself to walk into the pathway of the three-sided structure that housed the blacksmith. The forge was warm, and she knew without looking that Seth's face would be red from the heat. At first he didn't see her, but the late afternoon sun cast her shadow in his path. Both of them held back a greeting as though any utterance of words might be interpreted as cold or angry.

"Did you want to see me?" Seth said, breaking the deafening silence.

"Yes, if you aren't too busy," Katie said.

"No, Katie child, I always have time for you. Please come inside and warm yourself."

Now she comprehended the reason he always referred to her as Katie child. She stepped farther into the blacksmith, welcoming the warmth and praying for her words to come easily.

"I've been thinking and talking to Peyton about what you told me," she began. "The news is still a shock, but it doesn't or shouldn't change how I feel about you or those who raised me. I love you dearly, and I don't want uncomfortable feelings between us. If forgiveness is what you ask, then I forgive you. The things you told me will take some time to get used to, but I'm willing to accept them as part of the past."

"I can't ask for more than love and forgiveness," he said. "I wish I could make what happened easier for you to bear."

"It's just going to take time. . .I gather you won't want anyone else to know about this, so I won't tell a soul."

"I don't want things to remain the same. Is that what you want?" he said. A furrow inched across his brow.

Katie shook her head. "I don't know. I mean, you are my father, not my uncle, and my head is filled with questions about my mother."

"I know this is soon, but would you consider calling me Papa, maybe not right now, but later on, when you are more settled about it all?"

Katie searched his face. *This is my father, my real father.* "I like the sound of it, especially when Jacob calls you Papa," she said. "I called my—other father—Pa, so Papa would be different. What if folks ask why I stopped referring to you as Uncle?"

"I don't care about other folks. Too many years have gone by without me being able to claim my daughter, and I intend to make up for lost time."

"All right, then, Papa it is. And what should I call Aunt Elizabeth?"

He smiled. "Perhaps simply Elizabeth?"

She nodded. "Will you still give me away at the wedding?"

Tears formed in his eyes. He set his tools aside, peeled off his gloves, and welcomed her into his arms.

Over the next few days, Katie experienced sadness and grief as she dealt with the truth. She mentally rehearsed calling Seth Papa, but her resolve didn't stop tense moments when she allowed her mind to slip back to the mother she never knew. At those times, she sought out her newfound father and together they laughed and cried about Hannah Colter. Katie learned from Elizabeth some of Mary Colter's own words regarding the love she held for Katie. To the best of Elizabeth's knowledge, Mary never knew Elizabeth had been told the truth about Katie. For certain the Colter brothers grew into men of integrity.

Events and happenings of Jeremiah's last days now made sense. He rightfully sent her to Seth when he realized impending death would not allow him to fulfill his responsibilities. His instructions to find her rehoboth meant learning the truth about her parents. If so, Katie's search had ended.

She recalled when Papa learned of her arrival, he left his blacksmith and welcomed her into his home. Now his emotion, his patience with her struggle with God, and his careful discernment of a proper suitor. Elizabeth had encouraged her to seek his council on matters of importance. Now it all made sense. She smiled each time she recalled the night he stood ready to thrash Peyton if he talked or acted in an inappropriate way. It was also the night he referred to Peyton as a good son-in-law. At the time, Katie thought he merely used the term as a way of expressing his fondness for Peyton.

Christmas and the wedding rapidly approached, and Katie willingly pushed aside the confusion of her origin. She frantically stitched and fashioned Christmas gifts for Elizabeth, Papa, the children, and Peyton. After much deliberation, she decided to sew Peyton a deerskin jacket from the pile of hides in the bottom of her trunk. She was so pleased with the results that she took another piece and made a vest for Papa and a smaller one for Jacob. There were embroidered handkerchiefs and a bonnet for Elizabeth and a muslin face doll for Emily. The gifts might have been a bit extravagant, but this was her first real Christmas since Mary had died, and it was the Christmas of her wedding. Next year she and Peyton would be living in Illinois and unable to spend the holiday with her family.

Always, in the darkest part of Katie's mind, there lived the threat of Lone Eagle destroying all their hopes and dreams. Only Peyton shared her fears, and the two planned for their future as though the warrior's threat was hollow. She wondered if she should speak more with Peyton about Lone Eagle, but she didn't want to spoil the excitement or dampen his enthusiasm. The Kiowa had not shown his face in weeks.

Chapter Sixteen

*I*s everything finished for tomorrow?" Elizabeth said as she stirred a bowl filled with batter for honey cakes.

"Yes, ma'am, I've got things in order at the cabin and here," Katie said. "I'm all ready to take up housekeeping."

Elizabeth went through the list of all the items that needed to be in place and completed for the wedding and the reception.

"Tonight I'll finish the pies, and Martha says she has two cakes ready. Lauren and her sisters will help serve, and oh, I nearly forgot—Mrs. Ames brought by a huge apple cobbler. Let's see now. . .tablecloths are clean, and so are all the cups for the punch."

"Hopefully it will warm up a little tomorrow. I detest the thought of guests leaving early, but I'm afraid they are going to get cold," Elizabeth said. "Of course, having the reception at your cabin will help with a roaring fire."

"It's simply going to be wonderful," Katie said. She picked up Emily and whirled her around the room. "Won't it be grand? And then Christmas is the very next day! Oh, Elizabeth, I am so happy."

"Your mother—both your mothers—would have loved seeing you so beautiful and full of life," Elizabeth said with a sad smile.

"They can see me," Katie said. "We just can't see them."

"I guess you're right. For certain, you are going to be the loveliest bride this fort has ever seen. Seth is about to burst, and he's invited absolutely everyone."

Katie laughed. "Well, he didn't invite Mrs. Ames, because I did. She promised me she would be here."

Katie danced across the room with Emily, all the while humming a lively tune. "You know what? I'd like to go riding this afternoon."

"Child, it's too cold for a pleasure ride."

"Not really. That's how Pa and I used to celebrate Christmas. We would go for a long ride; then he would give me my gift."

"But it's not possible. There's no one to go with you," Elizabeth said. "Seth is working long hours to finish shoeing horses for the colonel, and Peyton is busy with drills."

"Peyton is off duty from this afternoon through Christmas Day. Colonel Ross called it a wedding present." Katie continued to dance across the room, and Emily enjoyed every minute of it.

"Is Peyton aware of your riding adventure?" Elizabeth said in pretended annoyance. "Or is this a surprise for him, too?"

"He knows, although his reaction was similar to yours. He will be here shortly to see if I am allowed to go."

Elizabeth shook her head and pointed to Emily's need to be changed. Snatching up clean clothes for the toddler, Katie proceeded to clean her up.

"I don't suppose there is any talking you out of this idea of yours?"

"No, ma'am. Please don't be unhappy with me. We won't be gone long, I promise. When I get back I'll bake the pies, and then we can spend the rest of the evening together."

Elizabeth smiled. "Katie, you bundle up warm, or you will be sick for your wedding day. And take my scarf. It's warmer."

The sun shone down long enough to send the temperatures up a few degrees, and it beat warm on Peyton's and Katie's backs as they left Fort Davis. Peyton rode his bay mare and Katie rode her spotted horse. She hadn't ridden since coming to the fort, but Papa had made sure the animal had been exercised and properly groomed. Elizabeth fussed and scolded over Katie's choice of riding bareback, but it did little good. Elizabeth's parting words to Peyton warned him of his headstrong bride.

"Don't let those green eyes and angelic face fool you, Sergeant Sinclair. She will be a handful, mark my word. It's not too late for you to postpone the wedding and let me train her right for you," Elizabeth said, attempting to sound angry, but Katie saw right through it.

"I think you want to mother me a while longer." Katie laughed.

Peyton promised to send her home on a regular basis for training, and Elizabeth appeared satisfied.

The two galloped out over the valley beyond Wild Rose Pass and across the prairie. Although the land looked brown and barren, Katie could easily imagine the green and color of spring. The wind whipped their faces, and Katie was glad Elizabeth had insisted upon a scarf. A quick glance back showed the fort clearly in the distance.

"Slow down, Katie," Peyton called to her.

"I'm enjoying my last day of freedom," Katie shouted back, but she did bring the horse to a trot.

"You will need to improve on taking orders," Peyton said, bringing the bay to her side. "This time tomorrow, Mrs. Peyton Sinclair will be expected to do her husband's bidding."

"And if I don't?" she said, pretending insolence.

"The stockade. That's where all unruly wives learn military discipline."

"It probably won't do a bit of good," she said. "What comes next?"

Peyton gave her a devilish grin. "I'll tell you tomorrow."

She warmed at falling for his wit once again.

He leaned up against the saddle horn. "We may have company."

"Who?"

He slowed his horse to a walk, and Katie followed his lead. "I saw the Kiowa this morning. I made sure he knew our plans. So if he has a message from Lone Eagle, we will find out shortly."

"Oh, I don't think we have to worry." She looked for signs of the scout. "The wedding's tomorrow. Lone Eagle would have sent word by now. Surely he's forgotten about me and won't waste his time."

"I hope so," Peyton said, but she heard doubt lacing his words.

Her gaze met Peyton's. "I don't believe he has decided to leave me alone, either. But he's nearly run out of time."

"I agree, sweetheart." Peyton pulled his horse to a stop, and Katie did the same. "We ought to start back. The air's getting colder, and there's no sign of the Kiowa."

"Does anyone besides Colonel Ross and myself know you speak Comanche?" she said.

"No, and I don't intend for anyone to find out. Too many times it's helped me get out of trouble."

"Or into trouble."

"Well, that, too."

The horses picked their way through the terrain toward

Fort Davis, and Katie allowed Peyton's teasing to keep her mind from the Kiowa. She wanted to savor every minute alone with Peyton so she would always remember the afternoon of December 23, the day before their wedding.

A gust of northern wind blew a harsh chill against their faces, and she shivered.

"Are you thinking the Kiowa may not have a message for me?" The idea of Lone Eagle setting her free was precious, even if it did sound like a fool's dream.

"Sweetheart, I've prayed for that very thing," he said. "I want it all to be over, just like you do—perhaps more so. I don't care how selfish it sounds, but our wedding needs to begin without any fear of Lone Eagle's influence in our lives. When we're married, I will relax."

"We haven't talked about it for several weeks," Katie said. "Once I worried he would make his demands after we were married, except. . .oh, never mind."

"What, Katie? This time tomorrow we will be husband and wife. I think you can tell me what's floating around in that blond head of yours."

She patted the neck of her spotted horse then tightened the scarf around her neck. "I don't think Lone Eagle would want me after I had a husband. For then his aggression would look like revenge instead of asserting his power," she said. "Unless he intended to punish me."

"He won't have much time to plan anything of the sort. I'd like to head back to Illinois before the spring. He can't follow us there."

"True, and he's not about to let up on the raids. We're foolish to think otherwise. The Kiowa spoke true when he pointed out the Comanches wouldn't fight over a woman," Katie said, finally voicing her fears. "Pride and honor might send him after me, but nothing else. Lone Eagle won't give up until the army stops the whole Comanche nation."

"You can be certain of that," Peyton said. "The army will have to send reinforcements before any security is made in this territory, and. . .look up to the ridge, Katie!"

She fastened her gaze on a ridge to the west of them. The afternoon sun provided a backdrop to the party of over fifty Comanche warriors. Their horses pranced, eager to run, and fear ripped through every part of her. Black war paint, the color of death, fairly glistened on their faces. Lone Eagle's horse stepped out in full view.

Lone Eagle would kill Peyton for sure. "What do we do?" she said, not once taking her eyes from Lone Eagle. "They are far too close to the fort. Oh no, Lone Eagle is planning to attack while everyone is preparing for Christmas. Peyton, we're just in the way."

"We could run for it." Peyton turned in the saddle to take a better view of the country around them. "Can we outrun these Comanches? There are another forty or fifty Comanches on the other side, and they are moving in around us. The Kiowa is behind this, I'm sure."

She focused on Lone Eagle. "He can't see my fear," she whispered. "But I am afraid."

"Me, too, sweetheart. We fooled ourselves into believing our wedding could take place without problems from Lone Eagle. I really wanted to spend the rest of my life with you."

Katie peered into his face. "I love you, Peyton, and I'm sorry to have brought you to this." She looked to the ridge again. "Perhaps I should try to talk to him. Maybe—"

"Don't put your own life on the line for me. I'm a soldier, remember? We're supposed to be heroes." He paused. "You know, I can't picture myself letting Lone Eagle take you from me without a fight. And we're close enough to the fort that rifle fire will warn the others of the attack. This bay has won a few races, and your horse is sure-footed. I want to bet on outrunning them."

"I'm ready when you are," she whispered. "God be with you, Peyton, because Lone Eagle will try to kill you first." She wanted to add her apology, that this was her fault. But the race for their lives stopped her.

Chapter Seventeen

Katie silently cried out for more time. She needed to tell Peyton all those things dear to her heart—those words she'd savored for their wedding night. This was all her fault! She had been the one to insist upon riding so far from the fort. Her own selfishness had gotten them into this death trap. Too many words were left unspoken, and she feared she would never have another chance to tell Peyton how much she loved him.

Dear God, I'm scared. Lone Eagle will kill Peyton. I don't care what happens to me, but please watch over Peyton. He's the innocent one. I'm sorry for being so selfish and stubborn. It's my fault, and I know it. All Peyton has ever done is try to protect and love me. Oh God, he can't die because of me!

Peyton spurred his horse north, away from the trail toward the fort. Katie dug her heels into the sides of her horse and joined him. They raced side by side as the warriors sped down from the ridge. Comanche war cries echoed in every direction, and the foreboding screams urged her mount on faster. She leaned low against its neck just like Pa had taught her and vowed not to look behind. It would only slow down the escape. She stole a glance at Peyton. Like her, he bent over his horse's neck. Even with the weight of the saddle, the bay ran like a bolt of lightning. Their horses' pace made her think they might have a chance. Both animals lunged into the wind as though they sensed the impending danger. Every muscle was conditioned to respond to the rider, but so were the Comanche horses.

Peyton had led them north, then he circled back south around the ridge. The Comanches didn't expect him to head away from the fort, and their braves were concentrated on the south side. The warriors would have to race down the ridge and across the flat terrain to catch them. The sound of advancing Indian horses pounding against the hard ground met her ears. The hooves hammered louder, and she knew Lone Eagle and his warriors were not far behind. Peyton's move had bought precious little time.

The crack of rifle fire broke into the chase. She smelled the pungent odor of sulfur and heard the bullets whiz past her. Katie tensed. She *could* endure a rifle shot and not slow the horse's pace. A prayer flashed across her mind: *Dear Lord, please keep Peyton safe from Comanche fire, and don't let me slow him down.* She refused to be the cause of the Comanches overtaking her and Peyton. Determined to outrun the Indians, Katie's focus saw the flesh rip away from Peyton's shoulder slightly above his previous wound. The sight of blood and the anguish that must be riding with him intensified the gravity of their situation. Fright blinded her from seeing anything but a vision of Peyton lying mutilated, like the bodies of the Lawrence family. He didn't dare allow the Comanches a chance to torture him.

She hurried her horse closer to his mare's side. Their mounts heaved heavily with the speed, and a sheen of sweat glittered from their sides. A steady stream of blood soaked his shoulder down to his wrist.

"Get out of here," he said. "Pull away from me."

"No!" Katie cried against the piercing cold. "I won't leave you."

Her eyes fixed on the path ahead of them, and she could see several of the warriors moving around an outcropping of rock to position themselves in their path. It would only be a matter of moments before she and Peyton were overtaken. Only an angel of God could save them now. Silently she prayed death would come quickly to Peyton. Lone Eagle knew how to make him pay greatly for her foolishness.

She remembered the times when she heard God's whisper calling for her to trust Him. *Have Peyton and my lives existed for this moment? Are we to die together, or will Lone Eagle force me to watch Peyton's slow torture? Lord, please save him from this.*

Another bullet tore away the lower skirt of her dress. For a moment, she wished the warrior's aim had ended the pursuit. She quickly pushed the thought aside. She would not be known for inviting death as an easy way out.

Up ahead, something diverted the warriors' attention. Comanche braves scattered in different directions. What were they planning? The band clearly dispersed, providing a clear path ahead. Katie didn't understand their strategy. It seemed useless to ambush when they held her and Peyton in the midst of them.

Katie strained to hear a peculiar sound. Was that rifle fire to the front of them? In her delirium, could it be the Comanches' shots merely echoed in an endless circle? She squinted to see beyond the warriors. Were those images really riders headed this way? Could it be blue uniforms racing to meet them? She recognized the stance of one of the colonel's scouts. God had heard her prayers. Soldiers rode toward them at breakneck speed, firing straight into the Comanches. Katie saw two warriors drop and another lose his horse. The hope must have given Peyton strength to continue on because he rode faster.

They were going to make it to safety.

The brush of an unseen rider alarmed her. In the next instant, an arm snatched her from the horse's back. It happened too quickly for her to fight or scream. She flew suspended in the wind with only the arm of her captor balancing her between life and death. Terror numbed her senses as a scream rose and fell in her throat. Helpless, Katie watched her horse travel straight into the path of safety without her. The warrior pulled her quivering body in front of him. He angled his horse away from the pursuing soldiers and raced toward the hills. She stared down at the scarred arm wrapped securely around her. She recognized the markings. Without a doubt Lone Eagle held her captive.

The struggling proved useless. The more she fought against Lone Eagle, the tighter he pulled her body to his until the pressure against her stomach forced her to cry out. Consciousness escaped her as she fell prey to momentary blackness. How well she understood the plight of a snared animal, and visions of Pa's traps tore across her mind. The agony of enraged animals would cower to pitiful whimpers from the pain of the trap's teeth. Death would be welcomed in the face of hideous pain.

Each time she twisted or tried to peel away from the warrior's arm, he gripped her waist and drew her body closer to him. She fell limp into periods of darkness where only her sense of sound prevailed with the steady labored panting of the animal beneath them.

The horse slowed to a gallop. . .a trot. . .then a walk. Wearily she fought the suffocating blackness. . .if only Lone Eagle would release his hold upon her. But didn't she want death? Wouldn't the grave be a warmer place than surrendering to the warrior?

"Would you like to live?" Lone Eagle whispered in her ear. His breath against her neck sickened her. She stiffened. His words brought her back from a haze.

The sound of Comanche words flooded her mind with memories. She recalled a little girl hanging on to Pa's hand. Quickly the child transformed into a girl who played with the Indian boy. Then she became a young woman. She held the hand of Lone Eagle and walked with him up a mountain path. What had happened? Pictures of the Lawrence family lying in grotesque positions in the back of their wagon flashed vividly before her. Lone Eagle's imperative question pressed against her senses, but she failed to reply. She didn't want to live, except the God who gave her life must be the One to take it.

"Would you like to live?" Lone Eagle repeated. His anger clearly tipped his words. He lifted a knife to her throat. The icy sharpness against her skin sealed any desire to die at his hand.

"Yes, I want to live."

"My wife will not run away?" Lone Eagle said.

The blade deepened across her throat. "No, I will not run away."

"Two warriors die because of you. But the white soldier is dead. He fell from his horse when hit by another bullet."

He was wrong. She had seen Peyton ride straightway toward the soldiers. *Lone Eagle wanted her to believe Peyton had died. He must think she'd not try to run away if there was no one to return to. Lone Eagle might rule her future, but he would never rule her heart.*

Exhaustion played upon her body, and the cold cut through to her bones. Her stomach ached and cramped from the force of Lone Eagle's arm. She attempted to ignore the pain so she could think. She had to pray.

The Comanche village came into view. Being here seemed like a lifetime ago; for sure she was a different person. She stretched to see if anything had changed. It looked as peaceful as she remembered, but the friendly people who once looked at her as one of them no longer existed. Lone Eagle had lost warriors in getting her back. She knew the plight of Comanche slaves. It would be a life worse than death. Men and women alike would beat and torture her for no other reason than to claim their superiority. She wanted to know the plans Lone Eagle had for her. He'd called her his wife—but in what fashion?

Lone Eagle slid down from the back of his horse. A crowd formed around the warriors. Some cheered, and others looked sullen due to the deaths of the two men. Katie's appearance brought no reaction. Perhaps they thought she wanted to return to them.

Lone Eagle pulled her down from his horse. "Go to my teepee."

Katie did not protest. What good would it do?

She waited inside until the need to relieve herself became too great. Her stomach hurt from Lone Eagle's rough treatment, and all she really wanted to do was sleep. No one stopped her outside the teepee, but she felt the eyes of everyone piercing through her.

She waited for him until dusk, preparing food for him as were her duties.

Lone Eagle lifted the flap of the teepee and stepped inside. His presence filled the small dwelling, but she didn't feel his domination drawing her to him as in the past. She took a deep breath and lifted her eyes warily to see his response.

A look of contempt and hostility challenged any rebellion

she might have fostered. If Katie had wondered if the Comanche still held any feelings for her, the question vanished in a single glance. Why had she thought he might have mercy?

"I have food for you." She was determined he would not see her fright.

A silent, angry stare served as a reply. He took a position near the food and began to eat. She hesitated then kneeled beside him.

"Lone Eagle, I can't stay here with you tonight," she said.

His hand instantly flew to the side of her face, sending her sprawling to the side of him. She tasted the blood trickling from the corner of her mouth, but she refused to cry out. It would only invite more of the same.

"Please let me explain," she said. "It's my woman's time."

His hand raised to strike her again, but she buried her face in her hands. "You liar," he said in a low voice. "Tomorrow you were to marry the white soldier."

"A woman doesn't always know about such things," she said, forcing herself to look at him. The warm flush of humiliation crept up her neck.

"If you lie, I will peel the flesh from your bones."

"I am telling you the truth."

"Get out of my teepee until your time is over."

Chapter Eighteen

Katie followed the familiar path to Desert Fawn's teepee. Their relationship began when Katie first came to the village. After Mary Colter's death, Jeremiah entrusted Katie to Desert Fawn's care. He could not be consoled, neither could he care for the child properly. The Indian woman sheltered and nurtured her in those early years, and the little girl soon attached herself to the old woman. Katie called her Grandmother, and the two formed a bond of love and companionship. Now what were the feelings for Katie as Lone Eagle's captive?

She understood Pa's intense grief over losing his wife and infant son. The couple had put their mistakes behind them to build and share a future together. In his mind, he had lost everything he treasured. By burying Mary's Bible, he marked his desperate rebellion against God. For a time, it looked as though he had gone mad, especially when he left Katie with Desert Fawn and took to the mountains. Upon his return, he adopted the Comanche ways. He passed the test of a warrior by proving himself in battle and earned a title of distinction when he saved Swift Arrow's life. She did not ask how he obtained the title of a warrior, but later she learned what Jeremiah had done.

He abandoned and seemingly forgot the customs of his

own people. He loved his little girl, but he devoted more time to the traditions and culture of the Indians. She saw him cast aside the practices of the white man and take on all the characteristics of a warrior. During this significant transition in his life, Katie learned many lessons about Indian life from Desert Fawn. If not for Comanche children teasing her about the color of her skin and hair, she would have forgotten her white heritage.

As she deliberated upon those days, the truth settled upon her. The biggest difference in Pa's and her life lay in how they reacted to tragedy. He turned from God when her mother died, and she drew closer to Him when he died. Katie would not be disillusioned over the Creator of the world.

Confusion mixed with gratitude met her as she pondered over her unexpected woman's time. Never had she considered it a blessing, but it did provide a few more days of freedom before Lone Eagle claimed her. Not that it changed the inevitable, except she could spend the days in prayer for strength and grace to endure the future. Comanche culture demanded she not sleep in her husband's teepee during these days. It also stated she could not eat meat, comb her hair, or wash her face. Before Katie resumed normal activity with her husband, culture demanded she bathe in the icy river.

Perhaps God intended to better prepare her for the role of Lone Eagle's wife. Oh God, please speak to me. Help me to accept what You plan for my life and to be content in all circumstances.

She couldn't fulfill her responsibilities to Lone Eagle alone. He was so angry, and according to his customs, he had a right to punish her however he chose. Different scriptures came to mind. She could recall the words but not always the books, chapters, and numbers of the verses. Papa and Elizabeth had done their best by her, and she'd go to her grave loving them. . .and Peyton.

She stopped in front of Desert Fawn's teepee. Trepidation halted her steps. Had Lone Eagle expressed his anger and distrust to everyone in the village? Would the grandmother she loved now be turned against her?

She hesitantly opened the flap of Desert Fawn's teepee. The old woman labored over a pair of winter boots made from buffalo hides. The woman rolled moistened sinew on her knee until it formed a point and could be threaded through a bone needle. Desert Fawn had made many pairs of winter footwear and beaded moccasins for Katie. As a child, she had watched the old woman sew garments, and her skill still fascinated Katie.

"Desert Fawn," Katie whispered.

The old woman turned in disbelief, and with open arms they reached for each other and shed quiet tears. Katie fondly remembered her many wrinkles, and the leathery hand stroked her hair as though she was a child again.

"I've missed you," Katie finally said. How good to have someone who loved her when life seemed torn apart.

"Why are you here, little one?" the old woman said.

Katie didn't know how to tell her without showing disrespect for Lone Eagle. "Lone Eagle brought me."

Desert Fawn merely nodded. She knew the truth.

"Can I stay with you for a few days?" she said. "It is my woman's time."

The old woman smiled. "Sit by the fire with me. You can watch me stitch moccasins like you were a child again."

God had granted Katie peace for a little while.

The following day would have been her wedding day. Katie tried to center her thoughts on the meaning of Christmas and not the ugliness separating her from Peyton, but it didn't stop the continuous lump in her throat.

The next two days passed quickly. One of Desert Fawn's sons invited them to follow a buffalo hunt, and the two trailed behind with the other women. When the warrior had killed the animal, she and Katie skinned it, dressed the meat, and packed it on a pony to return to camp.

"It seems like a long time since we have prepared buffalo for winter," Katie said. "You always work faster than me at jerking out the pieces. My fingers are weak, and yours are swift and strong."

The old woman smiled, and Katie watched the sun glisten off her silver hair.

"When you are as old as I am, then you, too, can work faster," Desert Fawn said.

"Yes, but you are the best teacher. Look, we will finish pulling the meat apart today. Tomorrow it can lie in the sun."

"And the next day we can slice it into thin strips so it can harden. My teepee will have plenty of meat during the winter."

Desert Fawn and Katie reminisced about the past and repeated stories about Katie as a child. She did not mention life at Fort Davis. She should forget all of it, but isn't that what she told herself when she arrived at the fort? The two laughed and talked. They mourned Pa.

"Lone Eagle is a brave warrior," Desert Fawn said. "He is fearless in leading warriors against the whites. Jeremiah should not have told you to return to them. You could have died with all the whites."

Her stomach whirled. "Yes, Lone Eagle is a brave warrior."

"Are you now afraid of him?"

"A woman should always fear her husband," Katie said, and nothing more was said.

That evening as the two sat around the fire warming

themselves, Katie felt an urgency to talk to Desert Fawn about God.

"I have learned many things about the Great Spirit," Katie said. "Not the god of the sun, mother earth, or the moon, but the one and only Great Spirit."

Desert Fawn tilted her head and leaned closer to hear Katie's words.

"The Great Spirit loves all of us, and He wants us to live in peace. He loves us so much that He sent His only Son to teach us the ways of love and how to live in peace. The people of earth did not want to learn these things. They wanted to be warriors and grew angry with the Great Spirit's Son. They plotted and killed Him, but they did not know the Great Spirit had planned for His Son to die for their evil ways. After three days, the Great Spirit raised His Son from the dead to show all people of His love and power. The Great Spirit said, 'All who believe My Son died and rose again to life will live with Me forever.'"

"Ah, the *Habbe Weich-ket* death song." The old woman sang softly. "How great his people were. How great a patriot he was. How he loved his country and his people. How he fought for them with no thought of the Happy Hunting Ground until his people thought of it for him."

Desert Fawn understood a little of what she was trying to explain. Comanches did not concern themselves about death until it happened. It would take more than one meeting for her dear friend to understand the Almighty God, and the thought of peace among the Indians would crumble the strongest Comanche. Katie wished she had her Bible. Her own instructions had barely begun, and there were many things she didn't know.

The day of her ritual bathing came. Unlike the previous

days of bleak, gray clouds, the sun shone and shimmered upon the water. Katie stepped into the cold river. Its frigid temperatures took her breath away, and she was certain her heart had stopped beating. She hurried through the task while her body numbed in the cold. For a moment Katie considered the irony of catching pneumonia and facing death. She'd much prefer death than marriage to Lone Eagle.

Wrapped in a thick blanket, Katie sat upon the riverbank and watched the ripples break across the water. It felt strange to be clothed in the pale yellow deerskin again, and the winter boots lined with buffalo fur warmed her icy toes. Yet the softness and scent of her Comanche clothes brought back a happier time when she shared a teepee with Pa and Desert Fawn.

She used her fingers to comb through the wet tresses; then she braided her hair in one long braid. Her thoughts drifted to those near to her heart and especially for those she would never see again.

She didn't want to be an emotionless woman. If her life was to be there, then she must find joy in small things. She must do everything possible to be a good wife to Lone Eagle—not just cook and do chores or bear his children but devote her life to making his days happy. She didn't have to agree with what he did or dwell upon what could have been with Peyton. God walked with her, and she was not alone.

Taking a deep breath, Katie reluctantly stood. The day would proceed as planned with or without her approval. She needed to collect firewood and prepare food for Lone Eagle's evening meal. A delay set the evening for his anger toward her to worsen.

She sensed someone's presence. It sent chills up her spine to think a warrior had watched while she bathed. She turned to see a familiar figure standing in the brush behind her.

"Lone Eagle," Katie said. "I didn't see you."

The Comanche strode alongside her. "I haven't been here long. Desert Fawn told me you were at the river."

"I am returning to your teepee today." She observed him closely for signs of hostility, but he appeared calm.

He nodded, and his gaze passed by her and onto the river.

She carefully chose her words. Fright did strange things to a woman. "I meant what I said to you before—I'll never try to leave you, and I will do my best to be a good wife."

His gaze rested upon her face. It took all her courage to stare into his ebony eyes, but she feared condemnation by avoiding him. Better she show bravery than shy away like a coward.

"Sit beside me," he said. "We haven't talked for many months."

Katie shifted the blanket around her and resumed her position on the riverbank. Her heart beat so fiercely that she felt certain he heard it pounding.

"I never thought you wouldn't want to come back," Lone Eagle said. "And I never thought I would see fear in your eyes. The white man has turned you against the Comanche, for now you see me as the enemy."

She rejected the urge to lie. Lone Eagle would read the deceit and despise, punish her for it.

"While I waited, you chose a white soldier to take my place. You planned to have two husbands," he said. "My anger against you and all the whites could not be satisfied. I wanted you dead. I wanted to cut out your heart for what you had done to me."

He sat stoic, the pace of his breathing proving she'd provoked his temper. "My father told me about your promise to Jeremiah, but it didn't matter," Lone Eagle continued. "He had accepted the gifts of many fine horses. Why did he ask you to leave?"

His words were demanding, and Katie's refusal to answer the warrior only invited punishment.

"I didn't know then, either." She breathed a prayer for help. "It took some time for me to understand and accept what he wanted for me. Please believe me when I say I didn't want to leave here. My heart belonged to you and no one else. I wanted the people at the fort to send me away—back to you. Instead, Pa's brother and his wife welcomed me into their home. They loved and took care of me. Neither one of them criticized me for living among the Comanches. They accepted me as one of their own."

"You are Jeremiah Colter's daughter and Lone Eagle's wife, a Comanche." His voice rose.

Katie sighed heavily. "No, I am not Jeremiah Colter's daughter. I found out he wasn't my father. His brother is my real father. I'm certain that is why he made me promise to return to Fort Davis. He wanted me to be with my true father."

"And you did not know about this?" His harsh tone cut through the air.

"No," she whispered. "It was very difficult for me to hear those words and forgive them."

"Is this why you agreed to marry the white soldier?" Lone Eagle said.

Lone Eagle could very well be sympathetic to her if he thought she agreed to marry Peyton out of unhappiness. Her reply determined her future, her life. It looked tempting. . . . "No, I agreed to marry before I found out about my parents."

He stiffened, and she braced herself for him to strike her.

"You could have lied to me," he said. "You know the penalty for an unfaithful wife."

"I did not consider myself your wife because we had not lived together. I knew what it meant when Jeremiah accepted your gifts, but I returned them to you."

"Your actions didn't change our arrangement," Lone Eagle said.

Lone Eagle could have her killed, mutilated, or the tip of her nose cut off. He could do anything because she was his chattel. Her hope lay in the fact that he owned her. Would Lone Eagle want to destroy his own property? The answer came from the many past deliberations about her relationship with the Comanche warrior. He had to maintain his pride and honor among the tribe. The other Comanches respected his position, but it was up to Lone Eagle to keep it.

Katie didn't like surprises. She desperately needed to know the warrior's intentions. Lone Eagle must have decided her fate, or he wouldn't have sought her out.

"What are you going to do with me?" She again fought the trembling in her body. Did he plan to punish her there by the river?

His hardened features told her nothing. His eyes stayed fixed on the water gurgling peacefully. The warrior stood, and she instantly rose beside him.

"I want to kill you," Lone Eagle said, glaring straight into her eyes. "Every white man, woman, and child I killed held your face. Their screams became your screams. Their blood became your blood. I watched them suffer through torture after torture, wishing they were you. Do you think I want you to live?"

Chapter Nineteen

The sun parted the clouds of winter and seemingly mocked Katie's anxiety as she viewed its slow descent. The hours moved by swiftly, yet not quickly enough. Let the evening come soon but not too soon. Confusion twisted and turned her thoughts and emotions. Terror danced across her mind as though Lone Eagle's hatred pressed into what the night might hold. Agonizing turmoil erupted again, pushing her further into a state of panic. Hopelessness. Reality.

If Lone Eagle planned to kill her through some hideous means, then why had he waited to make it known? Did his satisfaction come in devising the torture to make her pay for leaving him? Stories about tortured victims repeated until each accounting sounded like the last, and all the tales rolled into one. Visions of the Lawrence family focused before her eyes. The scent of blood-soaked bodies filled the air, and she knew not where the stench came from. Cries of terror echoed all around, calling out her name to join the spirits of the dead.

Waiting produced its own gruesome nightmare.

Katie hugged Desert Fawn close to her and said goodbye. The old woman asked her to visit often, and Katie agreed. She couldn't tell this precious woman of Lone

Eagle's words. Desert Fawn could do nothing, and Katie refused to alarm her.

As she expected, Lone Eagle's teepee stood cold and empty. He had not said when he would be returning, and she feared too much to ask. Gathering firewood and preparing food for him kept her hands busy but not her mind.

Her thoughts drifted back to a time soon after Mary's death. She and Pa had worked since sunup packing their belongings for the journey to the Comanche village. As he sorted through the last of the things they needed, she had ventured into the garden to search for any remaining vegetables. She'd finished one row and started another when the distinct hissing of a rattler met her ears. Panic seized her, and she couldn't move or speak. Holding on to a cornstalk, she watched the snake coil and poise to strike. In the flash of an instant, a knife pierced the rattler's head, ending its deadly mission. Pa grabbed her and held her tightly.

"How did you know to come, Pa?" Katie had said.

He looked at her strangely. "I heard you call for help, child."

"No, Pa. I was too scared to talk or move."

He looked deeply into her eyes and shook his head, incredulous of what had happened.

Now Katie felt the familiar tug at her heart, missing him. He couldn't protect her now. No one could. Not Papa or her dear Peyton. She pushed aside the recollection. Like so many times in the last days, her faith wavered. Unbelief whispered taunting words to a mind desperately needing something to grasp. Her senses became cold and numb, yet did she hear a faint whisper?

"Trust Me, Katie."

Evening shadows had stolen away the reflections of late afternoon when Lone Eagle arrived at the teepee. Wordlessly he peered down at her with no expression of anger or hatred. She met his scrutiny by challenging him with her own unemotional stare. Once, her greatest fear of Lone Eagle rested on living the rest of her life as his wife. That same fear became her one hope when he disclosed his passion to kill her. Now she waited for him to choose in which manner she should die.

He moved with confidence and power, reminding her of a mountain cat cautiously picking its way across a canyon wall. Beneath his heavy buffalo robe dwelled a mass of defined muscle and trained nerves ever alert to kill at a moment's notice. She wanted to deny any memories of loving this man. Even at this moment fear took precedence over hatred. He removed the robe and sat beside the fire. She sat back from the blaze while he ate the quail, pecans, and dried berries that she'd roasted for him.

Odd and peculiar thoughts floated through her mind as she focused her attention on a burning log. Why hadn't she used a knife on herself? Ultimately, she would have denied him the pleasure of watching her die. Weary of the waiting and anxious to be free of the unknown, she felt a surge of courage to step into the black haze of his mind.

Katie breathed a quick prayer. "What are you going to do with me?"

His whole body appeared to respond to her words. He placed the food on the dirt floor and pulled out his knife. It glittered wickedly in the firelight. How many other victims had fallen under his blade?

"Why do you not fear me?" Lone Eagle turned the knife over in his hand.

"I am afraid. But in death there is life."

"Your words make no sense."

"I have a God who will take my spirit with Him to live forever," she said. "I cannot fight you. I cannot resist you. I can only draw strength from my God to endure whatever you choose to do."

"You speak white man's words."

"No. These words are for all people. God loves us all and longs to save us all from the evil in our hearts."

Lone Eagle shoved her against the dirt floor. He jumped to his feet and threw the knife, snaring the sleeve of her garment to the ground. He stormed from the teepee.

She pulled the knife from her sleeve. Bewildered by Lone Eagle's actions, she laid the weapon by his unfinished food. *He wants to kill me, but something is stopping him. Has he enjoyed the hunt for so long that my capture is disappointing? How long will this go on?*

Long after the village rested quietly and the sounds of darkness cradled the night creatures, she listened for Lone Eagle to return. Exhausted, she lay beneath the buffalo robes too tired to weep or think. Her body relaxed and she slept.

She woke with the early morning sounds of singing birds and busy insects. A faint trickle of dawn filtered in through the teepee opening, and she smelled the aroma of a freshly built fire. Lone Eagle had returned and didn't waken her. God had delivered her one more time from certain death.

When she reflected upon the last week, God had protected her since Lone Eagle pulled her from the racing horse.

Her gaze rested upon the place where she had set Lone Eagle's knife. It was gone as well as the food. She didn't understand the warrior's behavior, but before she could further deliberate on all the unusual happenings since Lone Eagle brought her to the village, he stepped inside.

"We're leaving," he said. "The horses are ready."

Katie instantly obeyed. With a hint of sleep still dulling her senses, she wrapped a buffalo robe around her and followed him outside. The cold, crisp air against her face alerted her senses to the early morning confusion.

Within moments the two rode from the Comanche village and headed south. At one point, she started to ask him where they were going, except she thought better of it. The warrior would unfold his plans as he saw fit, and she didn't want to displease him.

Under any other circumstances, Katie would have reveled in the beauty of sunrise. Behind a backdrop of towering mountains, the sun emerged, pulling purple and orange banners from a navy blue sky. She smiled at the scene spreading color and light to a sleepy world. Lone Eagle's gaze studied her. She felt it, but she ignored him. Best now she pray and concern herself with him later.

The two stopped beside a narrow stream to refresh themselves and their horses. Katie kneeled beside the water and cupped her hands to drink. She hadn't eaten the day before, and the cool water helped fill the gnawing in her stomach. Again she felt Lone Eagle's eyes boring into her. This time she took a deep breath and boldly met his ebony eyes. Perhaps it was the serenity of a new day or the knowledge they were the only two people for miles around, but a trace of tenderness met her. It shocked her. That quickly, he concealed his vulnerability and ordered her back on the spotted horse.

They rode another hour until she saw the ridge where she and Peyton first viewed the Comanche warriors. What was Lone Eagle planning?

He brought his horse to a halt, and she did also.

"You can ride the rest of the way by yourself," he said.

"Are you letting me go?" Did she dare believe him?

"Yes. I owe Jeremiah Colter this one favor, even if you are not his daughter. I still want to kill you, but the spirits won't let me. I've been tormented since this place." Lone Eagle pointed to the land around them. "You are my wife and my enemy, and I will free you this one time to return to your people and the white soldier."

It was God who'd interrupted his plans, but she couldn't bring herself to tell him.

"Lone Eagle, we aren't enemies. Two people who loved each other can't be enemies."

"You don't know the ways of men and war," he said. "I will never spare you again. Now go."

She wanted to say more, but she chose to heed his words and urged the horse south toward Fort Davis.

The sun played in and out of the clouds, first bringing light and warmth then casting a dismal shade of gray. Katie paid no mind to the weather because her heart and mind sang praises to the God who delivered her. When she reflected upon the miracles since her abduction, they brought tears to her eyes. She wondered how many others had been praying for her. She asked for forgiveness in doubting Him and not having the courage to tell Lone Eagle who had stopped him from killing her.

Peyton was alive! Lone Eagle told her to return to the white soldier. He hadn't been killed but had ridden to safety among the soldiers. Had Peyton believed she died also? What would he feel now that she'd been set free? After a week's time, he might not welcome her as before. He might think the worst. Katie shuddered, contemplating the hideous tortures Lone Eagle could have inflicted. But he hadn't, and to some folks her unharmed body might indicate she had submitted to other things. She'd let them think whatever they chose. She knew the truth. The only persons who deserved to know what happened were Peyton, Papa, and Elizabeth, and she planned to tell them everything.

Lone Eagle. . .he admitted to being tormented by spirits since the afternoon with Peyton. The warrior tasted defeat by a power he didn't know existed. Katie remembered the hatred in his eyes and the bitterness in his voice. He wanted to kill her for the humiliation she had caused. He had administered immense suffering and slow agonizing torment to others, but he stood defenseless before a mighty God.

For an instant, Katie had seen a flicker of the warrior she once loved. Pity ruled her heart, for he forced himself to deny any feelings of caring or compassion. Fortunately she read more in his eyes than he could ever confess. Perhaps Desert Fawn would tell him about God.

Katie squinted and viewed an outline of Fort Davis. She focused her attention on Black Mountain and Wild Rose Pass. Such a refuge for those who needed a haven in the midst of a troubled territory. She clearly recognized the cultural differences between her own people and the Indian. In many ways, the battle over the land was unfair. For as many Indians who vowed to rid the territory of the whites, there were hundreds and thousands more whites to come. The weaker would concede to slaughter and be driven from their homes, and that would be the Indians.

Jeremiah Colter had permitted Katie to see both worlds. He left a legacy of love and compassion to a child he loved as his own. An adopted people, and an adopted daughter. He

◀

wanted Katie to find her rehoboth, a well of blessings and peace in a place provided by God. Katie couldn't have asked for more from any father.

A sensation of being watched or followed nudged her. She tugged at the horse and paused to look around. Several feet behind her she surveyed the figure of Lone Eagle sitting proud and erect upon his horse. She would never fully understand the Comanche warrior. She lifted her hand and waved good-bye.

Chapter Twenty

Peyton moved slowly about the fort, fulfilling his duties while his heart ached for Katie. Guilt assaulted him for riding to safety that day, only to find Katie's horse was riderless. Lone Eagle had taken her from him. He'd won. Peyton had turned his horse to go back, but Miles had grabbed the bridle.

"Peyton, you're hurt. You can't help her now."

"I can't let that killer have her."

Miles face saddened. "There's nothing any of us can do."

Many times, Peyton wished he'd died. What kind of life did he have without her?

What had Lone Eagle done to her? Was she still alive?

Colonel Ross had forbidden him to leave the fort, and soldiers watched to ensure the orders were carried out. But tonight he planned to leave. If he was killed in finding Katie, at least he'd have done his best to save her.

"Sergeant Sinclair," a soldier called from his post looking over the valley.

Peyton looked up from his position below. "Yes, soldier."

"Rider headin' this way, sir. Can't make out who it is."

Folks were jumpy and irritable with the Comanches raiding and murdering every chance they took. "One of the scouts?" He winced, momentarily forgetting his wound. The shoulder throbbed, the second time it had been injured.

"No, sir. It's an Indian. . .no, it's a white woman dressed in Indian clothes."

"Open the gate." Peyton hurried toward the fort's entrance.

"What if it's a trap?" the soldier said.

Peyton smiled broadly. "Then I welcome it."

Clutching his wounded shoulder, Peyton rushed through the gate. The pounding of his boots against the earth started a throb up and down his arm, but the pain would not hold him back. It had to be Katie; no one else could fit that description. Once he saw her blond hair around her shoulders, he ran. Tears of relief and joy stung his eyes. Katie was alive and nothing else mattered to him.

Her horse broke into a slow gallop until it reached his side. She slid to the ground, crying and calling his name. The purple bruise on the side of her face infuriated him. He reached to touch it gingerly as though she might break.

"Are you all right?" Peyton peered into her face.

Katie smiled. "Yes, I'm fine. He didn't hurt me, Peyton, only my face. He wanted to—Lone Eagle wanted to kill me, but he couldn't. God stopped him, and Lone Eagle sent me back to you."

Again Peyton searched her face and slipped his fingers through her hair. "God brought you back to me." He drew her close until his lips touched hers.

"Are you ready, Katie child?" Papa called.

Katie emerged from the evening shadows of Papa and Elizabeth's room, where she had dressed for the wedding. A smile spread across his face.

"You take my breath away," he said. "You are your mother,

Katherine Grace Colter, a beautiful angel. I hope Peyton realizes how precious you are to me."

"Oh, Papa." Katie lifted her face to plant a kiss on his cheek. "I love you so very much."

Elizabeth dabbed her eyes with a lace handkerchief. She reached to Katie's shoulder and adjusted a row of pearls.

"My wedding dress is so beautiful," Katie whispered through sparkling eyes. "Thank you for everything you've done." She touched the ivory satin gown that hugged her slender waist and flared to the floor.

"Hannah and Mary both wore it, and someday your own daughter will wear it on her wedding day," Elizabeth said. "And I have something else for you. Since you decided to wear your hair down, I thought you might like this." She placed a wreath of dried wild roses into Katie's hand.

"It's so lovely," Katie said and swallowed her emotion. "And so perfect. When did you make this?"

Elizabeth laughed. "Katie, you have been so busy with the wedding that it was really quite simple. Now, I'm not finished. I know you wanted to carry your Bible, so I decorated it for you."

Papa handed Katie her Bible adorned with additional dried roses and white ribbons nestled in a crocheted doily.

Katie held her breath. "I don't know what to say."

"Thank you will do just fine," Elizabeth said. "What a fine day for a wedding."

"I look so grand. Oh, do put the wreath in my hair."

Elizabeth fastened the rose wreath with two hairpins and stood back to admire the bride. "Let me give you one last hug before you become Mrs. Peyton Sinclair."

Katie embraced her with love in her touch. Oh, how God had blessed her life. He'd performed one miracle after another, and she knew no end to her joy.

Papa placed Katie's coat around her shoulders and fastened the first button. "I can't have my little girl taking cold, now can I?" He stood back and gave her one last look before reaching out to link his daughter's arm into his. "I am blessed richly to see you marry. Let's not keep Peyton waiting any longer."

In the twilight shadows, many people waited outside the small church. Such dear friends had come to see Sergeant Peyton Sinclair wed Katie Colter. A nervous twinge tickled her stomach as she smiled and nodded at those watching her pass by. Already there were voices from inside the church, indicating that it was full. Stepping into the doorway, she slipped off her coat and handed it to Elizabeth.

"I want Peyton to see me without this," she whispered. Smiling from her heart to her face, Katie caught a glimpse of the room where she would become Mrs. Peyton Sinclair. "Oh my," she said, trembling. "Everything is so beautiful."

Candles flickered in metal braces hung from wooden poles and lining both sides of the center aisle and the sides of the church. Dried wild rose bouquets were gathered with white ribbons and tied to candlesticks at the front of the church.

"I'm not worthy of this," she said. "Papa, I've never done a thing to deserve such a beautiful wedding."

He patted her hand. "Yes, you have, child. If I name them all, then I'll cry like Elizabeth."

Peyton entered through the side door of the church and took his place alongside Reverend Cooper. She could see the smile upon his lips, and it lifted her heart.

A soldier began to play his fiddle—a soft, sweet tune unknown to Katie. Slowly she and Papa walked down front to greet Reverend Cooper and Peyton.

The reverend opened his Bible.

"Heavenly Father, as You have ordained marriage as a holy estate, we humbly ask Your blessings upon this man and this woman as they stand before You to pledge their love. As You have commanded, a man shall leave his father and mother and cling to his wife, and they shall be one flesh.

"Into this holy estate this man and this woman come now to be united. If anyone, therefore, can show just cause why they may not be lawfully joined together, let him now speak, or forever hold his peace."

Reverend Cooper paused, looked out over the crowd, and smiled. He turned to Peyton.

"Wilt thou have this woman to thy wedded wife, to live together after God's ordinance in the holy estate of matrimony? Wilt thou love her, comfort her, honor and keep her in sickness and in health, and, forsaking all others, keep thee only unto her, so long as ye both shall live?"

Peyton's voice boomed over the quiet crowd. "I will."

Thank You, Lord, for delivering me unto You, and for this man.

Reverend Cooper gave Katie his attention.

"Wilt thou have this man to thy wedded husband, to live together after God's ordinance in the holy estate of matrimony? Wilt thou love him, comfort him, honor and keep him in sickness and in health, and, forsaking all others, keep thee unto him, so long as ye both shall live?"

Katie wanted to shout, but her voice failed her. "I will."

"Who giveth this woman to be married to this man?"

"Her father." Papa placed Katie's right hand into Peyton's and gave her one last kiss on her cheek.

Katie felt the firm grasp of Peyton's hand and his gentle squeeze. She turned to smile, meeting warm gray pools of endless love. Reverend Cooper's voice boomed out over the crowd as he read God's directions for a Christ-centered marriage.

As Peyton repeated his vows, she clung to every word, determined to remember the sound of his promise forever.

When Katie's turn came, emotion laced her voice, and she struggled to keep the tears from trickling down her face. Her hand trembled as Peyton slipped a gold band on her finger.

"God Almighty send you His light and truth to keep you all the days of your life. The hand of God protect you. His holy angels accompany you. May the Lord cause His grace to be mighty upon you. Amen.

"I now pronounce you husband and wife," the reverend said. "Peyton, you may kiss your bride."

Months later

Colonel Ross walked outside his office with Peyton. He extended his hand to the young man before him.

"Well, you are officially a civilian now," the colonel said. "I wish I could convince you to stay. The army needs good men like you."

"Thanks, Colonel, but I'm heading home to Illinois. Katie has everything packed, and we're leaving with the supply wagons in the morning. I'm mighty grateful for the army escort."

"Glad to help. You take care of yourself and that fine wife of yours," the colonel said. "What are your plans?"

"I'm planning to finish medical school," Peyton said. "A few years back I wanted nothing to do with it, but times change. Now that I'm going to be a father, I want the best for my family."

Colonel Ross grinned. "I'm expecting you and Katie to write when the baby is born."

"Most certainly. You will probably hear me shouting all the way from Illinois."

Katie Sinclair watched her husband walk away from Colonel Ross, his discharge papers in hand. *God is good. He gave me life, a spirit of truth, a loving husband, and my rehoboth.*

DiAnn Mills is a bestselling author who believes her readers should expect an adventure. She combines unforgettable characters with unpredictable plots to create action-packed, suspense-filled novels.

Her titles have appeared on the CBA and ECPA bestseller lists; won two Christy Awards; and been finalists for the RITA, Daphne Du Maurier, Inspirational Readers' Choice, and Carol Award contests. *Library Journal* presented her with a Best Books 2014: Genre Fiction award in the Christian Fiction category for *Firewall*.

DiAnn is a founding board member of the American Christian Fiction Writers; the 2015 president of the Romance Writers of America's Faith, Hope & Love chapter; and a member of Advanced Writers and Speakers Association, as well as International Thriller Writers. She speaks to various groups and teaches writing workshops around the country. She and her husband live in sunny Houston, Texas.

DiAnn is very active online and would love to connect with readers on any of the social media platforms listed at www.diannmills.com.

Song of the Dove

PEGGY DARTY

Enjoy Your Bonus Story!

Prologue

Morning Dove crept through the inky darkness to the tall red rocks and gazed into the valley below. The smoldering embers of a campfire gave a feeble glow to the circle of wagons. As Morning Dove's dark eyes moved over the sleeping camp, she thought of the palefaces and the evil spirit they had brought upon Ute land. Her eyes burned with anger.

Her anger was quickly tempered, however, by the gentle breath of the sleeping baby in her arms. Slowly, her eyes dropped to the child, and she lifted the rabbit skin and peered impassively into the face of the newborn girl. New fear thundered in her heart as she stared at the pale face, as pale as the moon overhead.

She had brought shame and disgrace to her people. This was not a cherished Ute whose birth would have been a joyous occasion. No warrior had brought firewood to her lodge in her final days. Nor had she gone to the birthing lodge where she could kneel on a straw-covered mat for the birth. Instead, she had fled to a secret cave when the ravaging pains began. She had begged the Great Spirit for death, but death had not come; instead, she had given birth to a healthy baby. Afterward, she had hobbled to the icy mountain stream to bathe herself and the baby; then she had wrapped her in a rabbit skin and crept to the high red rocks. She had intended to offer the baby to the Great Spirit to purge her sin, but when she reached the jagged rocks, she had spotted the wagons in the valley, which sparked a new thought in her mind.

As she stood gazing at the settlers' wagons, Morning Dove's mind drifted back to happier days when the Utes had roamed the land freely, from the bubbling springs to the open plains. But then the palefaces had come, over Ute trails and across Ute valleys, their greedy eyes seeking the buffalo and the beaver, their careless axes felling the big cottonwoods for reckless fires that blazed high in the night skies.

Tears filled her dark eyes as she recalled the evil man—the strong, fair-skinned man with his hairy face and eyes the color of the forest pine. Her search for piñon nuts had led her into their camp, and too late, she had remembered the warning of her brother, Black Hawk, who had cared for her since the death of their parents in the Winter of No Sun.

The man who rode the white magic dog had motioned to her, holding out a shiny wristband of silver. He had dropped down from the magic dog, speaking in a strange tongue. Curiosity chased the fear from Morning Dove's brain. Her moccasined feet stilled as he approached. Then his green eyes changed; his lips turned downward. She sensed danger, and she turned to run. But it was too late. . . .

A deep, wrenching sigh shook her now as she stared at the wagons. She suddenly knew what she must do. She would return the baby to its people, the nation of palefaces. But life would not be easy for the child—she was neither Ute nor paleface. Morning Dove's eyes lifted to the sky, again seeking guidance from the Great Spirit. She prayed for the baby girl's life, that somehow she might survive in the strange world to which she was going. The little squaw must have a spirit that would sing even when it suffered. Like her own spirit, like the name she had been given: Morning Dove. In her heart, the baby girl would always be Little Dove.

With new resolve, she began to pick her way down the rocky path leading to the valley of wagons. Soon the sun would set fire to the mountain of rocks; soon the palefaces would build their morning fires. Her steps quickened.

One wagon was swathed in darkness far from the fire and the guard. This would be the wagon she would choose for Little Dove. Her feet inched forward as drumbeats of fear pounded in her chest, and her stomach heaved as if she had drunk firewater. Still she pushed on, moving like a wispy shadow that melted into the darkness of night as she crouched to place the baby beside the rear wheel of the wagon.

She knelt, removing the blanket from her own shoulders to make a bed for the baby. Gently, she took the tiny bundle from the rabbit skin, and she began to whimper. That was good; it was what she wanted. She pinched the tiny foot until the whimper became a stronger cry of protest. Morning Dove turned and fled through the darkness as the cry sharpened to a high, thin wail.

She did not look back until she reached the high red rocks. Below her, the camp sprang to life as the small and distant cry of the baby filled the night.

She crossed her arms over her shivering shoulders and hesitated one last time to glance downward. The pale yellow flame of lanterns wavered in the darkness as loud voices drowned out the baby's cry.

As she watched the baby being lifted from the ground, Morning Dove's body began to tremble even harder in the biting cold. She had not wanted the baby who could bring evil to her village, yet her body had nourished it. And her heartbeat had quickened when she felt it *move* within her. In a strange way, she had relished the new life, and now she felt as though a piece of her soul had been torn from her and cast into the night, into the arms of the strange palefaces.

For a few more seconds, she stood as still as a spirit, watching the distant camp. . .and the sadness in her soul carved a trail of tears down her frozen cheeks.

Chapter One

Elisabeth

"W ake up, Elisabeth!" Mary Greenwood called from the living room of a small cabin at Greenwood's Trading Post. When there was no answer, Mary wandered to the door of her daughter's bedroom and gazed with pride at the young woman sleeping peacefully in the narrow iron bed.

Sleek black hair was swept back from an oval face in one long, gleaming braid, which, during her sleep, had wound itself around her slender throat. A high forehead, slim, small nose, and delicate lips were balanced by prominent cheekbones over hollow cheeks.

Sunken cheeks, Mary thought, shaking her gray head. *The girl is much too thin!* As she looked at her daughter, she felt a sudden remorse for being unable to provide a better life for Elisabeth, but she'd done the best she could ever since the baby had been left at their wagon. A baby when her womb was barren!

"Wake up, Elisabeth," she repeated, speaking with a rare tenderness. Mary was usually too busy herding stray chickens, dogs, errant children, and drunken traders from her doorstep to stop for such affections, but today for some reason she lingered, gazing at her beautiful daughter. "We're still running this trading post, remember? I'm goin' on to the kitchen to build a fire. We gotta fix a bigger breakfast today. More riders came in from Taos last night."

She paused to seize a strand of steel gray hair that dared escape the fierce bun at her nape. "That Missouri family staying in the last cabin has been prowling since daybreak. The kids are probably hungry. We've got dough to knead, hoecakes to mix, and fatback to fry." Thoughts of hard work sharpened her tone. "Wake up, you hear?"

"Mmmm-hmmm." The dark head tossed on the feather pillow and one long, slender leg twitched beneath the mound of quilts.

"I'm goin'," Mary said, stomping back through the cabin and slamming the front door to underscore her command.

Mary paused on the doorstep, looking around her.

Fresh snow covered the dome of Pike's Peak, blanketed the canyons, and piled up against the fence posts at their trading post. The post contained ten square, one-story buildings of slab pine with a large courtyard in the center.

Mary thrust calloused hands on her plump hips and squinted up at the sunny sky. Eighteen years of Colorado weather told her that the week's snow had ended, at least temporarily. She heaved a sigh of relief as her eyes fell to the post, scanning with pride the general store, the blacksmith shop, the guest cabins, and the kitchen–dining hall. She and her husband, Jed, had built every square inch of the place, starting from nothing. Although Jed would never admit it, his general store had drawn trappers and traders from the foothills, but it had been Mary's good cooking that kept them coming back. Now the post was the center of activity between Pueblo and Colorado City.

"I don't want to get up!" Elisabeth's voice echoed through the empty cabin as her inky lashes parted and dark eyes roamed the dim room. The thought of leaving her warm nest for another work-filled day brought a heavy sigh to her lips, yet she forced herself to toss back the covers. In her own way, she was as conscious of her duties as her mother.

She was slim and tall, with long, fine-toned legs. She made a swift leap to the small rag rug that offered a patch of warmth to her feet. Shivering into her long flannel gown, she leaned over the chest and plunged her fingers into the cold pan of water. As she splashed her sleepy face, a blur of hungry faces filled her mind. She could easily envision the crowd at breakfast, elbowing each other around the ten-foot table, grabbing food and talking with their mouths full.

She reached into the chest for her underclothes.

Fifty-niners. They had been so named for the year they started pouring into the territory. Ever since gold had been discovered at Cherry Creek, they had stampeded into the country, riding on wagons, mules, and horses. Some walked; others rode in sleek prairie schooners. Their clothes were mud crusted, and their faces were covered with beards, but all had that same dazed look in their eyes when they talked about their diggings. "Gold fever," it was called. She shook her head, mentally scolding herself for complaining. After all, it was the miners' money that put food on their table and clothes on their backs.

Her mother's departure had admitted a gust of cold air into the small drafty cabin, and the cold quickened her movements. She yanked on her camisole and wound her long braid into a thick coil at the nape of her neck. From a peg on the wall, she lifted her gray muslin dress and tugged it over her head. The soft folds of the skirt draped over her feminine form, slid down the tiny waist and gently rounded hips, and then fell to the floor, covering her only decent petticoat.

Her cold fingers moved stiffly over the buttons of her dress as she glanced down at her shivering body, suddenly recalling those awkward years when she had been all arms and legs, as gangly as the undernourished colts in the crowded corral. Unlike her mother, most Colorado women were as thin as a blade of prairie grass as a result of their long, work-filled days. Elisabeth had finally rounded into curves at breast and hip, yet her five-foot, seven-inch body registered only a dozen or so notches over the hundred mark on the scale at the post, and her mother nagged her constantly to eat more.

She hurried into the living room, frowning at the disorder that neither she nor her mother had time to straighten. She pulled on her kid leather boots, threw her black woolen cape about her shoulders, and took a deep breath. It would be weeks before the winter broke, but to relieve the monotony, her mind seized images of the columbine that would bloom in the meadows, the crystal streams thick with trout, the golden sunshine glinting over the mountain peaks. Those images were precious treasures to her during the long, harsh winters, and yet she loved Colorado.

She lifted the door latch and stepped outside, blinking into the morning sunshine. The bright light filled the depths of her dark eyes, and they gleamed like polished onyx in contrast to the pristine snow.

The creak of the gate drew her attention to the guard who was admitting an early visitor. Her eyes widened. She had always loved horses, though she had never owned one, but now she was looking at the most beautiful horse she had ever seen. It was a black stallion, about sixteen hands high, with a white stocking extending to the left knee. Its dark coat gleamed as though oiled in the morning sunlight. After a few seconds, Elisabeth lifted her eyes from the horse to the rider.

When she did, she was even more startled.

He sat tall in the saddle, wearing a fringed buckskin shirt and patched trousers. A cap of the same buckskin sat on his dark head. His face was clean shaven, and his eyes, as dark as his hair, were turned toward the general store. To her disappointment, he never once looked her way.

"Elisabeth, Elisabeth!" Tommy Ashbrowner had jumped up from his game of marbles and was racing over the snowy courtyard to her doorstep. "Are you gonna think up some kind of game for us today?"

A gentle smile touched Elisabeth's lips as she looked at Tommy, bundled to the chin in his heavy coat yet already missing his fur hat. Pale blond curls toppled over his thin face, a face lit by a pair of twinkling blue eyes. He shifted from one foot to another, eagerly awaiting her answer.

"If I have time, Tommy." She reached out and playfully mussed his curls. "I have a busy day and—"

"You better!" He thrust his small lips into a pout. "There ain't nothing else to do at this stinking post. Your pa won't let us have a snowball fight or do anything that's fun."

Elisabeth's smile faded as she glanced toward the general store where the tall, dark-haired man had dismounted and was quietly observing the argument in progress on the steps of the store.

Jed Greenwood, Elisabeth's adoptive father, stood haggling over a team of mules with a small, desperate-looking man. Jed was a skinny, rawboned man with thinning gray hair and an angular face.

Tommy sidled up to her. "He ain't really your pa, is he? Momma said he ain't."

The words brought a sharp ache to her heart. She had never ceased to wonder who her parents really were. Kidnapped from one wagon train and left at another by Indians, her mother had always told her. Still, she searched the faces of everyone who came to the post, wondering...always wondering.

"I'm sorry." The small, cold hand touched hers.

Elisabeth looked down into the boy's sympathetic face, and she sighed. "He raised me, Tommy. He's the only father I've ever known. Listen,"—she forced a smile—"you be a good boy, and I'll try to think of a fun game for this afternoon."

"Yippee!" Tommy shouted, racing back across the court-yard to spread the news.

Watching him bound off, Elisabeth's smile faded as she pulled her hood up against the cold. Jed had never wanted her; she had always sensed that. A son would have pleased him, but he considered a girl a luxury he couldn't afford. He seemed to forget the long hours she worked in the kitchen and the time she spent entertaining the children whose parents were staying at the post until the spring thaw. But her mother always defended her, and it had been her mother's love that sustained her, providing the comfort and security she needed when she felt confused and bewildered. And she felt that way more and more as she grew older and wondered where her life was heading.

"Them mules is worth more than you're offering, Green-wood!" the little man shouted angrily.

"Take it or leave it," Jed countered, raking his hand through his tousled gray hair.

"I'd leave it." The handsome stranger who had been lean-ing idly against a post now took a step forward, towering over the other men. "If this man won't pay you a fair price, Ben Williamson up at Three Mile will."

Elisabeth's breath caught, and she stared in amazement. Few men challenged her father.

Jed spat a stream of tobacco juice into the snow. "Fella, what business is it of yours?"

"I'm a missionary from the Denver area, sir. And I take offense when I see people treated unfairly. It isn't right."

"Then maybe you'd better head on back to Denver," Jed countered, "because your missionary services ain't needed here."

Elisabeth stopped walking and stared at the stranger, wondering what he would do.

"All right, sir. Good day." He unhitched his horse and climbed up in the saddle.

"Reckon I'll take that missionary's advice," the other man said with a sneer, as his eyes followed the stranger riding out of the post on his black stallion.

Elisabeth stared after the tall dark stranger for just a moment. He seemed so handsome and mysterious as he rode away, tall in the saddle. She would like to meet someone like that someday. A missionary, he had said he was. Now *that* was interesting. But she never had the chance to meet anyone interesting, and even if she did, Jed's sharp eyes were always watching her, scorning any man who was halfway friendly to her.

She turned back to the path and hurried to the one-room kitchen, lost in thought. She hated the tactics Jed used with the traders. She was secretly glad that he had failed this time. If not for the stranger, the missionary, Jed would have bought the man's mules for half their worth, fattened them cheaply, and then tripled his investment when the next wagon train pulled in.

Glancing back toward the gate, she saw that the stranger had already disappeared. She sighed, feeling a sadness settle over her as her boots made crunching sounds in the hard-packed snow. The deep, stinging cold brought to her the familiar smells of the post—hay, leather, wood smoke. The smells of home. And yet, a part of her had never accepted the post as home, or the Greenwoods as her family. Of course she knew she was adopted; her mother had told her when she was four years old. Something more basic than that knowledge haunted her, however; it was a sense of not belonging here, or anywhere, for that matter. While she had spent her life in the shadow of Pike's Peak, she had never felt at home there. And yet she had tried to tell herself any girl would feel the same way, growing up at a rowdy post rather than in a civilized place like Colorado City or Denver.

The tall stranger had said he was a missionary from the Denver area. *What is Denver like?* she wondered. *And what does a missionary do?* The only missionaries she had ever known were a man and woman from Denver who had stayed at the post two years ago.

Reaching the kitchen door, she scraped her boots on the step and tried to dismiss the man from her thoughts. Considering the way Jed had behaved, she was certain she would never see the man and his beautiful horse again.

Chapter Two

"It's about time!" Mary glanced at her.

"I'll catch up." Elisabeth removed her cape and dropped it on a peg by the door. She was never intimidated by her mother's strong voice. It was just her mother's way. Elisabeth couldn't remember her mother ever spanking her, although she had received some harsh scoldings at times.

"Ma, he was arguing with a man just now, trying to buy his mules too cheap," Elisabeth said. It was obvious who the *he* was. "And a stranger was out there." Elisabeth automatically glanced over her shoulder, although she knew the stranger was gone. "He was a missionary. Ma, what is a missionary?"

"You remember the Tillotsons who stayed a few days with us. They were missionaries."

"I know. I remember them. But what I mean is, exactly what do they do?"

"Well." Mary paused from her work, staring thoughtfully into space for a moment. "They're usually sent by their home church to spread the Word of God, to deliver Bibles, help those in need. That sort of thing."

Elisabeth thought about that as she grabbed an apron and whisked it over her head. The man had kind eyes, she remembered; he would be good at his work, she was sure. "Missionaries go to different parts of the country?" she asked.

"I think they have certain territories they're responsible for." She glanced back at her daughter. "You must have been quite taken with the man."

Elisabeth nodded slowly. "I was. He seemed like a gentleman," she said, tying the apron strings as her mind drifted to the normal flow of people at the post. "Ma, I'm tired of all these drifters," she said impulsively. "They're rude, they spit tobacco juice on the walk, and they stare and use bad grammar."

"That's why I'm paying that uppity eastern lady to teach you. Lucky for us, her husband got down on his luck and they ended up here instead of Pueblo. She's been a real blessing."

Elisabeth nodded, thinking that Alice Stacker had influenced her life more than anyone she knew. Mrs. Stacker was soft spoken, cultured, and once a beauty, though she was quickly aging here in the West.

"I want a better life for you," Mary said, her hand resting on the dough as her eyes stared dreamily into space.

"Maybe I'll meet a rich man," Elisabeth teased, feeling the oppression of the morning pass as she and her mother engaged in one of their dreaming sessions. "That man will fall in love with me and then we'll—"

"*Indians!*"

The hoarse shouts of warning reverberated over the peaceful posts, bringing Mary and Elisabeth to the door.

A dozen Indians were galloping into the courtyard, scattering snow, dogs, and children in a wave of panic. They wore fringed buckskin and beaded headbands. One man, obviously the leader, wore a headdress of white feathers.

"They threatened to attack if they can't trade!" the guard at the gate was yelling.

The leader edged his white horse ahead of his braves as his eyes, black as midnight, scanned every building. There was something about him that commanded attention. He held his head high and proud, and his face bore a stony expression. It was an arresting face—lean, taunt skin over rigid bones, a prominent nose, and piercing black eyes. He drew up before the hitching rail of the general store as his braves fanned out around him.

Jed Greenwood threw open the door and scrambled onto the boardwalk, gaping at the startling sight before him. The cold black eyes that swept Greenwood flashed contempt as Black Hawk shifted on his horse and coolly surveyed the gawking crowd. A few men took a step closer, curiously inspecting the formidable Indian chief as he motioned to a young brave.

The brave dropped down from his horse and removed an armload of buffalo hides. Jed's jaw sagged at the sight of the hides, so hard to come by now. Another brave followed with beadwork, water-jug baskets, and wooden flutes.

"You want to trade, Chief?" Jed yelled, a wicked gleam rising in his narrow-set eyes.

Black Hawk sat rigid on his white horse, whose muscles rippled beneath the firm hand of restraint. "The young squaw." Lone Eagle's deep voice boomed over the courtyard, quiet as death. "We trade for young squaw."

"*Squaw?*" Jed croaked. "We got no squaw here!" His greedy eyes returned to the buffalo hides and the handmade pieces that would tantalize the miners into parting with their gold dust and coins. But this crazy Indian wanted a squaw!

"What about some white lightning from Taos, Chief?" Jed asked with a sly grin.

Black Hawk glared at him. "Trapper John tell us papoose left at your wagon. Papoose belong to Morning Dove."

Jed sucked in his breath as his eyes slid to the kitchen

where Mary and Elisabeth watched from the open door. Elisabeth! They wanted Elisabeth. Jed clawed at the tight collar of his flannel shirt as he forced a hollow laugh from his tight throat.

"Chief, you got me confused with someone else. Why, I ain't been in no wagon train. I been at this post for eighteen years."

The muscles in Black Hawk's face clenched as he ground his teeth together, and a murderous warning leaped into his black eyes.

"Morning Dove leave a papoose eighteen winters ago," he countered. "Morning Dove dying. She want squaw."

Shocked whispers flew over the crowd. Heads turned, eyes shot to the kitchen door, which suddenly closed. The old-timers had heard how the Greenwoods' daughter had been left at their wagon, wrapped in an Indian blanket.

"You take," Black Hawk said, motioning toward their offering placed on the steps of the store. "When the sun rise again, we come for squaw. No squaw,"—he touched the pouch of arrows strapped to his side—"we fight."

He swung the big horse around and motioned to his braves. The hard-packed snow flew into the air, settling again into wet clumps as the horses thundered through the gate. As soon as the gate slammed shut, shouts of panic erupted across the post. Men cursed, women cried out in fear, and Tommy tore across the courtyard for the kitchen, yelling for Elisabeth as he ran.

The sound of wood striking wood captured the attention of the shuffling crowd as the kitchen door was flung wide and banged against the wall. Mary marched out into the courtyard, her long skirts billowing in the wind, her plump hands still floured and thrust in determined fists on her large hips.

"Nobody's proved Elisabeth belongs to this Indian woman!" she yelled, her pale blue eyes moving over each face in the crowd. "Why, she's lighter skinned than half of you! They just want her, that's all. They've seen her and they want her."

"Mary, why start a war over it?" someone yelled. "Couldn't Elisabeth just visit the old squaw? Be nice to her, then come on back to the post?"

"No!"

"Are you askin' us to fight 'em off, then?" A small, scowling man stepped forward. " 'Cause we got a war on our hands come sunrise if we don't figger somethin' out."

"I'll not turn my daughter over to them!" Mary shouted, her voice and her eyes daring anyone to challenge her. "And that's final!" She whirled and lumbered back inside, her large body stiff with pride. But her spine felt the cold breath of terror, a terror that surpassed all other terrors of her life.

Her steps quickened until she was almost running by the time she reached the kitchen. Her hands trembled on the door latch, trembled even more as she slammed it and shut the bolt. She turned slowly, dreading to face Elisabeth, who was now pacing the floor, wringing her hands.

"Here now," Mary laid a protective arm around her shoulder. "Don't look so scared, honey. Nobody's taking you away."

"Is it true?" Elisabeth demanded. "Am I the daughter of Morning Dove?"

"Course not!" Mary began to pace the floor with her. "They just watched you from the cliffs and want you—like all red-blooded males!" She yanked a stray hair back into her bun. "Why, the Cheyennes and Arapahos are attacking wagon trains and taking the women home as squaws. The Utes are getting ideas now. But they'll not get you, baby."

Pulling her daughter close to her, Mary could feel the

erratic pounding of her own heart. Fear clutched at her chest, choking the air from her lungs. She drew a slow, measured breath and forced a smile to her stiff lips. "I love you as my own. They'll not get you!"

"Ma, I don't want anyone killed because of me," Elisabeth protested, anxiously rubbing her forehead, trying to think. "Maybe I should go."

"No! You're not that squaw's daughter. And they'll keep you once they get you into their camp. I've heard the miners and trappers talking. The Indians want white women."

She paused to catch her breath. "You were kidnapped from another wagon train," she said forcefully, her tone more rational. "We all knew that."

A fist pounded the door. "Open up, Mary," Jed yelled. "We gotta do something."

As she unbolted the door and he burst into the kitchen, a torrent of words spilled from his mouth. "Them savages may not wait until sunrise. They may get a hankerin' to come back tonight."

Jed rarely wore a hat, and his thinning gray hair now stood on end. He tugged at his nose, marbled with broken blood vessels. "Her features ain't Indian, and her skin ain't real dark, but her hair and eyes. . ." He was muttering his thoughts aloud, distressing Mary even more.

Her hands clutched and unclutched the folds of her apron. "It's the craziest thing I ever heard, Jed. Elisabeth, an Indian."

"Well, she was wrapped in an Indian blanket, remember? You always figgered she was stolen, but. . ." His voice trailed off as he stared at Elisabeth's features then the shape of her long, slim body, examining her as though she were a stranger. "How did that Indian know a baby was put at our wagon if the ma didn't tell him?" he asked Mary.

"They just want her and they'll lie to get her," Mary snapped, beads of perspiration breaking over her upper lip. "All that matters is, she's *our* daughter now. So help me, they ain't getting her."

Jed's eyes narrowed on his wife while his mind pondered the value of those buffalo skins, buffalo so hard to come by now! And the trinkets and beads—why, he could make a hefty profit in no time.

His eyes shot back to Elisabeth. If she belonged to the Indians by blood, why start a war over it? He scowled and shook his head. Then turning to open the door, he stormed out.

"He'll trade me." Elisabeth's voice was a mere whisper as she stared at the space where Jed had stood.

"He'll do no such thing!" Mary cried. "I'm going to find Trapper John and get to the bottom of this."

Trapper John was a slight yet hardy man in his sixties. A grizzled gray beard and sideburns covered most of his thin, weathered face. Straggly white hair fell from beneath his coonskin cap, brushing the collar of this rabbit-skin jacket. He had survived blizzards, famine on a wagon train, and had even been trapped in a cave to escape a hungry mountain lion—and it all showed in his leathery face.

But nothing equaled the threat in Mary's face as she poked a loaded musket into his chest, backing him against the slab wood of the horse corral.

"Tell me what you told them, and for once you'd better get your story straight!"

Constant exposure to bitter wind and summer sun had weathered and darkened John's skin to the bronze hue of the Cheyennes. All color drained from his face, however, as the tip of the barrel slammed against his breastbone.

"I been tradin' with Black Hawk for years, Mary," he sputtered. "His camp's half a day south of here. He's been pestering me lately about a young squaw that one of his braves seen here at the post. I just figgered the brave was hankering after her, that's all. I thought. . ." His teeth ground into his bottom lip as though he struggled to reason out the words before he spoke them.

"You thought what?" Mary challenged.

Trapper John took a deep breath that made a choked hiss in the night silence, tense with the shocking news. Everyone seemed to be waiting with bated breath to see what the Greenwoods would do.

"I thought if he knew she was forsook by her parents like there was something wrong with her. . .Mary, you know how superstitious them Indians are. I figured if he thought something' was wrong with her, he'd stop asking."

"So did he?" each word was like a stone hurled in his face.

"No." A heavy sigh wrenched John's thin frame. "Then Black Hawk told me his sister was dying. That she thought all her pain was coming from the Great Spirit for leaving that baby at the palefaces' wagon." The words fell over his tongue, unchecked. "The squaw never could have babies after that, he told me. He said. . ."

"He said what?" Mary poked the gun farther into his chest. Her face was ashen, her heart hammered.

"He said the squaw Morning Dove wanted him to bring that baby back. She knew about you folks. She must have kept an eye on your wagon. She knew you were here."

Mary slumped, defeat registering in her eyes as she stared blindly into space.

Seeing her grip on the gun lighten and the look on her

face, as though someone had dealt her a blow, John grabbed a breath and made another attempt to rectify the situation.

"Black Hawk said the squaw wants to see the girl before she dies. Maybe that's all there is to it, Mary," he finished lamely.

She sank back against the wall of the corral as a hard pain tore through the center of her chest. She lowered the musket.

"Mary, you better get ahold of yourself," John said, suddenly concerned. "You look like your heart's about to take out on you."

"Not yet," she hissed. She had to think what to do. She had to save Elisabeth. But how? She lifted a hand to her heart, pressing against the persistent ache. The damage was done, and of course she had no intention of shooting John, although she felt tempted. But he would pay for his mistake later; she would see to that.

"I'm sorry, Mary," he muttered softly. "If only I could have done something—"

"You can do something now," she snapped. "You can take her to Denver tonight."

"Tonight?" John choked, his eyes shooting to the mass of dark clouds rolling in on a northern wind.

"You can take the best horses, and I'll pack food and coffee."

"Denver," he repeated limply. "That's all night and into tomorrow."

"You'll do it, John, and don't tell me you won't. You got that poor girl into this mess and you're gonna get her out." She raised the musket again.

John gulped and nodded. "All right, Mary. Get her ready. We'll head out within the hour."

Mary heaved a sigh of relief then glanced worriedly at the

clouds in the night sky. "The Tillotson family lives on this side of Denver. They're missionaries. They spent some time here, and I nursed his wife through a bad stomach ailment. They said if I ever needed anything. . ."

"Mary, what'll happen if Elisabeth ain't here when the Indians come back?" John didn't want to get killed, but he didn't want to be responsible for an Indian uprising at the post, either.

Mary shook her head. "I don't know, and right now I don't care. I have to think of Elisabeth."

"Does Jed know you're planning to sneak her out?"

Mary glared at him, her fingers closing over the trigger of the musket.

He sighed. "I'll take her anyway."

Chapter Three

*E*lisabeth huddled into her fur coat, her teeth chattering, her mind dazed with shock. In the darkness outside the corral, Trapper John led out a gentle mare then turned back to a frisky roan, raising the stirrups to accommodate his short legs.

"Now, don't waste any time," Mary whispered through the darkness, tucking a bundle of food in John's saddlebag.

"I'll send you a message from town," John said, pulling up into the saddle and lowering his cap against the wind.

"You'll be okay, honey," Mary said, her eyes hungrily searching Elisabeth's face as though memorizing each feature.

"Yes, I know. Don't worry about me," Elisabeth answered, trying to be brave.

"Elisabeth, you keep a tight rein on that mare," John warned from behind her. "We'll just mosey quiet-like out the gate and across them foothills. That's the best way to slip outta this valley."

Mary's plump hand shot up to grip Elisabeth's arm. "The Tillotsons are good people. They'll take care of you, and I'll come as soon as I can."

Elisabeth's teeth were chattering, more from nerves than cold, as she nodded in agreement, glancing one last time at the log buildings huddled in a dark mass against the falling snow.

"Take care of yourself, Ma," Elisabeth said, her eyes returning to Mary, always so strong, yet reduced to heaving sobs now. The sight brought tears to Elisabeth's eyes, but she sank her teeth into her lower lip, refusing to break down. She gripped the reins and kneed her mare into line behind John.

The guard opened the gate, a sad smile on his face as he quietly waved them through.

Elisabeth shivered even in her coat, her eyes stinging from the tears she fought to control. Her bottom lip ached from the hard thrust of her teeth as she centered her thoughts on getting to Denver. Her eyes were focused determinedly on Trapper John, whose cap was drawn low over his head. Just beneath the bottom edge of the hat, his earlobes glistened, fire red from the cold.

The mare plodded along, its slow, easy rhythm a soothing distraction to her turbulent thoughts. For the past hours, her mind had been frozen in shock. She was relieved that her mother had taken charge, making all the decisions for her. Now, as she rode along in the darkened night, the cold air had a sobering effect, mobilizing her thoughts again.

What if Black Hawk spoke the truth? How could she know what to believe? Her mother seemed certain that the Indians had kidnapped her from another wagon train, but was that what had *really* happened?

They had ridden in silence for almost an hour when Elisabeth sensed a change in the quiet night. She studied John up ahead of her, huddled against the cold. He seemed unaware of any change, yet her skin prickled. What was wrong, what was different?

The silence was no longer complete. That was it! She pushed her hood back and strained to hear. Then the change she had tried to identify became apparent even to John, who wheeled his horse around. The leather of his saddle creaked as he shifted his weight to survey the darkness that enclosed them, a darkness feathered by gently falling snow.

Elisabeth pulled her mare to a halt, following Sam's searching gaze into the black night and seeing nothing. But here was a sound drifting through the darkness, a thudding that grew stronger—hoofbeats, muffled by snow.

"Someone's after us," John called at the moment the realization struck her. "And we ain't hanging around to find out who! Kick that mare and ride like the wind!" he yelled. "We gotta reach them rocks up there so we can hide."

Wordlessly, she obeyed, slamming her booted heels into the mare's sides. The horse lunged forward, and the snow spun a white web around her as the mare tore across the frozen earth. Elisabeth's pulse drummed in her ears as she struggled to hang on, while the cold wind stung her face and blurred her vision.

The night was suddenly rent with shouts, words that were foreign to her. Then suddenly a body had landed on top of John, knocking him from his horse and into the snow.

"John!" she screamed, jerking the reins. At her panicked tugging, the mare reared then plunged again, throwing Elisabeth headlong into the snow.

She was half-buried in a mound that froze her face and matted her lashes. She struggled to get up, impatiently brushing the wetness from her face.

Hoofbeats and wild shouts filled her ears as she shook

loose the clumps that clung to her clothes. A rough hand yanked her to her feet, snapping her head back, and suddenly she was staring into the dark face of an Indian brave.

"John!" she glanced back over her shoulder, trying to see what had happened to him as more faces crowded in. Dark eyes peered at her as though she were a creature from another world.

She glanced across the snow, looking for Trapper John. They had not harmed him, she was relieved to see that. Two braves were merely restraining him as a hand gripped her and strong arms returned her to her horse. There was no point in asking where she was going, for she already knew.

Black Hawk had won after all.

Chapter Four

Moonlight streamed over the mountains, turning the peaks to a gleaming silver as the Indians led Elisabeth's mare into a wide meadow enclosed by dark pine forests and jagged boulders. This was the land of the bubbling springs that she'd heard about, where Utes left trinkets for the Great Spirit. She remembered a trapper who had once stolen one of those trinkets and had come to the post with it. Jed had traded some flour and sugar for it, put it in a jar, and told everyone it was a valuable good luck charm from a medicine man. A Kansas mule skinner turned gold seeker had paid a fortune for it.

Half-frozen and numb with shock, Elisabeth stared through bleary eyes at the small, silent village where a campfire threw flickering shadows on the buckskin lodges clustered in a wide circle.

The lead Indian broke from the group and loped into camp, shouting hoarsely as he tumbled from his pinto and raced to a lodge in the center of the village.

Flaps were thrown back, faces peered into the darkness, before torches were lit to flare in Elisabeth's terrified face.

Black Hawk appeared, wearing a furry robe and a long, elk-tooth necklace. His black hair hung in thick braids bound by rawhide, which swung about his shoulders as he broke through the gathering crowd and approached her. His dark eyes held a look of triumph.

"Come!" he commanded.

The deep voice rumbled over her, sending chills down her spine. She dismounted, pulling her coat tightly around her. Every bone in her body ached and throbbed from the long, punishing ride and the freezing cold. Still, she held herself erect, not wanting the staring kidnappers to sense her fear. She followed Black Hawk to a tall lodge that held colorful drawings of elk and deer. A large painting in the center featured a huge eagle and a young warrior.

Nearby, a smaller lodge held only one painting, that of a sad Indian maiden staring up at a dove on a tree limb. *Morning Dove,* she thought. Black Hawk threw the flap back and motioned her inside.

Elisabeth hesitated, growing apprehensive. Then, feeling Black Hawk's black eyes urging her on, she forced herself to enter the lodge. A flickering candle offset the darkness within, as she blinked and glanced around her. A young girl sat beside a small, thin body that lay still as death on a bed of animal skins.

"Morning Dove." Black Hawk pointed, stepping toward the sick woman.

Elisabeth's feet were like stones as she edged toward the small woman whose gaunt brown face was as shriveled as the prunes they sold at the trading post. Her gray hair was swept back from her face in a single braid, and curiously, Elisabeth took a step closer, carefully studying the blunt nose, pale lips, and sunken cheeks. *This person could not possibly be my mother,* she thought, sighing with relief.

The woman appeared to be sleeping, but, as though sensing her presence, the sunken eyes began to open.

The big bronze chief leaned down and touched his sister's shoulder. He spoke in a low voice, words Elisabeth did not understand. Then suddenly the woman struggled to sit up; dark, pain-filled eyes flew to Elisabeth.

Elisabeth froze as a gnarled hand flailed through the air and the woman began to babble incoherently. The words died away and the woman lay with her mouth open, gasping for breath, as Elisabeth stared.

"Little Dove. Your name is Little Dove." Black Hawk's deep voice broke through Elisabeth's thoughts. "She say your spirit sings even when you suffer. Like the little dove."

Elisabeth's mouth dropped open as her eyes drifted back to the sick woman who was staring at her with a wide, toothless smile.

"But there's been a mistake," she burst out. "I'm not Little Dove. I'm Elisabeth Greenwood. And I'm not her daughter."

Black Hawk's dark eyes were as sharp as eagle eyes, and he glared threateningly at her. "Tell her you forgive."

Elisabeth gulped and looked from his stern face to the suffering woman. "I forgive you," she said, staring into Morning Dove's pain-filled eyes.

Black Hawk translated her reply, and the woman listened carefully as tears filled her eyes and rolled unevenly down her creased cheeks.

Watching her, Elisabeth felt a sudden surge of pity for this woman, Morning Dove. Even if she wasn't her mother, Elisabeth decided it would do no harm to be kind. She was obviously dying. Elisabeth studied the brown hand, dangling in midair. Shyly, she reached out and grasped the cold fingers. New strength seemed to flow into the woman's feeble body, and Morning Dove began to speak again.

Elisabeth frowned, carefully studying the sunken eyes,

the nut-brown skin. No, this woman couldn't possibly be her mother and yet—how did she know that Elisabeth had been left beside a wagon?

The trauma of what was happening seemed to center itself in one blinding pain behind her forehead. Elisabeth could no longer think straight; how could she know what to believe?

Morning Dove's strange murmurings had ceased, and the grasp on Elisabeth's hand weakened. An expression of peace settled over Morning Dove's features as she closed her eyes and slept again.

Black Hawk nodded approval at Elisabeth then turned and swept out of the lodge.

Elisabeth's eyes cautiously followed. As the flap closed behind him, she gently removed her hand from Morning Dove's grasp.

The flap opened again, and the girl who had been keeping vigil returned with a clay pot of steaming broth. Elisabeth's eyes dropped to the thin liquid, and her mouth began to water as her empty stomach reacted to the flavorful aroma. She was motioned to a corner of the lodge where a smooth rock served as a table. She sank down on a buffalo skin, her weary glance moving from the broth to the dark-skinned girl, who gave her a shy smile before she darted out again.

Elisabeth filled her stomach, trying not to think. But one worry after another raced through her mind. What happened to Trapper John? Did he return, or had he lit out in another direction, afraid to admit his mission had failed? What was going to happen to her?

She glanced around the small lodge, walled with buffalo hides sewn together between long, rigid poles that narrowed into a chimney at the top. The lining of the skins helped insulate the lodge against the harsh weather, but Elisabeth continued to shiver. As her eyes moved curiously about, she could see doeskin dresses, moccasins beaded in flower designs, and baskets shaped like jugs attached to the poles. Along the floor, there were more baskets of various sizes and shapes, and a clay bowl and crude wooden spoon.

Elisabeth sighed and returned to her broth. As she was finishing, the flap parted and the Indian girl returned, carrying a buckskin dress, a pair of moccasins, and several animal skins, which she indicated were to be Elisabeth's bed.

Bone weary, Elisabeth sank onto the skins, too numb in mind and body to care what would happen next. The warm broth had filled her hungry stomach, and with only the snores of the sick woman to distract her, she pulled the extra skins over her and quickly fell asleep.

Elisabeth huddled before the morning fire, staring glumly at the interior of Morning Dove's lodge. Absently, she counted thirteen slim poles that held the dried buffalo hides together. Her eyes roamed to the opening covered with a flap of skin held by two rigid poles. If only she could walk through that opening and leave this village behind. But an Indian brave stood guard outside, making her their prisoner.

She sighed and turned to stare into the fire. She was trapped within this lodge, this village. And to complicate matters, one of the braves had become a suitor of sorts. Still, she had refused to wear the clothes of an Indian maiden, had chosen to eat and sleep in her one rumpled dress until this morning when Black Hawk had demanded she wear the dress and moccasins they had given her.

Her eyes ran down the soft buckskin dress now, ending on her moccasined feet. She was beginning to feel like one of them, and she had noticed that her hair was as dark as many of the other maidens. Was it true that her father had been white, had actually raped Morning Dove, who had then left Elisabeth with the white people?

She had been told this over the past week, and at times she half believed it. But another part of her mind argued that this could not possibly be true.

She sat brooding, staring listlessly into the fire. Homesick tears welled in her eyes. Five days had passed, and the tense waiting had drained her energy. The Utes interpreted her silence as submission to this strange life, but they were wrong.

Her pent-up tears overflowed and streamed down her cheeks when she thought of the post and her adoptive parents. Surely by now they had heard from Trapper John that she had not reached Denver—if John were alive to tell them! Surely Ma knew they had not reached the Tillotsons, for there would had been no telegraph back to assure her. Elisabeth expected little from Jed Greenwood, but her ma. . .

She wandered over to lift the flap, trying to push those thoughts from her troubled mind as she studied the inhabitants of Black Hawk's small village. On this cold morning, the men wore animal-skin robes over their breechcloths and moccasins. The women wore loose dresses fashioned from animal skins. Some of the dresses held painted decorations; a few were embroidered with beads. The women talked in low voices, smiling at one another, apparently happy in their work.

Near the fire, some of the women were skinning a large buck brought in from the morning hunt. Two squaws had cradleboards strapped to their backs. The dark-eyed babies appeared content, obviously accustomed to this kind of activity. The children roamed freely. A few were clustered together in some sort of game with a stick and a rock. Their dark braids bounced against their rabbit-skin coats as they raced merrily about.

Strange, Elisabeth thought, *how the children here seem happier than those at the post.* None cried or begged at their mother's side. Suddenly, one of the children let out an excited shriek and jabbed a small finger in the direction of the trail leading into the camp. The other children joined in the excitement, laughing and yelling as they raced toward the road.

Elisabeth's brow knitted in a curious frown, and she ventured outside to investigate. Everyone's attention was centered on a man riding a black stallion into the village.

Recognition flashed in Elisabeth's eyes. It was him! The missionary who had come to the post. Had her parents sent him to speak with Black Hawk? For the first time since her capture, her hopes soared.

The children crowded about him as he swung down from his horse and reached into his saddlebags. Hands shot out, eagerly awaiting the contents. Obviously, this man was no stranger here; certainly he must have been generous in the past. The children shrieked with delight as their small hands were filled with peppermint sticks and assorted trinkets.

She studied the man more closely. A friendly smile touched his lips as he spoke to the children. Elisabeth stepped outside, staring curiously at this man who had stood up to her father, as few men did, yet who could be generous and caring to the Indian children.

"How!"

The deep voice of Black Hawk rumbled as he swept past her. For the first time, there was a pleasant expression on his face as he looked from the man to the children who were jumping up and down with glee.

"How!" the stranger called back, lifting his hand. As the

missionary returned Black Hawk's greeting, he did not seem intimidated by the Indian chief. Still, he spoke with respect, half in English, half in the Ute language, as Black Hawk approached his side.

As the sunlight filtered over the man who had so fascinated her, Elisabeth took in every detail of his appearance. His rugged features and buckskin clothes made him the epitome of the western man, yet the brown eyes held a look of humility as he spoke words of kindness to the children who flocked around him. As she stood staring, he glanced in her direction, and she saw a look of surprise flash over his face. But then Black Hawk spoke, reclaiming his attention.

Elisabeth's brave smile began to waver. She had expected him to acknowledge her in some way if, indeed, he had been sent to take her home. But then she recalled his disagreement with her father. What, she wondered, had Jed offered him to come here for her? Maybe it was part of his plan, to appear casual, conceal his real intention.

When he turned to walk with Black Hawk to the center lodge, Elisabeth motioned to Deer Woman.

"Who is he?" she asked, pointing to the tall, handsome man.

"Friend. . ." The old woman spoke the word slowly, reverently, as she touched a thin silver bracelet on her wrist.

Elisabeth's eye jumped from the bracelet back to Black Hawk's lodge, into which the men had disappeared. Just then a wail of pain pierced the air, and Elisabeth turned back into Morning Dove's lodge. The woman's agonizing battle for life appeared to be coming to an end. Her dark eyes rolled back in her head, and her mouth that had issued moans of agony now sagged as Morning Dove sank into death.

Elisabeth stared down at her, dumbfounded at the reality of death, even a death that had been obviously imminent. She heard someone speaking rapidly, and she turned to see Deer Woman's aging eyes widening in stunned comprehension as she stared at Morning Dove's lifeless body. Then she dashed out, shrieking the news.

Gently, Elisabeth pulled the buffalo robe over Morning Dove's still face; as she did, she was surprised to feel sadness welling up inside of her. She thought of what Black Hawk had said, that Morning Dove was her mother. She shook her head slowly, dismissing that unlikely possibility. There was not the slightest resemblance. It had all been a mistake, as her mother had insisted.

Black Hawk burst into the lodge, his dark face filled with sorrow at the sight of his sister's covered body. Elisabeth could see the buckskin trousers of the stranger at the edge of the flap, as he politely waited outside. She glanced back at Black Hawk, who was momentarily caught up in grief.

Seizing the opportunity, she slipped from the lodge and motioned the stranger out of earshot of Black Hawk.

"I'm Elisabeth Greenwood from Greenwood's Trading Post," she spoke breathlessly, eagerly awaiting his reaction.

"I'm Adam Pearson. The people here call me Walks Tall." He smiled. Removing his skin cap, he looked into her face. Elisabeth's eyes ran over his slim, smooth features—thick brows over deep-set brown eyes, straight nose and sculpted lips, and a firm jawline. His skin was deeply tanned, and she noticed a slight cleft in his chin. Her eyes moved down the muscled neck; swept broad shoulders; narrow torso; and long legs, ending in dark leather boots. She shook her head slightly, trying to pull her thoughts back to her reason for speaking to him.

"Did my parents send you?" she whispered.

"Send me?" he tilted his head, obviously unclear as to what

she was talking about.

Elisabeth swallowed, fighting the sick disappointment overtaking her. "I've been kidnapped," she explained desperately. "I'm Jed Greenwood's daughter from the post. You were there. I saw you!"

"Kidnapped?" he repeated, as though nothing else she had said registered in his mind. "I can't believe Black Hawk would allow—"

"There's been a terrible mistake," Elisabeth interrupted, glancing impatiently toward the lodge. "I haven't time to explain but you must believe me." Her hand shot out, grasping desperately at his fringed sleeve. "You must help me. *Please*."

His eyes widened, taking in every inch of her, from her tangled hair down to the buckskin dress and her dusty moccasins, as Black Hawk emerged from the lodge.

"She has gone to the Great Spirit," he said, heaving a sigh.

"Black Hawk, may I say a prayer for her?" Adam asked gently.

Elisabeth stared at him. Why did he want to say a prayer for her? Did missionaries act as ministers also?

"Would you allow me to do that?" Adam persisted.

Black Hawk nodded, and Adam stepped inside the lodge. As he did, Black Hawk turned his attention to Elisabeth.

While their dark eyes locked, she heard the gentle tones being spoken inside the lodge.

"I want to go home," she spoke in a small yet firm voice. "I have cared for her as you asked; I have told her I forgive her. Now my people will be worried."

At that moment, Adam had stepped outside the lodge again and was looking curiously at Elisabeth and then Black Hawk.

"I think this man will be willing to see me back to the post.

Please let me go!" she cried, her eyes filling with tears.

Black Hawk merely grunted and turned to motion Adam toward the lodge.

Adam stared at her for a moment, obviously puzzled by all he had encountered. When he turned and strode after Black Hawk, Elisabeth suddenly realized she hadn't even asked him to take her home. Surely she could persuade him to do that; her parents would pay him well, she was sure of that.

But what if he was going in another direction? What if he refused?

Chapter Five

Elisabeth stared after them as they disappeared into Black Hawk's lodge. Gripping her hands tightly against her waist, she suddenly became aware of the dirt on her skin. She looked down at her broken, grimy nails. No wonder Adam Pearson was reluctant to help her. She yanked a strand of hair from her head, examining its dull, lifeless color. Why, she looked like a vagabond, she looked. . .like a squaw, only these squaws were cleaner than she was.

Footsteps whispered behind her, and she whirled to see Deer Woman returning to Morning Dove's lodge. Sighing, Elisabeth stepped inside, determined to find a way to say good-bye and leave with Adam. Deer Woman was gathering up Morning Dove's clay bowl, her beaded moccasins, and doeskin dress.

"What are you doing?" Elisabeth asked curiously. Deer Woman motioned to the lifeless body then held the articles up and indicated through hand motions that these would be buried in the crevice of the red rocks with Morning Dove.

Elisabeth nodded. Unlike their Cheyenne neighbors who buried their dead high above the ground, the Utes buried their people in rock crevices, and they particularly favored the high red rocks.

A low, mournful wail broke over the camp. Other voices

joined in, and soon the sound of dozens of stamping feet filled her ears. A chant swept over the village; this was the mourning dance she had heard about at the post.

The tent flap was thrown back, and two braves entered.

Elisabeth quickly looked away, unable to watch as they hoisted the lifeless body and carried it from the lodge.

Watching them go, a strange emotion began to sweep over her. She had developed a feeling for this woman over the past days, one she had not yet identified. When she first came here, she had known that the woman's death might permit her to return to the post; now, there was an odd, hollow feeling, an emptiness welling up inside. Why did she feel this way? Her mother had once told her that folks didn't always understand what went on in the heart. She had thought the words strange at the time, but now they made sense to her.

She frowned, following the men from the lodge. As she stood on the edge of the crowd, her eyes met those of the brave who had been boldly watching her all week. Her breath caught.

She had to do something; she had to act now before the brave persuaded Black Hawk to keep her here.

Her decision propelled her feet into action, and she flew up the path to Black Hawk's lodge and burst in, surprising Black Hawk and Adam as they sat quietly smoking the pipe.

She clenched her fists at her sides, summoning all her courage. "Let me go," she said, her voice shaky yet determined. "Please let me go. She's dead now. There's nothing more I can do here."

Black Hawk's face was a bronze mask.

Adam Pearson laid down the pipe and rose to his feet. "Perhaps I can settle the problem," he said pleasantly. "The God I worship does not believe in holding people against their will. If you will let her return to her people who care for her, I am willing to make a trade." He reached into his pocket. "I panned many streams for this." He withdrew a gold nugget, offering it to Black Hawk.

Black Hawk's dark eyes glowed as he turned the nugget over in his palm, studying its soft gleam in the glow of the fire.

For a moment, Elisabeth's eyes were frozen in shock as she, too, stared at the nugget. How humiliating to be traded for a. . .a piece of rock!

"You don't have to do that," she said sharply, her eyes relaying her offense.

Adam did not respond; he merely looked back at Black Hawk.

"Do we trade?" he asked.

Black Hawk's eyes swept Elisabeth. "You want to go back to them?" he asked sharply.

"Yes, I do. They raised me. They're my family now."

With a sigh he began to nod. "Then we trade."

Chapter Six

The sun was not yet midway across the sky when Elisabeth climbed on her horse again and rode off with Adam. She had changed back into the rumpled clothes she had worn for days, but she had managed to bathe and redo her hair.

Neither she nor Adam spoke as their horses plodded away from the camp. She dared not look back, though many eyes followed them.

"Where do you come from?" she asked, shifting nervously in the saddle. She hoped to make conversation and put the unpleasant situation behind them as soon as possible.

"I was raised in the South." He looked across at her. "But I've been in Colorado for three years. I ride the circuit, visiting people throughout the territory. I also pan a little and trap a little to make ends meet."

"My father will repay you for the nugget." She pushed her chin forward stubbornly, still embarrassed by the incident.

His dark eyes returned to her, and she could see that he was puzzled by what she said.

"What really happened?" he asked, turning back to straighten the reins in his hands as their horses walked at a leisurely pace through the deep snow.

"You mean why was I kidnapped by the Indians?" She

sighed. "I was hoping you had been sent by my father."

She glanced at him and saw that his head was tilted; the dark eyes were sweeping over her curiously once again. She felt her skin flushing beneath his gaze, and she looked away.

Her mother's stern protectiveness had discouraged most of the single males who came to the post. Mary didn't consider any of them good enough for her daughter. There had been only two who may have proved acceptable suitors, but the trains had moved on, and there had been no time for a friendship to develop.

Now she felt painfully vulnerable and inexperienced.

"I wasn't sent," he answered her. "Sorry to disappoint you. I stop in on Black Hawk's camp when I am in the territory. Part of my mission is to help the Indians."

She bit her lip, considering his words. What would he think if he knew they considered her to be Ute? As though reading her thoughts, he spoke again, shocking her with his words.

"My mother was a Cherokee in North Carolina; my father was a pioneer. They married and I was their only child. We lived in the wilderness until my mother died. Then he moved into town so I could attend school," he spoke matter-of-factly, as if this bit of information was old news. "My father's brother was a missionary to Colorado. I was fascinated by his stories when he came back to visit. I began to do some missionary work among the Cherokees. Then later I came here."

She turned to stare at him, amazed by what he had told her. Then, before thinking, she spoke her observation.

"You seem proud to be—" She bit her lip, hating herself for so blatantly revealing her emotions.

"To be part Cherokee? Yes, I'm proud of my heritage," he said, looking across at her. Then slowly a dark shadow seemed to pass over his face. "One of the most tragic things I can think of is being ashamed of the life God has given you."

"My life hasn't been that good," she said, fighting back the sudden rush of tears. The dense woods bordering the road blurred before her as she fought to control her emotions. "I never knew who my real parents were. I was left at a wagon train, wrapped in an Indian blanket. . . ."

"How did your parents explain that?" he asked.

Her stomach fluttered. It felt as though every nerve in her body were in a war in her stomach. She swallowed and tried to keep her voice calm as she spoke. "My mother said I was kidnapped from one wagon train and delivered to another by the Indians."

He was thoughtful for a moment, staring at the snow-packed trail as they rode along. "I've never heard of that happening," he said quietly. "Usually if the Indians take a baby, they keep it. Many of the women lose their babies to sickness and are lonely for children."

"Well, that isn't what happened to me," she answered quickly. "Listen, I'm worried about the man who was taking me to Denver. Everyone called him Trapper John. Do you know him?"

"No, I don't believe I do."

"I wonder what happened to him. Either he died there in the snow or he lit out to Denver, afraid to tell Ma what really happened."

"And what did?"

Slowly, she began the story, telling him everything. As she did, she recalled how the people at the post had reacted when Black Hawk announced she was the daughter of Morning Dove. Despite her mother's stern rebuttal, she had felt a change in the attitude of those around her. She sensed their doubt and suspicion, even among those she considered her friends. For as long as she could remember, people at the post scorned half-breeds. But this man didn't seem at all worried about that. He said he was proud of his heritage. She finished her story, leading up to this morning when he arrived. "So you see why I was desperate."

He looked at her. "Did they treat you well at the camp?"

She shrugged. "I can't complain." She was ashamed to admit to him how well she had been treated. Everyone had been kind to her, bringing her food and fresh clothing if she had wanted a change, but she didn't. She had even started refusing food.

"They were only kind to me because they thought I was her daughter," she said.

"They've always treated me very well." He said nothing more, but it was apparent to Elisabeth that he had great respect for Black Hawk and his people. Possibly more respect than for Jed, whom he had caught trying to cheat a man.

"How far is it to the post?" she asked, shading her eyes against the white glare of sun on snow.

"We're half a day. If you want to, we can move at a faster pace."

"I want to," she said, kneeing her mare. "I'm eager to get *home*," she said, adding new emphasis to the word.

Elisabeth's heart was lodged in her throat when finally her eyes scanned the valley and came to rest on the trading post. Her hand automatically gripped the reins tighter, slowing her mare.

"What's wrong?" Adam asked. Elisabeth swallowed. "I don't know. I'm just nervous, I guess."

As they neared the post, she began to smooth her wrinkled dress. Then she removed a comb from her saddlebags and
whisked her hair into a bun at the nape of her neck. Although
Elisabeth would not admit it, she was trying *not* to look like
the Utes.

"I feel anxious about returning," she confessed. "I don't
understand why Ma didn't send someone to Black Hawk's
camp. I didn't expect Jed to do anything, but Ma. . ." Her
voice trailed away as her eyes focused on the approaching pine
buildings. Smoke curled high in the sky on this sunny morning. *Perhaps the sunshine is a good omen,* she thought.

As their horses trotted through the gate, Elisabeth's face
fell at the meager greeting offered by a small group of stunned
faces.

Adam's eyes drifted over the men, reading something more
than shock in their expressions. Pity? Embarrassment?

Elisabeth drew rein at the post kitchen and dropped down.

"Ma!" she called, throwing open the kitchen door. She
stopped in her tracks as a Mexican woman, years younger than
her mother, looked up from the stove.

"Where's Ma?" Elisabeth asked, glancing around.

The kitchen was different in a way she couldn't immediately define. The smells were spicier; pots and pans cluttered
the countertops. This was a stark contrast to Mary's neat
kitchen.

She turned questioning eyes to the woman, who stood
twisting her plump hands in her apron.

"You are. . .Elisabeth?"

She nodded, puzzled.

The woman dropped her head. "Your mother. . .is not here."

Elisabeth whirled from the kitchen and hurried across the
courtyard to the cabin, her eyes flicking from right to left.

Where were the children? Where was Tommy? Where was her mother?

"Ma?" she called, bursting into the cabin, ready to hurl herself against the bosom of the woman who had given her so much love. After what she'd been through, she felt that she needed Mary more than ever in her life.

Clothing was scattered carelessly about the cabin. On the wooden floor, snow clumps had melted to puddles of water. Lifting her skirts to sidestep the water, Elisabeth peered into the bedroom. She found only an empty, unmade bed. Frustration mounted as she flung open the door to her room. Her mother was not there. A strange comb and brush and a black-lacquered hand mirror cluttered the tiny dresser.

Shocked, Elisabeth walked over to peer into the closet. The heavy perfume of the Mexican woman clung to the unfamiliar dresses hanging here.

A gentle rap sounded at the front door, and she found Adam standing on the slab step, his eyes filled with concern.

"May I come in?" he asked.

She nodded blankly, glancing back at the disheveled room. "I don't know what's going on. Ma's not here. . . ."

The sound of quick steps crunched over the snow beyond the open door, echoing in the tense silence that hung between Elisabeth and Adam. Then Jed Greenwood poked his head in the door.

"Thought you were in Denver."

"No. Didn't Trapper John come back and tell you? We never made it. Black Hawk's braves were waiting for us. They took me back to his camp. I don't know what happened to Trapper John. Either he died, or he rode on to avoid trouble with you."

Jed looked shocked at her words; he obviously knew

nothing of what had happened.

"Where's Ma?" Elisabeth asked, as her eyes traveled nervously over the cluttered cabin. Behind the forced smile, her words held the echo of fear, a fear too horrible to identify.

Jed rubbed his hands down the front of his faded flannel shirt, casting a curious glance at Adam.

"Gone to Denver?" she asked. "Did she go to the Tillotsons looking for me? She said she would."

Jed coughed uncomfortably and loosened the collar of his shirt. "Girl, I don't know how to say it, other than straight out." The silence in the room lengthened; only the steady drip of snow melting from the eaves outside could be heard for several seconds. Elisabeth's eyes darted to Adam as Jed took a step toward her.

"Your ma's heart gave out the night you left," he finally blurted. "We buried her the next day."

"Buried her?" Elisabeth gasped, horrified. *Buried her. . . ?*

Her hands flew to her mouth to stifle the sobs. Through a blur of tears, she saw Adam reach for her hand while Jed backed out the door.

"We never heard nothin'," Jed argued. "Figured you were safe in Denver. Thought it was best not to send for you, all things considered."

"What things?" Elisabeth gasped. "You should have known I'd want to be at Ma's funeral." She couldn't believe that the one person who had loved her was gone. She felt an arm slip around her shoulders, and she leaned against it, fearing her legs would buckle. Her ma. . . *Gone. Buried.*

Wiping the streaming tears, Elisabeth struggled for words. "Did she. . .suffer?"

Jed shook his head. "She just come in here"—his eyes slid to the door of the room that had belonged to Mary—"laid down on the bed. . .and died."

Fresh tears stung Elisabeth's eyes, and then as her gaze dropped to the floor, she saw a tattered black lace petticoat. Her grief burst into rage. She snatched the petticoat from the floor and hurled it against the wall. Then she spun on Jed. "And you moved that Mexican woman into Ma's house?"

"Elisabeth," Adam warned gently.

"Watch your mouth, girl," Jed snarled. "I had to have a cook."

"I can cook," she cried. "If only you'd sent for me—"

"I ain't gonna stir up war with them savages! Can't you get that through your head?" His eyes raked her in a slow, contemptuous manner. "Besides, from what that Indian chief said, you may be the daughter of that squaw."

The room was spinning around her. She felt as though the earth had given way and she was being sucked down into the recesses of it. She would not let Jed Greenwood destroy her— she would not!

She forced herself to meet Jed's hard eyes. This was no longer her home. She knew that now, but she had to make an effort to stand her ground.

"I have spent the past week at Black Hawk's camp," she answered, her voice taking on a calmer tone. "That squaw could not possibly be my mother." She waited for Jed's reaction, but his expression remained unchanged. "Anyway, she died yesterday."

Jed said nothing; he merely glared at her.

Elisabeth studied his face with the wisdom of eighteen years spent cringing under his scowls. She stumbled across the living room and sank into a chair.

"I'd like to have something to remember Ma by," she said dully, staring at the dirty floorboards. "Then I'll be leaving."

If she had looked at Jed, she would have caught the faint sigh of relief, followed by the twitch of satisfaction on his mouth. Adam, however, missed nothing.

"Her things are in a trunk in the other closet," Jed answered slowly. "Reckon you can have whatever you want." He paused to clear his throat. "Where are you going?"

Elisabeth lifted her tearstained face to him. Where indeed? She tried to think, but her mind was locked in disbelief.

"I could take you to Denver to the home of those folks you mentioned," Adam offered.

Jed's eyes flew back to Adam. He was obviously curious about this man who had brought her back, who dared to speak up to him that day. But he certainly wasn't going to make a fuss; if the man was willing to get her off his hands, then so be it.

Elisabeth took a deep breath and looked at Adam. "Do you know the Tillotsons? They're missionaries and—"

Adam began to nod. "I know them well. I'll take you up to the Tillotsons' home."

"You'll be better off there," Jed said, not meeting her eyes. "With all this business about Indians, some folks feel kinda uncomfortable about you bein' here."

Elisabeth ignored the inference as her eyes moved toward the open door.

"Where is everyone?"

Jed kicked at a loose board. "Half the post left after your ma died, and Carlotta—"

"We'll be leaving as soon as Elisabeth gets whatever she needs," Adam interrupted.

Jed merely grunted and stalked out.

Elisabeth stared after him. "How can anyone be so cruel?" she said dully, still unable to believe all that had happened.

PEGGY DARTY

"Elisabeth, he is an evil man. Sorry, but that's obvious to me. The sooner you're away from here, the better. Now let's pack your things."

She turned pain-filled eyes to him. "You're not evil. You're very good," she said, bewildered. "A stranger whom I've just met is kinder to me than a man I've called Father for all these years."

"There is a big difference, Elisabeth," he answered slowly. "I am a man of God."

240

Chapter Seven

*I*n a daze, Elisabeth opened her mother's trunk. More tears filled her eyes at the sight of the rumpled dresses, the sturdy work shoes, the heavy wool cloak.

Her hands scooped up the dresses, and she buried her face in the soft cloth, trying to find the lingering scent of her mother to forever etch in her memory. And it was there—the faint yeast-and-onion scent of Mary Greenwood.

Thank you, Ma, she thought. *Thanks for loving and caring for me. It couldn't have been easy. . .with him.* She quickly replaced the dresses, poking further into the trunk. Her fingers closed over a small object, loose among the dresses. She stared down at the cameo pin, lifting it gently to her lips. This was the treasure she sought, the one she would keep with pride.

She closed the lid and bundled up the last of her possessions in a clean flour sack from her mother's cupboard.

"I'm ready," she announced to Adam. Her face was pale, haunted, but her chin was set determinedly.

Elisabeth's eyes roamed over the cabin, silently bidding it good-bye. She hesitated in the door, remembering all the sessions with her tutor and the hopes and dreams of a bright future that she and her mother had shared. But the hand of fate had smashed those dreams, washed away everything that had been comfortable and secure. She was alone now, with only her own ingenuity to shape her future, and already she could sense how difficult that future was going to be.

Adam had brought the horses to the door. It would save her the embarrassment of having to walk across the courtyard beneath the rude, appraising stares of those who had once been her friends but now stood in judgment of her. She tied her knapsack on the saddle then climbed on her mare.

The afternoon stretched on as they rode in silence. Adam glanced worriedly at Elisabeth, who hadn't spoken a word since they left the post. Her eyes were distant and haunted, and yet her mouth was set in a determined line. He knew she was hurting, but he chose to remain silent. She would have to come to terms with her pain, and that was going to take time.

He turned the leather reins over in his gloved hands, absently studying them. He was beginning to feel responsible for her, but he was certain she would manage all right once they arrived in Denver. The Tillotsons were good people. They had retired from the mission field and seemed to be content living in town.

"Where do you live?" she asked, breaking into his thoughts.

"I have a cabin in a mountain valley above Denver," he said, looking across at her. "I have a large circuit to cover, and my cabin is situated about halfway between the areas I travel."

She frowned. "You said you were fascinated by your uncle's stories. When did you know you wanted to do this kind of work?"

Adam considered her question. "Funny, it was always something I knew I wanted to do. As soon as I got saved—"

"Saved? Saved from what?"

He smiled gently and began to tell her the story of the day

his uncle had come to visit and taken him to church.

"Between listening to my uncle, then the pastor, my heart was touched. I knew I wanted to belong to this Jesus I heard about, and I wanted to do something worthwhile with my life. My uncle was the best role model I had ever met." He grinned. "I even live in his cabin." A sad expression touched his dark eyes. "He died soon after I came out here. It seemed natural that I would try to take his place in the world."

"I'm sure you must do a very good job," she said, looking deep into his eyes. "I can see you are a man of God; you've proven that to me. And I'd like to hear more about your faith. I had a tutor once who read to me from the Bible. I liked the sound of the words, but—"

"But what, Elisabeth?"

She sighed, turning her eyes toward the mountain peaks, jagged against the afternoon sky. "I'm going to have to settle some things in my mind before I can take on this God of yours."

"You've got that backwards," Adam said. "First you accept God; then you'll find that things get settled in your conscience."

She shook her head, puzzled. "You're confusing me."

He reached over and touched her hand. "I'll pray for you."

Her head whipped around to look at him. He was going to pray for her—no one had ever made such an offer before.

She smiled warmly. "Thank you."

"Now, do you mind if we stop at the Castlemans' boardinghouse just up the road at Lone Peak? Mrs. Castleman is very nice; I think you'll like her. We can't make it all the way to Denver today. I stop over at Mrs. Castleman's to break up the journey. Is that okay with you?"

Elisabeth shrugged. "Whatever you think."

Her thoughts were not on the boardinghouse or the trip

to Denver; she was still thinking about this man who rode beside her and talked of being saved. The only kind of "saving" she understood at the moment was the way he had come into her life to save her from the horrible nightmare that faced her.

Elisabeth fell silent as the little community unfolded in a valley dominated by a jagged mountain peak. A row of rough pine buildings contained a mercantile, a saloon, a couple of eating establishments, and a stable and blacksmith shop. On the streets winding upward from Main Street she could see half a dozen log houses.

"We need to see to our horses first," Adam said, drawing rein at the log hitching rail before a large open-ended building that was a combination of blacksmith shop and stable.

A heavyset man was laying a hot iron to a horseshoe, but at the sight of Adam, he plunged the iron into a barrel of water and came striding forward.

"Afternoon, Jake," Adam called.

Elisabeth looked at the man who was well over six feet tall, with large, blunt features and shaggy gray hair. He shook hands with Adam then glanced at Elisabeth and nodded politely.

"Jake, we'd like to leave our horses to be rubbed down. We've traveled quite a few miles. Thought we'd stop over at Mrs. Castleman's." He grinned. "Does she still make those good buckwheat pancakes?"

"They're better than ever." The big man rubbed his sagging stomach then reached over to stroke the neck of Adam's horse.

As Adam helped her down, Elisabeth felt as stiff as the board sidewalk beyond the blacksmith shop. She was unaccustomed to riding a horse so many miles, and every muscle in her body ached. Still, she didn't mind. She had started a new life, and she was beginning to feel hopeful again, now that she had met Adam Pearson.

"No use trying to go farther on an empty stomach," Adam said as they turned to cross the street. "And I could use a strong cup of coffee. What about you?"

"I suppose," Elisabeth replied, thinking of her ma's coffee and the kitchen in which she had grown up.

Swallowing hard, she tried to keep sad thoughts pushed back as they approached a large log house with a restaurant on one end. Passing under a hand-lettered sign that read EATS, they entered the front door and were greeted by a cozy, cheerful room with red-checkered curtains at the window and half a dozen square tables and tall wooden chairs. Most of the people seated at the tables were men dressed in work clothes. Elisabeth dropped her eyes as Adam's hand touched her elbow protectively and guided her to a quiet table in the corner.

"Mrs. Castleman lost her husband to a mining accident two years ago. They had some money put back, which she used to fix up her place for a boardinghouse and an eating establishment."

A tiny brunette woman with a friendly smile approached their table and nodded in recognition as she looked at Adam.

"Well, hello! You've been a stranger to us lately."

"I haven't been in this area. Mrs. Castleman, this is Elisabeth Greenwood. I'm escorting her to Denver, but we need a couple of rooms tonight, if you have them."

The woman's little face registered her disappointment. "Sorry, Adam, but I only have one room, and it has to be shared with a Mrs. Martin from Denver."

Elisabeth's breath caught. *Now what?* she wondered.

"Then Elisabeth can take it, and I'll bunk over at the stable. It won't be the first time."

Elisabeth frowned across at him. "Are you sure? I hate to—"

"He won't mind, dear." The little woman laid a hand on Elisabeth's arm. "This is the most agreeable fellow I've ever met. Now, you two must be hungry. What can I get for you?"

"Do you have any of those good buckwheat pancakes made up?"

"So happens I do." She grinned, wreathing her small face in a pleasant glow. "Two orders?"

He looked at Elisabeth. "Sound okay to you?"

"Sounds fine." She had no appetite, but she knew she must force herself to eat something to make the long journey to the Tillotsons' house. Suddenly, she found herself thinking of her new life in Denver, and an unexpected feeling of excitement swept over her. Despite the tragedies she had faced, hope seemed to be building in her—perhaps it was having Adam's encouragement or maybe it was her own unstoppable optimism. Even in crises it seemed to surface as it did now.

"I'll get a job when we get to Denver," she said, thinking ahead.

Adam leaned back in the chair, appraising her thoughtfully. "What will you do?"

She hesitated. "I guess I'll find a job cooking. I know how to do that. Or maybe I could be a chambermaid at one of the hotels."

Adam nodded, studying his hands. Elisabeth sensed he was worried about something. "What's wrong?"

"Oh, nothing." A smile touched his lips, and Elisabeth found herself thinking of how handsome he was—so tall and masculine, yet he spoke in a gentle manner, and as far as she could tell, he seemed to possess a heart of gold.

"Well, actually, I suppose I should warn you, there are lots of women looking for work, and many of the jobs are taken."

Elisabeth frowned. "Where do the women come from?"

"Miners' wives whose husbands spend all their time up in the hills panning the streams or trapping in the woods. So many people flooded into the territory when gold was discovered at Cherry Creek. Frankly, I think that supply has been exhausted. Now they're having to range farther. Money is scarce, and most wives don't see their husbands for weeks, or sometimes months."

"That doesn't sound like a very good life for those women." But then she thought of her mother, and a pang of sadness touched her heart. "It's the way things are, I guess. All women have to work hard now," she said with a deep sigh.

The pancakes arrived—huge, round cakes drizzled with butter and honey—and Elisabeth's mouth watered. Maybe she was hungrier than she thought.

They fell silent as they began to eat; then Elisabeth asked the question that had been puzzling her for the past hour. "How long will you be in Denver?"

"Just long enough to get you settled, check in with my home church, rest a day or so, then head out again."

"Oh. And how long are you out on your circuit?"

"Well,"—he lifted his fork and speared into a huge pancake—"I'll be out a long time. I only come into Denver a few times a year to buy supplies and meet with my mission board. The rest of the time, I use my cabin as headquarters and branch out across the back side of the Rockies."

Elisabeth stared at him. "I guess it's a miracle we met."

A tiny smile lit his dark eyes. "Honestly, it is. I came to your post for the first time the other day when I had to make a trip down to Colorado City to meet with another missionary. I like to compare their method of witnessing and delivering Bibles to the way we do things up here. Also, they have news from other mission posts. I do stop in at Black Hawk's camp when I'm on that road. I'm hoping soon to deliver some Bibles to them and try to teach them something about the Word of God."

The pancake grew heavy in her mouth as Elisabeth stared at him, trying to imagine him out doing this kind of work. It was so different from anything she had ever heard about. "Do you plan to keep doing this. . .this mission work for the rest of your life?"

His eyes drifted slowly over her features, and she wondered what he was thinking. "Always," he said with conviction.

"Oh." She tried to suppress the sigh forming in her chest. He was such a kind, likable man. Why couldn't he be a merchant, or do some kind of work in Denver? That way maybe there would be a chance she could see him more often. But with his job, she knew she would rarely see him, and she found herself growing oddly sad.

"You'll like being with the Tillotsons," he said, shifting in his chair and looking around the room. "They're a very nice older couple. Since he retired, though, his health has not been good. I think the cold winters make him worse. They've talked of going south, but I don't think they plan to do that yet."

"Well," Elisabeth said hastily, "I don't want to be any trouble to them. As soon as I get a job, I can move into a boardinghouse like this one."

Adam nodded, yet there was a small frown gathering between his brows. Elisabeth wondered what he was thinking.

It was good she couldn't read his thoughts, for they were troubled. Jobs, like inexpensive rooms, were scarce in Denver. She was a beautiful woman who was going to attract a lot of men, and he greatly feared what could happen to such an innocent girl in this restless city.

He dropped his eyes to his pancakes and tried not to think about it now. His responsibility was to get her to the Tillotsons' then pray that she could make a new life in Denver.

A heavy feeling tugged at his heart. He was afraid he was going to have a hard time riding off, forgetting her. Already, there were strong feelings for this woman churning in his heart, although he didn't see how there could be a future for them. He couldn't expect a woman to share his rough life, and he could sense that Elisabeth didn't have the same faith in God that he did.

As he pushed his empty plate aside and sipped at his coffee, he knew tonight's prayers would last longer than usual.

Chapter Eight

Elisabeth's room was comfortable, even with only the bare necessities—two iron cots, two washstands, a couple of chairs, and a small rag rug that covered less than three square feet of the cold plank floor. She shared the room with an older woman who slept with her mouth open.

Elisabeth tossed and turned on her cot throughout the night, listening to Mrs. Martin's snore. It had been a relief when finally the morning sunlight slipped into the room and Mrs. Martin roused from her bed.

She was the matronly type, in her forties, whose gray eyes were filled with despair as she related her life's story to Elisabeth.

"We never should have left Texas! But Harold swore he'd strike it rich if we could just sell our little spread and join the wagon train heading to Pike's Peak." Tears welled in her eyes. "We've spent most of our money, and now Harold's living up in the mountains like an animal, waiting for the weather to break so he can strike it rich." She shook her head, her eyes betraying her bitterness. "We never should have left Texas!"

Elisabeth took a deep breath, trying to think how to console her. "Maybe your husband will find some gold this time."

The woman continued shaking her head miserably. "Either a fellow's lucky or he's not. My Harold's been unlucky all his life." The corners of her mouth sagged downward in a perpetual expression of defeat.

As Elisabeth looked at the woman, she felt a rush of pity for her. Were these the kind of people Adam was witnessing to up in the mountains and backcountry? If so, he was doing a wonderful work, for Elisabeth didn't think she'd ever seen anyone look so miserable. She'd tried to think what she could say to help. She thought about what the woman had said about her husband's bad "luck." It was a silly word. She wished she knew what kind of advice Adam would offer, so that she could speak the right words now to this woman who desperately needed hope and encouragement.

She remembered what Adam had said to her; the words had almost instantly made her feel better. She took a breath and looked at Mrs. Martin.

"I'll pray for you," Elisabeth said, although she wasn't certain what such a prayer would hold.

The woman looked startled; then she began to smile as she dabbed at her eyes with a worn handkerchief. "Thank you, dear. I know God can help; He is the *only* One who can help us now."

Elisabeth had changed into a long-sleeved, dark-print dress, hoping it would be fashionable enough for Denver. Winding her long hair into a braided chignon, she inserted the hairpins carefully, studying the dark eyes that peered at her through the looking glass.

For no reason she could think of, she was remembering the pain and agony she had seen in Morning Dove's dark eyes and the suffering she had endured.

Elisabeth closed her eyes, willing her mind to shut off the

memory. She had done what she could to help; now she must put the experience out of her thoughts. They had made a mistake, that was all. Even though her eyes and hair were dark, her skin was too light, her features too small. She was *not* the daughter of an Indian woman, she was certain of that.

Thinking she had put the matter to rest, she thrust her feet in her kid boots and went downstairs to meet Adam.

"Good morning," he called to her. He was waiting in the front hall, dressed in a clean flannel shirt and tan trousers. His thick, dark hair was neatly combed, and his brown eyes glowed as he watched her approach.

"Good morning." She smiled up at him.

Her eyes locked with his for a moment before he cleared his throat and looked around.

"Hungry?" he asked.

She shrugged. "No. Look, Adam, about this expense money—"

"I am allowed expense money in my missionary work. You can repay me once you get a job in Denver."

She frowned. "I don't know how long that will be." She had thought of something the night before, however, and she was quick to share the idea with Adam. "Once we get to Denver, will you help me sell my mare?"

Adam looked surprised. "Won't you need to keep her?"

She shook her head. "I can get another horse later on, and I need the money. Please, Adam, will you help me?"

He nodded thoughtfully. "If that's what you want to do. She's a stout little mare, and I'm certain we won't have any trouble finding a buyer. A good horse is always in demand."

Elisabeth breathed a sigh of relief, feeling a bit more

independent. Now she didn't feel so bad about taking money from him. *It's only a temporary loan until we reach Denver,* she told herself.

"Let's not worry anymore. Try to relax and let's get some breakfast."

Elisabeth nodded, realizing she was beginning to depend on Adam too much. And yet there was more than dependence involved. She had feelings for Adam; she had felt something the very first time she saw him at the post—she had to squelch those feelings.

Elisabeth forced herself to look toward Mrs. Castleman, who was entering the front door. She needed to thank her for her kindness and then say good-bye. She had a new life in Denver to think about.

As they rode toward Denver, Elisabeth enjoyed the view of sweeping mountains and open valleys. Occasionally, an antelope or deer bounded across the meadow or darted daringly in front of them. Her mind drifted back to the post and the years she had spent there. It seemed like another lifetime, and not a happy one.

They stopped for lunch at the home of a farmer whose wife served travelers as a means of helping with their income, or so Adam had told her. They dined on fried venison, creamed potatoes, and thick gravy in large bowls on one long table.

Two older men, traveling together, sat across from Elisabeth and Adam.

"What's going on in the outside world?" Adam asked conversationally.

"The war down south's heating up," one man complained.

A deep frown knitted Adam's dark brows. "Do you think

it will end anytime soon?"

"Don't know what will happen," the man answered. "But Governor Gilpin's letting too many deserters into our territory."

"What do you think of our governor?" Adam asked, looking from one man to the other.

"Gilpin's supposed to be an expert when it comes to civil government. He's already touring the mining camps, taking a census of the population of the Colorado Territory. There'll be an election to choose delegates to Congress and legislature."

"We're getting too civilized," the other man grumbled, taking a deep sip of coffee.

"There's been more trouble between the Utes and Arapahos," the more congenial man continued, undaunted by his friend's gruffness. "And the Cheyennes are giving newcomers out on the plains a hard time."

"I've yet to meet an Indian that wasn't a savage," the grumpy man put in.

"Oh, I don't agree," Adam drawled. "I travel around the territory, visiting some of the camps. They've always been good to me. But maybe that's because I'm part Indian myself."

A tense silence fell over the group. Elisabeth leaped to her feet.

"I'd like to go," she said quickly, glancing at the men who were watching Adam then her. Were they looking at her a bit differently, too? Did she look like a half-breed? *Was* she?

Her arm swept out, carelessly knocking her water glass to the floor. At the sound of broken glass, the farmer's wife scurried out of the kitchen with a broom and a dustpan.

"I'm so sorry," Elisabeth mumbled, feeling the blood rush to her cheeks. She glanced desperately at Adam.

"Could we pay for the glass?"

"Isn't necessary," the woman replied, busily sweeping up the shards of glass.

"I am sorry," Elisabeth said in a rush then hurried out the door.

Outside, she breathed deeply of the crisp, cold air, wondering what on earth had come over her. She was acting ridiculous, behaving as though she felt guilty about something.

She heard the door close as Adam rushed to her side. "Why are you acting this way?" For the first time Adam's tone held an edge of irritation.

"I can't help it. Their talk of savages!"

"Then, why not defend those *savages*, rather than run from the truth?"

She whirled around, glaring up at him. "And what do you consider the truth?"

He shrugged. "Does it matter? You're being unfair, not giving the Indians a fair chance to—"

"To what? Kidnap me again?" She turned and charged toward her horse. "Don't try defending them to me, Adam Pearson. Because of those savages, my mother is dead!"

Adam's expression changed from one of irritation to something more unreadable. He said nothing more as he strode to his horse and untied the reins, leaving her to do the same.

As she scrambled back into the saddle, she began to regret her harsh words with him. He was the kindest person she had ever met. But why did he have to be such a goody-goody, always defending the Indians?

But then, of course, he was half-Cherokee himself. And he was proud, not ashamed. Closing her eyes for a moment, she tried to think of a way to bridge the awkward gap. She had spoken too quickly, and she had probably offended him, as well. She cleared her throat, trying to soften her tone of voice. "I'm just anxious to get to Denver, aren't you?"

He hesitated for a moment. "Very anxious."

"At least you'll be rid of me," she said, testing his mood with a little smile.

He didn't smile back. He merely turned his horse up the road, and Elisabeth decided he wasn't the "goody-goody" she had thought him to be. He was a kind man, but it was obvious that he had a temper when someone offended him or the people he held dear.

Maybe that was not a bad thing. She sighed, realizing there was no one in her life left to defend. Her mother was dead. *Maybe both of your mothers are dead,* a thought whispered in the back of her brain.

As they rode in silence for the next half hour, she dared not look at him. She couldn't help how she had reacted. It had been a traumatic week for her. Still she had to get ahold of herself. The Utes had made a mistake, that was all; she was not one of them, she had no feelings of love for them.

She knew she should apologize for being so rude, but she couldn't seem to find the right words. She was glad he wasn't talking to her; she didn't want to talk to him, either.

She focused her eyes on the melting snowbanks that lined the sides of the road. She would be glad to get to Denver.

It was early afternoon when Elisabeth first saw the sprawling settlement of Denver, built out in the flats with the jagged, frost-glistened peaks of the Front Range as a backdrop. The mountains had given way to hills with table-flat summits and sandstone ridges as the country opened up, stretching out before them.

"That's Cherry Creek," Adam said, pointing to a narrow stream threading its way between two rows of cabins built of cottonwood logs and roofed with earth and grass. "It used to be the dividing line between Aurora and Denver. Folks fussed and occasionally fought each other for the miners' and settlers' trade. Finally they realized that the only way either could succeed was to join forces as one town: Denver City."

She took a deep breath, relieved that he seemed to have gotten over his irritation with her.

"You seem to know a lot about the area," she said, eager for a safe topic of conversation.

"My uncle lived in Denver when it was first being settled. He said it was like one giant ant heap. People were crowded into tents and crude shacks, even sleeping under wagons. Half of them were ready to turn around and head home. But they stayed and built this town, and now many are successful merchants. The only problem is"—he turned his reins over in his hands—"they seem to have forgotten the years when they had to do without; otherwise, I don't know how they could charge as much as fifteen dollars for a sack of flour. That's what I paid when I stocked up for my trip home."

Home. The word was like manna to her ears, and suddenly, more than anything, she wanted a home of her own.

"Tell me about where you live." She looked across at him.

He turned his face toward the mountains, and she could see that the subject pleased him. A smile tilted his lips, stretching to the crease in his cheeks.

"My cabin is on a stream on the back side of a mountain. Only a few cabins are scattered about in the small area called Aspen Valley."

"That's a pretty name," Elisabeth said, studying the log buildings they passed. "I suppose the aspens are pretty there in the fall."

"A beauty that takes your breath away," he said. "Well, here we are."

She was sorry they had stopped talking about his cabin. It sounded so peaceful and homey. But it was time to think about the Tillotsons and her new life here in Denver. She studied the brightly lettered signs over the doors of shops and on the sides of buildings. There was a gun shop, a carpenter shop, a hardware store that boasted stoves made of sheet iron, a meat market, bakery, saloon and gambling hall, and a barber shop. Graham's Drugstore offered watches and jewelry made to order from native gold.

"This is quite a town," she said, looking around and feeling a bit lost and out of place.

"It's fine if you like towns, I guess. We'll take this next street to the right. The Tillotsons live down at the end."

Elisabeth nodded, trying to force her mind toward what she would say to them. She hated to tell them why she was here; perhaps it wouldn't be necessary to tell them everything. She could say that her mother had died, but before her death, she had sent her to look up the Tillotsons.

It had been a long time since she'd seen the older couple. Perhaps they wouldn't even want her to stay with them. She glanced across at Adam's strong yet gentle features. She would never forget Adam; she had never met anyone quite like him. And rather than think of the Tillotsons, she found herself thinking of Adam. Again.

Chapter Nine

The Tillotsons lived in a small frame house located in a nice neighborhood and within walking distance of the shops. Elisabeth decided it would be a perfect place for her as they turned their horses in at the hitching rail near the front gate. The small patch of yard was covered with snow, but the little porch had been swept clean. White lace curtains fluttered at the windows, offering a cozy invitation. It had the look of home to Elisabeth, and she was desperate for one.

Almost as soon as Adam knocked, the door swung open, and Mrs. Tillotson, a tiny, birdlike woman, surveyed them beneath thick white hair and wire spectacles.

"Hello, Mrs. Tillotson." Adam extended his hand.

"Adam! How good to see you. And I know we have met,"—she looked at Elisabeth—"but I'm having trouble remembering exactly when."

"I'm Jed. . .and Mary Greenwood's daughter." She stumbled over those words then hurried on. "When you were at the trading post—"

"Of course! I would have recognized you instantly if I had seen you in that area. Just wasn't expecting you in Denver. It's good to see you, my dear."

"It's nice to see you," Elisabeth said, shaking her hand.

"Please! Come inside and let me make a pot of tea. You two must be half-frozen. It's such a cold day."

The little woman bustled ahead of them, down a narrow hallway, motioning them to a room off to the right. "Go into the parlor and warm yourselves. I have a fire going. I'll get that tea."

As they entered the small room and looked around, Elisabeth saw that it was filled with touches of home and family. Framed photographs of a man and woman dominated tables covered with crocheted doilies, needlepoint pillows graced the sofa, and sturdy rocking chairs were drawn near a cozy fire in a small hearth.

Adam looked around. "Mr. Tillotson must be out. Let's have a seat." He motioned her to the nearest chair.

As Elisabeth took a seat, enjoying the cheery fire, Mrs. Tillotson bustled back, carrying a tray with a china teapot and cups. "Luckily, I already had the kettle going so there's no wait," she called over her shoulder.

"We'll be glad to get some tea," Adam replied. "How is Mr. Tillotson?"

Turning to face them, the older woman's smile gave way to a terrible sadness as she put the tray on a table and sighed. "You don't know, of course. He passed away a couple of weeks ago."

Adam went to her side, hugging her gently. "No, I didn't know. I'm sorry to hear that. He was a wonderful man."

"Yes, he was," she sniffed, reaching into her apron pocket for a lace handkerchief. "We never had children and I am so lonely. But he died suddenly. I'm thankful for that." She dabbed her eyes and looked across at Elisabeth. "Young lady, what brings you to Denver?"

Elisabeth hesitated, looking at Adam.

"Could we get some hot tea first, Mrs. Tillotson?" Adam intervened.

"Oh, of course." She turned to fill the cups.

As she poured tea, Elisabeth tried to explain that her mother had passed away, and that before she died she told Elisabeth to come to Denver. "I plan to get a job here and—"

"Then, you must stay with me! I have a spare bedroom, and I need the company. I miss my husband awfully. You must miss your mother, too. She was a good woman."

Elisabeth nodded, sipping her tea to ward off the tightness that clutched at her throat. She was aware of both Adam and Mrs. Tillotson watching her thoughtfully, and she couldn't bear the thought of breaking into tears in front of them. Clearing her throat, she tried to think of the practical matters involved in living with Mrs. Tillotson.

"Mrs. Tillotson," she said, "I expect to pay for my room and board."

"We'll see about that."

"Please. It's the only way I'll feel comfortable about staying."

The little lady lifted her shoulders in a light shrug. "Well, since you put it that way. . . But only after you're settled into a job." She looked at Adam. "How is the mission field?"

He sighed. "Busier than ever. There are so many to reach, so much territory to cover—"

"You can't do it all. It's an impossible task. Which is why our missionary society has launched a campaign to get some outposts established. Aspen Valley is on our list."

"Is that right?" Adam smiled politely.

"Yes. It's only your youth and enthusiasm that allows you to cover so much territory, and we know there are many trappers and traders back there who need a church. And the

Indians desperately need to hear the Word of God."

Adam looked across at Elisabeth, who dropped her eyes.

"Are you two hungry?" Mrs. Tillotson asked suddenly.

"Oh no," Elisabeth replied, glancing at Adam.

"Actually, we have business to take care of. We're going to the livery to sell Elisabeth's mare. Then I have to be on my way home."

Elisabeth felt her heart sink upon hearing those words. She hated the thought of Adam leaving, but she knew there was nothing she could do about it. She felt guilty for taking up so much of his time, when Mrs. Tillotson had just pointed out how busy he was.

"You'll stay for supper, won't you? I won't hear of you riding back into the wilds on an empty stomach."

"Since you put it that way,"—Adam grinned—"I will be pleased to stay for one of your good meals. Then I'll be on my way."

The day passed all too quickly, for the knowledge that Adam was leaving lay heavy on Elisabeth's mind. He had obtained a good price for her mare and instructed her how to best stretch her money until she found work. Then they sat down to a tasty meal with Mrs. Tillotson. It was obvious that the tiny widow had missed having conversations with someone, for she began to talk as soon as she served them.

"I wish that crazy war down south hadn't started," Mrs. Tillotson complained. "Are you worried about your family down there, Adam?"

Adam sighed and nodded slowly, staring at his cup. "My father is still in east Tennessee."

Elisabeth stared at Adam, sensing his concern.

"Bless you." Mrs. Tillotson leaned forward, laying a small hand on his arm. "When did you last hear from your family?"

"I haven't heard from my father in years. I write him but he rarely answers." He took a deep breath and turned sad eyes to Mrs. Tillotson. "He wanted me to say in the South, but my calling was in the West."

Mrs. Tillotson was wiggling in her seat, her concern obvious. "Do you think he might get involved in this awful mess?"

"His health is poor and we have no family. I doubt that he will leave his farm if it's possible for him to stay there."

Mrs. Tillotson nodded and sighed. Then something else seemed to occur to her. "Don't you think men are warriors at heart, Adam?"

Elisabeth watched Adam grin at her and speak pleasantly, even though some men would take offense at such a question.

"Now, why do you say that, Mrs. Tillotson?"

"I'm not talking about you, of course, or my husband, God rest his soul. It just seems that so many men have to have a gun or tomahawk in their hands and drive their horses into battle. I think it goes back to something primal in our bloodline when warriors sat before the fire each evening discussing their victories and their losses."

Elisabeth's glance slid from Adam to Mrs. Tillotson then back to the vegetables on her plate. Each time the word *tomahawk* was mentioned, she found herself shifting or twisting or feeling uncomfortable. She had to stop acting this way. Adam was half-Cherokee and he didn't seem to take offense.

Adam spoke up. "About the war. . . I never agreed with slavery. I'm afraid the South is in for some hard times because a lot of people are resisting change. But it's too bad that there has to be a war to settle the differences between North and South."

"It's just terrible." Mrs. Tillotson shook her head.

"Well," Adam said, rising from the table, "I really must get started. I have a long ride ahead. Mrs. Tillotson, I'm grateful for your wonderful meal."

"You're more than welcome, Adam," she said as her eyes moved to Elisabeth. "And I'm grateful for my new companion."

"I'll say good evening, then."

"I'll walk with you." Elisabeth stood quickly, hating the thought of saying good-bye.

"I appreciate all you've done," she said as they walked out the front door. "You rescued me at the Ute camp, you took me to the post, and now you've brought me here. And thanks for selling my mare." As she looked up at him, she felt a ridiculous urge to burst into tears.

"I've enjoyed being with you, Elisabeth. And I'll be praying for you."

"I'll need your prayers,"—she forced a smile—"but I'll be fine here." She looked up at the sky where only the pale sickle moon rested against the clouds. "It's an awful dark night for you to be riding back."

"I'll be fine."

"Again, Adam, I don't know how to thank you," Elisabeth said, as they reached the hitching rail and he began to untie his horse.

"No thanks are necessary. On second thought. . ." He turned back to her. "There is something you can do for me."

Elisabeth was puzzled. He had never asked anything from her.

"What is it?"

"I want you to try and resolve who you are. It doesn't really matter who your earthly parents are. We all have the same Father, the same loving God. There's a verse in the

Bible that I sometimes give to the people who call on me for advice when they are having financial or family problems. I give them Matthew 6:33: 'Seek ye first the kingdom of God, and his righteousness; and all these things shall be added unto you.'"

She nodded thoughtfully. "So you're saying when I accept God I will have my heritage?"

"That's what I'm trying to say."

He couldn't really understand what she was going through. No one could. But she knew he meant well.

"You are a very special, lady, Elisabeth." Their eyes locked, and he seemed to read the conflict that raged within her. He turned to leave, saying no more.

Her hand shot to his arm, touching his sleeve lightly. "Have a safe trip back."

He nodded, gripping her hand. Then, as if on impulse, he lowered his head and kissed her gently.

Elisabeth's senses reeled. This was her first kiss, and she had never felt anything like the tenderness and gentleness that was Adam. When he drew back from her and their dark eyes met in the sparse moonlight, she felt her heart beating faster.

"I must go," Adam said, pulling up into the saddle.

Nodding, she waved to him and watched him ride off into the night. Then, as he disappeared, a terrible loneliness swept over her. It was only then that she began to realize she had fallen in love with Adam.

Chapter Ten

As Elisabeth sat at the kitchen table having coffee with Mrs. Tillotson, she related her frustration over not having found a job.

"Well," Mrs. Tillotson said, "I don't know if this would interest you, but there's a new photographer in town. He's set up shop in that little building next to the newspaper office. He has no help. Why don't you talk to him?"

"That's a good idea. Thanks for mentioning it, Mrs. Tillotson."

Photographer. How interesting. She couldn't wait to go and speak with him about a job. So far there was nothing available in the hotels or restaurants where she had tried. Adam had been right; many women had gotten in line ahead of her to get a job, and most jobs available were already taken. She had been looking for over a week now, but she tried to hide her discouragement from Mrs. Tillotson, who had been so encouraging.

"I'll go today," Elisabeth said, finishing her tea.

Elisabeth located the Gallery, as the sign read, and quickly decided to work for whatever he could pay her if he would just hire her. She needed the money; furthermore, she needed something to occupy her mind. Added to her sadness over her mother's death was the sharp ache of missing Adam, much more than she had dreamed possible.

She stood for a moment before the false-front shop, taking a deep breath. She'd never had any experience at this sort of work, and for a moment she felt rather foolish. Just then a funny little man opened the door. He was small, with brown eyes and hair, and a long nose above a handlebar mustache.

"Come in," he said, looking eager for business.

Elisabeth acknowledged his invitation and entered, glancing about at the cozy front room. An exhibit of photographs covered the wall. Elisabeth thought they were very pretty as she looked at views of mountains, miners at work, and for contrast, a busy eastern city.

"You do nice work," she said, glancing at him.

"Thank you! Allow me to introduce myself. I'm Seth Wilkerson from New York."

Elisabeth's eyes took in his slim, small frame—he was no more than an inch or two taller than she, which seemed quite short in comparison to Adam. Probably in his thirties, Seth was dressed in a dark suit, obviously tailor-made, because it fit him to perfection.

"How do you do. I'm Elisabeth Greenwood." She extended a gloved hand.

"You'll make a lovely photograph! I'd be most eager—"

"Excuse me, but I stopped in to see if you need someone to work for you." At his shocked expression, she glanced around the room, trying to think how to win him over. "Where do you make the pictures?" she asked.

"In here," he said, opening a door. "There's a tiny dressing room back there, the room just off the parlor, and this is my laboratory."

Through the open door, Elisabeth could see a darkroom

covered with orange cloth.

"I use orange light because it doesn't harm my glass plates," he explained.

"I see." Elisabeth nodded. "You have some expensive-looking equipment here. It seems to me you need someone to watch your gallery if you have to be away."

"Well. . .yes I do. I've been wanting to make another trip to the mining camps to get pictures of the miners. They love to send photographs home to show their families, displaying their working situations."

"Then I could take care of your gallery while you're away. I could keep the place clean, make tea for your customers."

"Yes. . .I suppose I do need a helper. . .but the wages would be very small in the beginning."

"It doesn't matter." She smiled. "I want a job. Do you know Mrs. Marjorie Tillotson? I live with her."

"Mrs. Tillotson?" His eyebrow hiked and his smile widened. "She's a lovely lady. We attend the same church." He withdrew a gold watch from his vest pocket, glanced at the time, and then returned it to his pocket. "Miss Greenwood, I'm due at the bank for a meeting. You can start to work right now. If anyone comes for a photograph, don't let them leave until I return!"

Elisabeth's mouth fell open as he grabbed his hat and sailed out the door. Then, smiling after him, she removed her cloak and gloves and looked around. There was a thin layer of dust on the board floor so she went in search of a broom.

That evening as she sat with Mrs. Tillotson, she let the older woman serve her tea and chat about a benefit cake sale the Ladies' Missionary Society was planning, but Elisabeth scarcely heard a word. She was thinking about Adam and feeling amazed that she missed him so much.

A knock on the door interrupted Mrs. Tillotson's constant flow of words, and she cocked her little head to one side, obviously startled.

"Now, who on earth would be calling at this hour?" She looked at Elisabeth, who found herself hoping that Adam had returned.

Mrs. Tillotson peered through the curtains and then gave a little cry of delight. "It's Star of the Morning!"

"Star of the Morning?" Elisabeth repeated, puzzled, as Mrs. Tillotson rushed for the door and quickly turned the key in the lock. "Star of the Morning, what a pleasant surprise! Do come in." Mrs. Tillotson opened the door.

Elisabeth watched a beautiful young woman, dressed in a white doeskin dress and matching moccasins, enter the room. Her hair was jet black, as were her eyes, and her skin a smooth olive. She had small, pretty features, and her clothes were immaculate. Elisabeth's breath caught. She was the prettiest Indian woman she had ever seen.

"Hello." She smiled at Mrs. Tillotson then looked toward Elisabeth, a question in her eyes.

"Dear, this is Elisabeth Greenwood," Mrs. Tillotson said, laying a hand on Star of the Morning's fringed sleeve.

"Hello." Elisabeth smiled back at her, her mind filled with questions.

"Hello, Elisabeth." The young Indian woman looked about Elisabeth's age and spoke English perfectly.

"Elisabeth, Star of the Morning was our best pupil at the mission school."

Elisabeth smiled. "Congratulations."

"Elisabeth is from down in the Pike's Peak region," Mrs. Tillotson continued. "Her folks have a trading post there. I'm sure her father traded with your people."

Elisabeth almost choked at those words, knowing how, given the chance, Jed Greenwood had swindled everyone who came through his door.

"I want to go to that area." Star of the Morning smiled. "I am hoping to be sent there to help my people."

"Star of the Morning is Ute and has a calling to return to teach. She had now completed her education." Mrs. Tillotson gave her a hug. "We're so proud of her."

"It has taken your prayers and your help." Star of the Morning returned Mrs. Tillotson's embrace.

Elisabeth was at a loss for words. This young woman was so pretty, so vibrant, and certainly seemed to be led by God. Elisabeth fell silent, not knowing what more she should say. Her mind whirled back to the time she had spent in Black Hawk's camp and the kind people she had met there. In retrospect, she knew she had never given them a chance, for she had made up her mind that these were not her people, and all she could think about at the time was leaving.

Mrs. Tillotson was busily seeing to her guest. "Here, dear, take a seat. Have you eaten?"

"Yes, thank you." Star of the Morning settled gracefully onto the sofa, tucking her moccasined feet together at the ankles.

"Then I'll make tea. I'm sure you could drink a cup of tea."

"That would be nice." She smiled gratefully at Mrs. Tillotson.

As the older woman hurried off for tea, Elisabeth couldn't help staring at the pretty girl opposite her.

"What brings you to Denver?" Star of the Morning asked pleasantly. Her dark eyes glowed in her smooth face as she looked across at Elisabeth.

"Well. . . ," she began then hesitated. Why try to pretend?

Something about this woman evoked honesty, and she felt much the same way she had when she first met Adam in that she could tell her the truth.

"If I am being too personal, you do not have to answer." Star of the Morning seemed to sense a problem.

"No, I was just thinking how to phrase this." Elisabeth glanced over her shoulder toward the kitchen." It's a long story. There was a. . .misunderstanding with my adoptive father after my mother died. My mother was a good woman, and she wanted me to come to Denver if anything happened." Her voice trailed as she felt grief welling up in her throat.

Star of the Morning began to nod. "I see. Then you could not choose a better home or a better person than Mrs. Tillotson. When I first came here to the mission school, she was my sponsor. I was a skinny, frightened little thing,"—she laughed softly—"and Mrs. Tillotson and the other ladies at the mission school were so good to me. They changed my life." She hesitated, studying her slim graceful fingers. "My parents were killed in a battle out on the plains. That was my home. I had nowhere to go, and my people were starving. The Tillotsons were missionaries at the time; they came to our village and brought some of the children back here to the mission school. They saved our lives, and I will always be grateful."

As her soft voice trailed into silence, Elisabeth nodded, seeing how her life had been shaped for her missionary work. "You seem to have made the most of a difficult situation. I respect that."

"Here we are, girls." Mrs. Tillotson hurried back, bearing her tray of teacups and teapot, steaming with the aroma of fresh herbed tea. "This will warm us up a bit on a cold winter night."

As she poured tea, Mrs. Tillotson began to pelt Star of the

Morning with questions concerning the mission school. The young woman answered each question, patiently and competently, as they sipped their tea. Elisabeth felt herself relaxing, enjoying the evening, and she realized this was largely due to Star of the Morning's radiant presence.

At they finished their tea, Star of the Morning put down her cup and stood. "I must go now. I only came to say hello. I have to get back to the school. I am preparing to leave at the end of the week."

"Must you go?" Mrs. Tillotson looked distressed. "Where are they sending you?"

"That I do not know,"—she smiled—"but it doesn't matter. God is with me; I will go where I am needed."

Mrs. Tillotson hugged her affectionately. "Bless you, my child. You are such a credit to your nation."

At these words, Elisabeth felt as though her heart were shrinking. She was torn with embarrassment because she had not worked toward being a credit to anyone—white or Indian. Seeing the way Star of the Morning had turned her adversity around to make her life count for a good cause, Elisabeth felt a wave of shame sweeping over her. When she thought she was linked to the Ute tribe, she had been appalled and embarrassed, and now she was sorry for the way she had felt. She wanted to change those feelings, and yet she couldn't seem to do that on her own.

"It was nice meeting you, Elisabeth," Star of the Morning was saying. "Maybe I will see you again."

"I hope so." Elisabeth smiled at her. And she did hope that their paths would cross again. She was more impressed with Star of the Morning than anyone she had met.

Except for Adam.

Chapter Eleven

The next day Elisabeth had a few minutes of spare time before going to work, and she sauntered into the mercantile store. Women shopping there were dressed in fine woolens and dainty bonnets. Patent leather gaiters peeped from beneath their crinolines. She tried not to stare, but she couldn't help wishing she did not feel so out of place in her old-fashioned cotton dress.

As she looked around, her eyes nearly popped at the endless array of items labeled PIKE'S PEAK. There were Pike's Peak guns, shovels, and picks, Pike's Peak boots and hats. An outfit displayed with a small sign proclaiming it to be the "New American Costume" was made of dark calico with a knee-length skirt from which peeped a pair of matching pantalets.

Amused by it, Elisabeth stared for a moment then wandered toward a long woolen dress, blue as a Colorado sky. She trailed her fingers over the soft nubby cloth, wishing she could afford such a dress. Now that she had a job, she could use some of the money from the sale of her mare. Did she dare? Her mind automatically raced to Adam. She would like to wear a dress like that when he returned. She wanted to style her hair, fix herself up pretty for him.

She tried to dredge up her logic, be rational, but she kept

thinking about Adam, and impulsively, she walked over to the counter. "I'd like to try that one on, please." She pointed toward the blue dress.

"Certainly." The older woman smiled. "There's a dressing room right back there."

Elisabeth dashed behind a curtain and changed into the soft blue dress. The tucked bodice molded to her tiny waist then swirled in a perfect circle around her feet. She stared into the looking glass. The soft blue accented the darkness of her eyes and hair. As she stared at herself, an odd thought struck her: she did not look so different from Star of the Morning. Her hair had the same dark radiance, her eyes. . .

She dropped her head. It was true, she knew it was. She really did possess Ute blood. Drained of her enthusiasm, she removed the dress and changed back into her faded clothes. Gingerly, she carried it back outside to hang it up again. "That color must be stunning on you." The helpful saleslady rushed up, obviously hoping for a sale.

"It's a very pretty dress," Elisabeth sighed. "I need to think about it."

"Don't think long," she replied, taking the dress from Elisabeth to rehang. "We just got it in, and I daresay it won't stay here long."

Elisabeth nodded. "Thank you." She walked out the door and headed to work, her thoughts whirling. What if it was true? What if she was Ute? Was that so bad, after all?

Confusion filled her mind like a winter fog. She had to think about her job, she had to get her mind on what she was doing.

Her steps quickened as she hurried to work, glancing around her at the people crowding the sidewalks. Some of the men were dressed in red shirts and buckskins, others in dark business suits. It was exciting to live in a busy town, in one sense, but she missed the wide-open views and fresh air of her home. She thought of Star of the Morning and then, of course, Adam.

She wondered about the place he lived. She must remember to ask Mrs. Tillotson more about him.

As she turned into the shop, she saw that her new employer was busily packing up his supplies.

"Since you can stay here today, I'm going into the mountains," he announced, carefully loading a camera into its case.

I'll take good care of things," she offered, removing her cloak and smoothing her cotton dress. Automatically, she headed for the broom closet to tidy up the shop.

That evening, she sat before the fire with Mrs. Tillotson, listening to more news of the benefit cake sale that the Ladies' Missionary Society was planning.

When the little woman had finally run down, Elisabeth ventured a few questions about Adam.

"He is a wonderful young man, don't you think?" Mrs. Tillotson asked, cocking her little white head to one side and studying Elisabeth thoughtfully.

"He is nice, and he seems dedicated to his mission work here."

"Yes, he is." She looked into space, remembering. "His mother was a Cherokee in Tennessee. He had a calling to help all Indians."

Elisabeth dropped her eyes. She had not told Mrs. Tillotson the full story of her life. She was waiting for the right moment or for a time when she had settled the issue in her heart.

PEGGY DARTY

"Adam has done so many kind things for his people."

"Tell me about the area where he lives." Elisabeth slipped to the edge of her seat, anxious to hear about him.

Studying her, Mrs. Tillotson smiled and began to explain what she knew. "Adam lives up in a lovely valley on the back side of the mountains. There are only a few rough pine buildings there, however—a small general store, a stable and blacksmith shop, a building that serves as a community hall for circuit doctors and ministers and anyone doing something for the community. The community hall needs work, and that's one of our projects with the Missionary Society. We want to equip it with facilities for starting a school and church. I think Adam will be an important part of our dream."

Elisabeth nodded, considering her words. Everyone seemed to have a "part" in something. Star of the Morning had her mission in life; Adam had his. She had nothing—no identity, no family, nothing but a blank future staring her in the face.

"What's wrong, dear? You look troubled."

Elisabeth put her teacup on the table and stood. "Actually, I'm pretty tired. It's been an adjustment learning my new job. I think I'll say good night now."

Mrs. Tillotson nodded. "Of course. Get a good night's rest. And, Elisabeth, I'd like you to accompany me to church on Sunday."

Elisabeth hesitated then nodded slowly. She had a real hunger to know more about the God who seemed to fill them with such goodness. She wished she were more like them.

"I'd like that," she replied. "Good night."

As soon as Elisabeth reached the quiet of her little room, the tears she had fought to keep back flooded forth, pouring down her cheeks. She sank onto the bed, burying her face in her hands. Her life seemed so empty and bleak, and she had never felt so lonely. Was God working in her life? Was He preparing her for some mission? Or would she have to live with this awful emptiness from now on?

Chapter Twelve

Adam

The muscles of the big black horse rippled beneath his satin-like coat as he pulled up the steep hill. Adam sat on his horse, gazing out across the snowy hillside, searching for animal tracks. He had seen some deer tracks, at least two days old, but yesterday's winds had practically obliterated them. His eyes traveled upward to the bald eagle soaring above a craggy peak. To Adam the eagle symbolized the wild, free beauty of Colorado.

He drew rein and sat back in the saddle. From his vantage point, he could see east to the dome of the mountain peaks, blanketed with fresh snow. His brown eyes returned to the valley below, to his rough, slab-pine cabin; food was scarce, so he had taken up hunting. Some folks thought it was wrong to kill animals, but his father had told him early in life the Bible taught that man was to have dominion over the animals.

"But dominion is different from waste," his father reminded him. "We never kill an animal just for the sport of it. We only take an animal's life when we need food." As he thought of his father, a deep sadness welled in his heart. He needed to make peace with him, particularly now with the conflict raging between the North and South.

The wind stirred through the pines, and Adam looked

around, thinking maybe the deer would be bedding down. He had always felt a kinship with the animals, with all of nature. He believed this was due to his Cherokee background.

Suddenly Elisabeth Greenwood came into his thoughts. His prayer for her was that she would come to terms with her background, as he had. In his mind, the Ute heritage was a heritage to be proud of.

He dropped down from his horse, looped the reins around a pine trunk, and sat down on a dead log. A bitter wind howled down the mountain, ruffling his dark hair, but he didn't notice the weather now. He was consumed with thoughts of Elisabeth, and he didn't know how to deal with his feelings. It had been a week since his departure, and she had scarcely left his mind. He knew there could be no future for them until she found peace in her soul, and that meant turning to God for help. She would have to do this on her own; he had said all he was comfortable to say to her while she was still unsaved.

He hoped by now she had found a job. His funds were running low, as well. He would have to start panning the streams as soon as the snow started to melt. He had one nugget left, and that wouldn't take him far.

As he scanned the woods, he began to realize that tonight's meal would consist of more canned beans if he didn't ride the extra miles into the tiny trading post at Aspen Valley. He hadn't planned to go until tomorrow when he had been invited to the community hall to discuss the letter sent by the Denver Missionary Society. It was a dream come true that at last the group was raising money on behalf of Aspen Valley. So much was needed here. He would simply have to make two trips—one tonight and one tomorrow. He was hungry.

He pulled his six-foot frame upright again, shivering against the cold settling into his bones. The animals had dominion over *him* today. He would go to the post to spend his last nugget.

Chapter Thirteen

The letter had been waiting for him at the post, and as he read it, it filled him with a combination of fear and dread.

Dear Adam,

I hope this letter reaches you soon. The North and South are at war. I need you here to help me hold on to the land. Please come home.

Your Father.

Adam had spent a sleepless night, and by morning, he had decided to take a leave from his mission work to go south. He couldn't ignore his father's plea for help. He felt certain the mission board in Denver would understand.

As soon as his decision was made, he began to pack. He found his heart growing heavy, however, as he stood in the small cabin, looking around, thinking about leaving.

Sunshine spilled over the plain furnishing—the iron bed holding his bedroll, the wooden nightstand where a kerosene lamp sat beside his Bible. Pegs on the wall held his clothes. His eyes moved to the opposite end of the cabin, to the dining table and chairs with the three shelves on the wall containing his tin plate and cup and a few eating utensils, the woodstove that kept him warm and cooked his food.

Beside the small horsehair sofa sat another wooden table with a kerosene lamp and more books. It was a simple cabin, crude by city standards, and yet it had been home to him for two years. He hated to leave it.

He felt he had accomplished a lot, but here was so much more to be done. How long would his work be delayed?

The smell of mountain air and fresh pine filled his senses, and there was a bittersweet ache in his heart, knowing he might be leaving for good.

But there was no delaying what he must do.

Chapter Fourteen

The trip into Denver seemed unusually long and tiring the next afternoon. He was weighted with the burden of resigning his ministry for a while, but he felt sure they would understand. And then he planned to drop by Mrs. Tillotson's to say good-bye to Elisabeth. It would not be easy, for he had thought of her often. She might be gone by the time he returned, or, considering how pretty she was and the inevitable suitors who would come calling, she could be married. That thought added to the heaviness growing in his heart.

As they sat in Mrs. Tillotson's parlor, Elisabeth was strangely quiet.

"You really feel that you must go?" Elisabeth asked.

"I do. It's a matter of duty."

"But Tennessee is so far way." She looked across at him, her dark eyes troubled.

"Yes. I'm taking the night stage out. I've made arrangements with a friend here to keep my horse for a while. I'll write him about my future plans."

"Adam, will you write to me?" she asked, turning to jot down her address on a piece of paper.

"Yes, I'll write. It will help to make the time pass more quickly. And I would like for you to stay in touch," he added softly.

"I'll write you back," she said, handing him her address.

He nodded, glancing at her handwriting before folding the paper in half and inserting it into his pocket.

He looked down into her round dark eyes, wondering what she was thinking. Did she care for him? He wanted to believe she did. But he could not ask her to wait for him; that would be unfair. He forced himself to look away, to try to think about his departure and the task ahead of him once he reached home.

"I pray that you will be well," he said, glancing down at her again, for he could not keep his eyes from her face.

Her soft lips parted and their eyes locked. He took a deep breath and told himself there would be no good-bye kiss. It was difficult enough to say good-bye to her; he couldn't bear the thought of her kiss lingering in his memory, torturing him as their previous kiss had already.

"I will be fine," she said, lifting her chin proudly.

He nodded. "I'm sure you will. Well, good-bye."

He reached out, taking her slim fingers in his own for a moment and squeezing her hand gently. Again, he resisted the impulse to lean forward, touch his lips lightly to hers. No, it would only make matters worse.

Quickly, he released her hand, turned, and walked through the door, out into the cold winter night.

The stage seemed to jostle on forever, and to break up the monotony of the trip, Adam decided to write to Elisabeth, as he had promised. He had purchased a tablet and pen at a stage stop the day before.

"Dear Elisabeth," his letter began. *"The trip has been long and hard, but uneventful, thank God. There have been no raids on the stage by the Cheyennes or by army deserters who seem to be everywhere. Two other men rode with me, each returning to their home state because of the war. One was a Southerner from Mississippi, the other a Northerner from Pennsylvania. Strangely, we did not argue over the issues that started this war. There was a common bond among all of us to reach St. Louis safely."*

He paused, staring out at the streets of St. Louis as they approached the next stage stop. There were Union soldiers everywhere, and he had already been told that Nathaniel Lyon had captured the rebels in the city, taking them prisoner and parading them through the streets of St. Louis. A small group of Confederate sympathizers had rallied back in anger, starting a riot that resulted in more people being killed and wounded.

He returned to the letter, thinking ahead. *"I am purchasing a horse and intend to start south today. Don't worry about me. I will remain safe, for I have no intention of letting anything stop my return to my father."*

Chapter Fifteen

Adam tried to push Elisabeth from his thoughts as he rode doggedly through the stormy spring night. He had never imagined he could miss someone so much, and yet her face was a sweet vision as he looked daily on the gaunt faces and disease-ridden bodies of the victims of war in Missouri and Kentucky.

He blinked his sleepy eyes and squinted into the dark night. There was only a pale quarter moon for light, and now that moon was obscured by wind-driven clouds. He blinked again and something scratched against his eyeball, a particle of dust from the back roads, which were a dense tangle of briars and vines.

His right cheek bore the slash of a sharp branch; his clothes were clotted with debris and broken vines. Still, he preferred this to the gunfire of Yankee troops, or the Confederate army. Every day men out of uniform were being shot from their saddles as deserters. Neither army could bear the sight of a deserter, or even a strong, able-bodied man not fighting or impassioned with this war fever that bordered on insanity, it seemed to Adam.

He sighed. Judging from his last stop, he had one more hard day of riding before he would make it to his father's small farm in Tennessee.

As he shifted wearily in the saddle, his worn pants and shirt, washed out in creek water, scratched stiffly against his sore body. He now looked like a deserter, too. His beard, like the other men's, was thick and unkempt. His dark hair grew long on his neck beneath his battered felt hat.

Hearing a rustle in the dense woods behind him, he turned in the saddle. He saw the crack of fire a second before a sharp pain tore through his side. Toppling from his saddle, he lay facedown on the hard, rough ground. Still and silent in total darkness, his assailant watched him.

He held his breath and lay motionless. The mold of decayed leaves and rain-soaked earth reeked in his nostrils, along with the sweat of his horse, nervously stamping the ground just behind him. At last he heard the cautious approach of another horse. Underneath him, his hand closed around a two-foot oak branch. His chest was nearly bursting from his indrawn breath.

The steps ceased. He heard the creak of the saddle as someone climbed down. Just as the boot of the assailant reached his side, he whirled over and swung the oak branch, knocking the soldier to the ground. Adam straddled the soldier, landing a hard right against his chin until the man slumped beneath him and lay still.

Peering through the semidarkness, Adam could see the rebel uniform and the gaunt face of a boy, no more than sixteen.

"Oh dear God," he moaned. "What has the world come to?" Sighing, Adam removed a strip of jerky from his pocket and shoved it in the boy's thin hand. Turning, Adam pulled himself weakly onto his horse, hoping the clouds would slip away from the moon so he could see how badly he was wounded. Gently, he probed his side as warm blood rushed over his hand. The bullet had penetrated just below the rib cage.

He yanked the ragged shirt from his back and ripped it up as best he could then bound himself tightly, hoping to check the flow of blood. If he could slow the blood flow, maybe he could get to a farmhouse. As he turned his horse to plod slowly down the muddy road, he prayed.

God, help me. Send someone to help me. . . .

For the first time since leaving Colorado, he doubted the wisdom of his long journey. He had underestimated the difficulty of escaping not only soldiers, but worse, the deserters and thieves who prowled the night for money, horses, and food.

The night grew darker—or was he about to faint? He squinted through the deep woods on both sides of the road, his ears strained, listening for the beat of horse hooves. Suddenly an acrid smell floated through the trees, wafting beneath his nostrils, already filled with thick breath from his tightly squeezed chest.

He cocked his head and sniffed again. Smoke! Had the Yanks burned a farmhouse, or was he getting the drift of a campfire? He stopped his horse and turned his head from right to left, trying to identify the direction of the smoke. His senses drew him to the right, to the depths of the woods bordering the road. He had no idea how deep he must go into the woods to locate the source of the smoke or who might be at the campfire. But he had no choice. He would bleed to death if he didn't get help soon.

He slumped over the saddle, hanging on by sheer determination as his mind drifted in and out of consciousness.

The sticky blood filled his shirt bandage, and the whirling dizziness in his brain was worse than the vine-tangled path. He caught sight of a tiny patch of orange through the darkness and plunged on, finally coming upon a circle of men seated around a fire. The men wore gray uniforms. Two soldiers had bolted to their feet, their rifles drawn.

"Don't shoot," he gasped. "I'm a Southerner."

The curious faces faded from his vision, along with the glowing fire that promised warmth and perhaps food. He could feel himself slipping from the horse, and in those dark seconds, Elisabeth Greenwood's face swam through the darkness in his brain.

Chapter Sixteen

A sharp pain seared Adam's side, a rotating pain that cut off his breath. His matted eyes dragged open, and he was looking into a lantern, then a bearded face above it.

"Lie still," the man commanded in a Southern drawl. "Jim's digging the bullet out of your side. It may hurt a mite, but if he doesn't get it out, you're gonna die."

"Thanks," Adam rasped, unable to say more.

He gritted his teeth as the sharp gouging continued. He hadn't the strength to tell them who he was, to convince them he wasn't a deserter or a spy. He knew he must show courage, and he ground his teeth into his lower lip, determined to hold on. As the man said, he might die anyway. He might as well die with dignity.

He opened his eyes again and concentrated on the face above him. Bold blue eyes above a dark beard showed keen intelligence. Adam sensed the man was not a low-ranking officer, although he couldn't see the chevrons on his uniform. Dark brows slanted over his eyes, and the black hair beneath his rebel cap was thick and curly. Adam had no choice but to trust the stranger, and as the pain swept over him, he gave in to a deep sleep.

A pleasant smell penetrated his senses. It occurred to Adam there was no pain now, and for a moment he lay reveling in the freedom from that torture.

Thank You, God.

A breeze rustling through the oaks picked up the drifting aroma, and his mouth began watering at the delicious scent. Slowly, he opened his eyes to a thin gray light. Dawn. In the distance, he could hear low voices, whispers. Again, his stomach twisted with the pain of hunger, and now he understood why starving men ate whatever they could find.

He pushed himself up onto his left elbow, but the right side resisted, and he felt the stabbing pain again. His eyes dropped to his bare chest beneath the frayed blanket, and he saw a neat row of bandages covering his chest. He lifted his head and squinted at eight men seated around a morning fire. With surprise he noted the men were no longer wearing gray uniforms. Had he merely imagined that they were Confederate soldiers last night with his vison blurred and his mind desperate? They were dressed in old clothes, similar to the ones he wore. Suspicion and doubt warred within him, until he remembered they had saved his life. Whoever they were, they were his only friends right now.

"Morning," he called weakly.

The men whirled at the sound of his voice, and the blue-eyed man rose to his feet. He was not a tall man, nor was he muscled, but he moved with the agility of a forest animal, bounding quickly to Adam's side.

"We were wonderin' last night if you'd ever see daylight again. Who are you, and what happened?"

He swallowed against his dry, scratchy throat, hoping to speak clearly.

"I'm Adam Pearson," he answered. "I've been in Colorado for the past three years. I had started to Tennessee to check on my father." His voice was so weak that Adam wondered how convincing he must sound to those strangers.

A muscle twitched beneath the man's thick beard, and his blue eyes were now as cold as frozen seas.

"You waited a long time to come home, mister."

Adam nodded. "Never thought of coming back, but after hearing stories of the war. . ."

"Well, I tell you what. . ." The man stroked his chin thoughtfully. "If you live, and I think you will, you can forget going any farther for a while. I doubt you'd get far alone. Anyway, you've just been drafted. I'm Captain Thomas Hines of the Ninth Kentucky. If you want to serve your country, you can start right now. We need you to help us push the Yanks back."

When Adam considered his circumstances, he wondered if he really had a choice. He had already heard too many stories about deserters being shot by their own men, and while Captain Hines's tone was soft, Adam had seen the cold look in his eyes when Adam admitted he was not a member of the Confederate army.

He nodded slowly, as if in agreement, then closed his eyes again. A sadness engulfed him as his thoughts drifted back to Elisabeth. He prayed that no man had won her heart.

Chapter Seventeen

Elisabeth

Winter finally dragged into spring while Elisabeth struggled to stay busy with her job. In the evenings, she and Mrs. Tillotson sat by the fire, discussing passages of scripture. Elisabeth could feel her life changing ever since she began reading the Bible Mrs. Tillotson had given her. After attending church for the past month, Elisabeth had accepted Christ into her heart, and now her world was changing.

The bitterness she had felt toward Jed Greenwood was fading, along with the sharp ache of missing her mother. One thing had not changed, however: Elisabeth still missed Adam and longed to see him. She tried to keep up with what was going on in the South, but it was difficult. And the more she heard about the war raging, the more she worried about Adam. One evening as she sat by the fire with Mrs. Tillotson, she voiced her concerns.

"God will be with him," Mrs. Tillotson said, staring thoughtfully into the fire. "He's a fine young man. I pray every night that God will keep him safe."

Elisabeth swallowed hard. She had been praying that as well, but she didn't tell Mrs. Tillotson.

"I wonder when he'll come back," she said.

"I don't know, but when he returns I expect we will see him

right away." Her eyes twinkled as she looked at Elisabeth.

"I hope so."

"I'm sure he will be calling on you."

"You're sure?" Elisabeth echoed, wondering what the little lady meant. It seemed to her Mrs. Tillotson knew a secret whenever Elisabeth asked her about Adam. She got a funny little smile on her face, and her eyes took on a mischievous twinkle.

"In case you hadn't noticed, Elisabeth, I believe Adam likes you."

Elisabeth's breath caught in her throat. "Why on earth do you say that?"

"A woman just gets a feeling about those things. And"— she paused, giving her next words significance—"he asked me to take special care of you. I knew then he was smitten."

Elisabeth felt color rush to her cheeks. She was thrilled by those words, and yet she had thought Adam was just being a kind person who would have helped *anyone* in need. And she had certainly been in need. Still, Mrs. Tillotson's words were encouraging.

The next day, after collecting her week's pay, she strolled into the mercantile and looked at the blue woolen dress again.

"Must have been meant for you," the salesclerk said. "There has to be a reason it hasn't sold before now."

Elisabeth stroked the nubby blue cloth, smiling with delight. "It *was* meant for me." She wished the same was true of Adam, but she tried not to let her hopes soar beyond reason as she took the dress home and hung it in her closet. This was her act of faith that she kept hearing about in church. She would not wear the dress until Adam came home, and then she would wear it for him.

While war raged in the South, Colorado was torn with conflict between Indians, settlers, and outlaws. Several thousand men had left to enlist in the army while Civil War deserters and refugees flooded into the territory. It was a poor exchange, for the mines and gold mills fell to skeleton crews, while stealing and shoot-outs became commonplace in the streets of Pueblo, Colorado City, and Denver.

Elisabeth went straight to work and straight home each day, sometimes accompanied by Seth Wilkerson. She feared he was starting to see her as a possible wife, but she tried to maintain the proper balance between her business and personal life. Still, she was grateful for his concern. And still the blue dress hung in the closet, unworn, untouched, waiting for Adam's return.

Chapter Eighteen

Adam and Elisabeth

*A*s Adam healed, he tended the horses, kept a good campfire, and cooked for the exhausted men. He had learned the reason the soldiers changed clothes as regularly as a company of traveling actors. They were a select group of General Morgan's men—rebel raiders, as they were known throughout Kentucky. Morgan had been a skilled cavalryman, but he excelled in more than cavalry tactics. He was a master at conspiracy, a trait that seemed to distinguish the magnetic Hines, as well.

Adam had not challenged the men or argued with them about their beliefs. He did what he was told to do, but evenings by the campfire, he took his Bible out and read it. There were sneers on a few faces, but one by one, the soldiers came around night after night, asking questions about the Bible. After a particularly bad day, they seemed eager to have him share the Word of God, so they would have promises to cling to in battle.

This is hard, God, Adam prayed one night as he lay awake staring through the warm darkness to stars twinkling overhead. *This is hard, but I know why You've placed me here.*

Spring stretched to summer. Then, as Hines's troops pressed into Ohio and fought bravely at Buffington Island, they were finally captured. Adam, ill with fatigue and exhaustion, felt only a numb relief when his part in the raids ended.

The relief was short lived, however, when the Confederate prisoners were loaded onto boats for a three-day journey to the prison at Cincinnati. As Adam huddled among the jostling bodies, the dull fog of exhaustion cleared from his mind, and the truth of his circumstances hit him with a startling clarity.

His chances of reaching his father's farm in Tennessee had been slim before, but now they appeared impossible. His group was met by jeering mobs in Cincinnati who shouted taunts of "Hang them. . .hang them."

A guard shoved him into an overcrowded cell, and in the privacy of midnight darkness, Adam prayed desperately. Some of the men who had been talking with him about the Bible were now eager for anything he could tell them. Everyone feared they would die soon. While they were not permitted to talk with each other, some of the men used their utensils to communicate, carving words in food.

Bible verse?

Psalm 21, he wrote back. *John 3:16*. He had taught them about Jesus during their campfires, and had quoted the twenty-first psalm for one desperate homesick young man. These soldiers seemed to remember everything he had told them, for sometimes he could see their mouths moving silently, and he would read the words on their lips. . . .

"Should not perish, but have everlasting life. . ."

On the third day in prison, the message Adam read in Hines's mashed potatoes brought hope to his heart. Hines had devised a means of escape—a tunnel to be dug under the dirt floor of the cell next to Adam's.

Adam knew it would take patience, determination, and

reckless disregard of the consequences to attempt the escape. But despite the obstacles, he felt that God was with them.

He moved his head in a cautious nod, and Hines grinned. Adam knew in his heart that somehow he would make it to Tennessee.

Chapter Nineteen

*E*lisabeth had taken to reading her new Bible nightly. After spending time in God's Word, she would extinguish her lantern and pray earnestly for Adam.

"God, please bless him wherever he is. And please return him safely to us."

She also prayed that she could fulfill Adam's one request of her: accepting her heritage. The important thing was that God was her true heavenly Father. Each night as she crawled beneath the sheets of her bed and extinguished the lantern, she felt a calm assurance that He was going to work things out in her life. And in Adam's life as well.

Adam's escape came in the wee hours, and to everyone's amazement, weeks of digging actually did pay off. The tunnel was tiny and cramped, but hope and desperation gave them the strength to force their bodies through to the far end where a patch of daylight waited. No good-byes were said; everyone fled into the dark night, hope in their hearts, a prayer on their lips.

Elisabeth awoke in the middle of the night, her heart racing, her forehead covered with perspiration. What was wrong?

Something was wrong!

Her dark eyes flew over the room, assessing her situation. She was in her comfortable room at Mrs. Tillotson's house. All was quiet and still. She strained her ears. Had Mrs. Tillotson called out to her?

She leaped out of bed and peered through her open door to the hallway, where she could see across to Mrs. Tillotson's room. The elderly lady preferred to have her drapes opened at night so she could lie in bed and look out at the stars.

Now the moonlight filtered through the lacy curtains, silhouetting Mrs. Tillotson, sleeping peacefully in her bed.

Elisabeth heaved a sigh. Thank God!

She stood for several minutes in the doorway, her ears training, her eyes searching every darkened corner. Soon she convinced herself that nothing was wrong; all was just as it had been when she said good night earlier.

Creeping back to bed and nestling under the quilt, the soft summer night flowed over her room, and she began to wonder about Adam. Was he in trouble? Had something happened to him? Had some inborn sense of alarm alerted her that he needed her prayers?

"Adam," she whispered into the darkness as new pain wrenched her heart. Tossing the covers back, she knelt by her bed, her hands clasped together. And she began to pray for Adam, a prayer that went on for an hour.

Chapter Twenty

Adam heard the words, and suddenly the world seemed to spin. When he reached out to grip the door frame for support, the woman's blue eyes were sympathetic.

"Sorry about your father, but he died peacefully in his sleep, I was told."

For a long time, Adam merely stared, scarcely able to believe that despite all he had gone through, it was still too late. Why had God allowed that to happen?

Tears glazed his eyes before he turned away. Before him, the rolling hills blurred through a haze of tears. He had always liked it here, but some part of his soul had never called it home.

He remembered his father's letter, asking him to come back and help him hang on to his land. He had failed.

"If it will make you feel better, he got your telegram," the woman said over his shoulder. "With the mail service paralyzed in places, it's a miracle word got through to him. But I found it among his possessions when we cleaned out the house. He knew you were coming home."

Those words were fresh inspiration to a man whose hopes were quickly dying in his heart. Adam turned back to face her, not caring that she saw his tears.

"Thank you. Who did you say you are?"

"We are the Canfields. My husband is a land speculator,"

she replied, "and we're from Washington. He bought up some of the land in this area by paying off the taxes. . . ."

Adam nodded, sick at heart.

"Where did you come from, young man?"

"Colorado," he replied, shoving his hands in his pockets. "And I will be returning there."

"Did you travel through the country with the war going on?"

He nodded, unable to say more. The past months were a nightmare for him. He had no idea how he was going to cross back through the same territory, particularly since he had escaped from a Yankee prison. Bitterness welled within him, but he fought back. He had to keep praying; he couldn't let hardship steal his faith.

"Listen, young man." The woman walked out to stand beside him. "It just so happens my husband is traveling with some men to St. Louis. You would be safe traveling that far with them. It's the least we can do for you. . . ."

He turned stunned eyes to her, scarcely able to believe what he was hearing. Just when doubt hovered like dark clouds, threatening to obscure all hope forever, here at last was a new ray of sun.

"I would be very grateful," he managed to reply. "I'm going to the family cemetery," he said. "And then I'll be back to talk with you."

"Thank you."

There was nothing left to do but visit his parents' grave and see for himself that they were gone. They were both Christians, and Adam knew they were in a better place.

And still the tears streamed, unchecked, down his face as he swung into his saddle and turned his horse toward the family cemetery.

Chapter Twenty-One

The return to Denver was surprisingly easy and without incident. With the help of Andrew Canfield, Adam reached St. Louis safely and was able to secure a horse and make his return to Colorado in less than a week. He had prayed throughout the journey that Elisabeth was still in Denver—and most of all, that she was not betrothed to another man.

When Adam appeared at Mrs. Tillotson's front door, Elisabeth was there to meet him. As her eyes ran over him, her breath lodged in her throat. She could hardly believe he was here. At home. Safe. At last.

He was a striking figure dressed in a dark broadcloth suit with a starched white shirt and gleaming black leather boots, gifts from the Denver Missionary Society upon his return home. His fashionable new round hat was dark, like his suit, and sat on his thick hair, which was trimmed neatly around his ears. His face was deeply bronzed from the summer wind and sun, accenting the vivid darkness of his eyes.

"Hello, Elisabeth," he said, removing his hat.

"Hello." She smiled up at him, delighted by the look of admiration on his face.

He had sent word that he would be arriving Friday afternoon and would like to see her. She was glad she had bought the dress.

"You look very pretty," he said.

"Thank you." She dropped her eyes to her hands, gripped tightly together before her.

Behind Elisabeth, Mrs. Tillotson cleared her throat, and Adam looked in her direction.

"Good evening, Mrs. Tillotson. Would you like to accompany us to Apollo Hall? I've been told the play is a good one."

"Oh, no, thank you," she said with a little laugh. "At my age, the hearth is the best place for me on a summer night."

"Have you been well?" He smiled at her.

"I have. And you? We've prayed for you daily."

He hesitated for a moment. "I am well now. My father passed away."

"Oh, I'm sorry." Elisabeth reached out, gripping his hand.

"Well, I want you to know that I've heard from the folks up in Aspen Valley. They're eager to have you back home. And your cabin is clean and waiting," Mrs. Tillotson informed him.

Adam shook his head. "How can I ever thank all of you?"

She waved the question aside. "Our thanks are to you. We decided not to replace you; you're irreplaceable. We're all excited that you'll be going back to the valley. Everyone up there sends you their regards. Now, you two have a good time," she said, letting her eyes drift back to Elisabeth as she stood waiting, her shawl on her arm.

"Here, allow me." Adam took her shawl and laid it lightly about her shoulders. "It's a warm night. I thought perhaps you would like to walk."

"That would be nice," Elisabeth replied, glancing back at Mrs. Tillotson "I won't be late, Mrs. Tillotson."

Mrs. Tillotson merely waved and retreated back into her parlor as Adam and Elisabeth stepped out into the pleasant evening.

A soft golden twilight was settling over Denver as they strolled along, and Elisabeth felt a rush of happiness at just being with Adam. She turned to look at him, eager to relay her news.

"I have something to tell you," she said, looking up from the corner of her eye. She was still trying to adjust to her new ruffled bonnet, but having studied it in the looking glass from every angle, she decided it complemented her face. Watching Adam, she thought he must like it, too, for he was smiling down at her with a huge grin on his face.

"What is it?" He reached for her gloved hand, inserting it into the crook of his arm.

"I became a Christian while you were away. Mrs. Tillotson gave me a Bible, and I'm reading it every night."

A wide smile lit his dark face. "Elisabeth, that's wonderful. How do you feel?"

"Much happier. And more at peace with myself."

He nodded thoughtfully, as his eyes trailed over her features. "You look different. I kept thinking it was because of your pretty clothes, but now I think it's the radiance from your soul."

He lifted her gloved hand to his lips and lightly kissed her fingers. "Elisabeth, I've missed you."

"And I've missed you, Adam," she said as their eyes locked. For a moment, they stopped walking until someone bumped into Adam at the street corner, drawing his attention back to their surroundings. "Well," he said, looking more serious, "we'd better hurry or we'll be late for the play."

The play was performed by a troupe recently arrived in Denver. Elisabeth and Adam had joined a large audience to see *Richard III* acted out on stage illuminated by candles, which added to the romance and intrigue of the story.

Afterward, Adam suggested a late supper at the Tremont House, and they dined on hot tea and roast beef sandwiches. It was the first time Elisabeth had eaten in an elegant restaurant, and at first she was nervous about which fork to use or breaking the crystal glass or chipping the fine china. Adam soon put her mind at ease, however, as he began to talk about his work up in the mountains.

"Do you want to talk about the war?" she asked gently.

Adam stared at her, amazed that she was so sensitive to his feelings. "I'm not ready to talk about it yet. Maybe another time. I just want to enjoy being with you, and try to put these past miserable months behind me."

"Then that's what we'll do," she said, smiling into his eyes.

"Elisabeth," he said then hesitated.

"What is it?"

He took a sip of tea. "Are you happy here?"

Her eyes drifted over the well-dressed crowd seated around them. "I should be. But there's an emptiness inside. Oh, it's much better since I became a Christian, but I want to do something more special with my life than working in the photography shop."

Adam leaned forward. "Do you have any ideas about what you'd like to do?"

She shrugged. "Maybe. I met Star of the Morning this past year, and she's been back to visit a few times. She seems so happy. . .so fulfilled."

"I know her,"—he nodded—"and she is a wonderful young woman. The secret to that happiness, however, is her dedication to her work. To God's calling." He looked deeply into her eyes. "Would you want to do something like that?"

Elisabeth's breath caught in her throat. She sat very still, unsure how to respond. The conversation seemed to be getting very personal, and she wasn't yet sure how Adam felt about her. She felt reluctant to answer his question, but then she decided the best answer was an honest one.

"I still have to come to terms with my identity before I can make a success of anything." She toyed with her fork, wishing life did not always confuse her so much.

"Is it so important to you?" he asked.

She nodded quickly. "Yes, it is. Wouldn't you feel the same way if you were me?"

He took several seconds to consider her question; then finally he responded slowly. "I suppose I would. In my case, I just always knew that I was part Cherokee, part white. I accepted it early, and it was never a problem."

"That's because you were loved," she said tightly.

His hand closed over hers. "Elisabeth, you are loved now. Can't that be enough?"

She stared at him, unable to believe her ears. Loved by Adam? Was it possible?

"I'm making you uncomfortable," he said, laying his napkin on the table. "Forgive me."

She wanted to tell him so much, to open up her soul to him, but for some reason she held back. Did he mean that *he* loved her? No, surely he was referring to Mrs. Tillotson, and maybe he meant that he loved her in the sense of brotherly Christian love. Something deep in her heart told her she was fighting with the truth, that the look in Adam's eyes was sincere. And yet, all the years listening to Jed Greenwood's rough voice, his constant belittling and scorning, had left her doubting that anyone could truly love her. Then when she returned to the post as practically an outcast. . .

"Shall we go?" Adam asked.

She hesitated, wanting to tell him how she felt, and yet the words were locked in her throat. She came to her feet, saying none of the things that filled her heart.

"When are you returning?" Elisabeth asked as they walked back to Mrs. Tillotson's house.

"On Sunday after services. Are you working tomorrow?"

She frowned. "I'm sorry to say that I am. Saturday has become our busiest day. But maybe you could stop by the shop," she suggested, turning hopeful eyes to him.

"I'll try to."

His tone was more reserved now, and she wondered if she had hurt his feelings by not responding. But they had been apart for months, and there was a deep sadness etched into Adam's face. She knew it was going to take time for him to heal from the war, and she wanted to be fair with him.

When they reached the doorstep, he lifted her hand to his lips, gently kissing her fingers. "I'll see you tomorrow," he said, almost as if he couldn't stay away.

The look in his eyes pulled at her soul, and she reached out to him, gently touching his cheek. "I hope so," she said.

He leaned down and kissed her, more passionately than before, and yet it was a brief kiss. And then he stepped back from her, and she rushed inside before she could have a chance to open her mouth and spill all the things at war in her soul out to him.

Chapter Twenty-Two

When she arrived at the shop the next day, Seth Wilkerson was standing in front of the Gallery, staring down the street, idly twirling his mustache.

"Good morning," she called.

"You're here." He whirled to her. "Good, I can leave." He grabbed his camera, slapped his round hat on his dark head, and almost ran over her. "I'm making pictures for the newspaper. Kit Carson has brought some Indians to town, and he's making a speech in a few minutes."

"Indians?" she repeated, following him out onto the sidewalk.

"Just some Utes," he tossed over his shoulder, hugging his camera under his arm and bounding down the board sidewalk.

Just some Utes. The words were like salt in an open wound, and she stared after him, startled by his indifference.

"Just some Utes?" she called after him, feeling an unexpected rush of temper.

She tilted her bonneted head back and gazed down to the next street corner. At the corner at Larimer, a crowd was gathering around two men dressed in buckskins and leather, with long hair and beads, and dusty felt hats perched low on their heads.

Elisabeth stretched her neck, trying to see the object of

everyone's interest. What if the Utes were from Black Hawk's camp? What if this was someone she knew, one of the women who had been kind to her?

She felt herself being drawn toward the crowd, and she completely forgot her job and the Gallery as she inched toward the corner, peering around the onlookers.

Two ragged Ute children stood beside the men, one of whom was introducing himself as Kit Carson. He was rather short with bold features and keen eyes.

"The Utes and Arapahos are at war," his voice rang out over the crowd.

Elisabeth searched the crowd for her employer; he was busily at work, focusing his camera. He wouldn't know she was anywhere in the background. She took a few steps closer.

"Last year when me and Jim Beckworth tried to persuade the tribes not to fight, we had no luck," Kit Carson's voice rang out. "Now, I'm askin' some of you to help these children. They were left without parents or a home, and the mission school is already crowded."

A hush fell over the crowd at first; then silence turned into a flurry of whispers. No one stepped forward, however. Elisabeth bit her lip. Surely someone would help those poor children. . . .

Elisabeth was frozen with horror at the words Carson had spoken. Her mind raced back to Black Hawk' camp. Were they being attacked by Arapahos or white settlers? Compassion tugged at her heart, and she found herself wishing she could do something to help the children. Jed Greenwood had instilled a lifetime of prejudice into her thinking, but she could see now that it was wrong, all wrong.

"God forgive me," she silently prayed as she stared at the gaunt faces of the Ute boy and girl, the hollow, dark eyes. They looked frightened to death. . .and hungry.

Without giving it another thought, she lifted her skirt and ran back to the baker, yanking open the stings of her purse. She hadn't much money left, but she certainly had enough to buy a loaf of bread. And that was the least she could do.

By the time she returned with the warm bread wrapped in newspaper, most of the crowd had dispersed. Only a few curious ones still lingered at the edge of the street, staring at the children as though they were from a foreign land.

Elisabeth pushed past the people, oblivious even to Seth Wilkerson, clicking his camera in the background.

"Here." She rushed up to the children, eagerly tearing the bread in half and giving each a generous piece.

The dark eyes were fearful as the children took the bread, while in the background she could hear someone whisper several words with one word more distinct: *savages.*

She whirled on the man who had stumbled out from the saloon peering at the children with bleary eyes. "Savages." He called out, louder than before.

"They're not savages," Elisabeth yelled back at him. "They're human beings who deserve some respect."

Suddenly she realized how loudly she had spoken, and how quiet everyone had become. Then, in the blur of faces, she saw the red face of her employer and wasn't sure if the emotion on his face was sympathy or anger.

Giving the children one last smile, she turned and rushed back to the Gallery and dashed inside, slamming the door behind her. None of the people were more surprised by her reaction than she was. Removing her bonnet, she hung it on the peg by the door, while her thoughts lingered on the poor children. She couldn't forget their sad, tormented faces. Her stomach was comfortably filled with tea and oatmeal from

Mrs. Tillotson's cozy kitchen. Her skin was covered with nice clothing, and yet those poor children were so in need. . . .

"Miss Greenwood,"—Seth Wilkerson burst through the door—"did you leave this shop unattended?"

She turned to him, still dazed by her thoughts. "What did you say?"

"I said. . ." He took a step closer to her, and she could see a hard glint in his dark eyes as he glared into her face. "Did you leave this shop unattended while you ran your goodwill mission? Obviously, you did. Do you have any idea how much of my money you risked by so carelessly wandering into the crowd?"

A frown marred Elisabeth's smooth brow as she struggled to make sense of his words. As she did, her eyes swept him up and down. He was as arrogant and uncaring as the drunkard she had yelled at.

"And you made quite a spectacle of yourself out there." His finger jabbed the air behind him. "It was an embarrassment to me."

"An embarrassment to you?" she cried out, horrified by his words. "Don't you even care that those children are cold and hungry? No, you don't," she said slowly, realizing for the first time what a self-centered little man he was.

"My concern is with my line of work and my business here in town, which you have just put at risk with your carelessness."

Elisabeth could feel her spine stiffen. "What do you consider most careless, Mr. Wilkerson?" she asked slowly, furiously. "Leaving your precious equipment unattended, which, by the way, nobody could work but you, and I'm not sure anyone wants to go around snapping that thing in people's faces." She pointed at his prize camera. "Or are you referring to my giving food to hungry children? Was that what you call making a spectacle of myself?"

"Boldly defending them against Tom Searcy, publicly embarrassing him?"

"The drunkard was doing perfectly well embarrassing himself. And he was drunk, in case you didn't notice."

"Tom Searcy spends a lot of money in this town. He's very successful in the trapping business. People don't yell at him."

Elisabeth took a step back from him, so furious she could hardly control the trembling that ran over her. And then a smooth, deep voice spoke up in the background.

"And no one is going to yell at Miss Greenwood," the man said.

Elisabeth and Seth whirled simultaneously.

Adam stood in the door, glaring at Seth, his fists balled at his sides.

Chapter Twenty-Three

Elisabeth ran to his side, throwing her arms around him. "Oh, Adam, it's all right." She turned back to Seth, who was boldly surveying Adam's fashionable broadcloth suit and round hat. "I'm not interested in working for you any longer."

She reached for her bonnet and cloak and linked her arm through Adam's. As soon as they were out the door, Adam gripped her hand and smiled down at her.

"I'm so proud of you," he said.

"For standing up to a mean little man?"

"And for defending the Indian children. I had just walked up to the Gallery to see you, when I spotted you on the edge of the crowd with the bread in your hand. I hurried down there and saw what you did. Before I could get to you, you had spoken your mind to the drunk and dashed off."

She looked at him sheepishly. "And you were proud of that?"

"Of course I was."

Elisabeth stopped walking and looked at Adam.

"Could we sit down and talk?"

"Of course."

They had reached a small park, and he led her to a bench where they took a seat. Elisabeth was oblivious to the people milling around as she looked into Adam's face and shook her head sadly.

"I've been so confused. But not anymore. Since I became a Christian and got my heart right with God, I feel as though the fog has cleared. It's been like a fog, you know. I was confused. . .lost. But you were right. My heavenly Father is the One who really matters."

"That's right," Adam acknowledged, "but still you must be at peace with your life and your past. How do you feel now about the Utes? Different, it seems."

"Different, yes. And ashamed for being so intolerant, so prejudiced. If I am half-Ute, these are my people who are being treated like animals, Adam."

He nodded and sighed, turning her gloved hand over in his and staring at it. "Many years ago, I felt the way you're feeling now. I knew I had to stand for something, to help those who were being mistreated. I've never regretted my decision."

She tilted her head back and looked at him. "Maybe that's what I'd like to do."

"Nothing would make me happier," he said, pulling her into his arms as they both ignored the stares of people around them. He hugged her against his chest, and neither spoke for several seconds. Then he gently pushed back from her and looked down into her eyes. "I want you to think and pray about that decision. And if you still mean it, when I come back to town, I want to take you home with me."

"Home with you?" she gasped.

"As my wife. It won't be an easy life, Elisabeth. I travel a lot, and you would be left alone in the cabin. Well, not alone"— he chuckled—"because I'm always taking in strays who need help."

"I wouldn't mind," she said softly, gazing up into his eyes.

For several seconds neither spoke. Then Adam stood and pulled her to her feet. "We mustn't do anything hasty. You think about this, and I will, too."

"I won't change my mind," she said softly as they walked back to Mrs. Tillotson's house.

"Just be sure. And to be fair about it, you need to come up to the valley and see what my life is like. Maybe we can persuade Mrs. Tillotson to accompany you."

She shook her head. "She won't travel until spring."

"Then I'll think of something," he said, leaning down to kiss her cheek.

"Maybe you should just take me home with you now. As your bride."

He stopped walking and stared down into her eyes, unable to believe his ears. "Are you sure about that?" he said, his voice choked with emotion.

"I've never been so sure of anything in my life!" she said and began to laugh.

It was true—all that mattered to her was being with Adam and serving God wherever He sent them.

Adam began to laugh with her as they quickened their pace back to Mrs. Tillotson's house.

"Mrs. Tillotson is going to be surprised," Elisabeth said as he hugged her tightly.

"I don't think so. I told her the day I brought you to her house that I might come back and marry you someday."

She whirled to stare at him. "How did you know that?"

"I didn't. I just asked God to work things out and He did."

Tears filled her eyes as she looked at Adam and smiled, "Yes, He worked things out just perfectly."

Peggy Darty authored more than 30 novels before she passed away in 2011. She worked in film, researched for CBS, and taught in writing workshops around the country. She was a wife, mother, and grandmother who most recently made her home in Alabama.